THE LONG JOURNEY

A story of divided loyalties, revenge and flight.

Clemens Lucke

First published in the United Kingdom in 2015 by CompletelyNovel.com

Copyright © Joan Angus

ISBN: 9781849148283

In memory of my father

"Keep your face always towards the sunshine - and shadows will fall behind you."
Walt Whitman

Part One

Family Feuds

Chapter 1   1644
Homecomings, Speyside

Dawn stole softly over the Scottish Highlands. The first of the sun's rays fingered their way into the rocky shelter to arouse the young men sleeping there. John Grant sat up, stretched and looked round at his four companions. They were a dishevelled bunch; blood-stained, with long hair and beards and tattered clothing. John staggered to his feet and went to survey their surroundings. Nearby, a rowan tree was ablaze with colour. Dew glistened on the heather and a mist was forming in the valley.

He turned to face the others. "'Twill be only a day's journey home, lads. Think of those maids and mothers waiting with open arms and clean sheets on the bed."

Hamish sat up. He examined his roughly bandaged leg and said, "I'll bide here. I canna goo another step."

The others protested. "You've come this far. We'll no' leave you here."

"I'd only slow ye doon. I'll rest here theday."

"Nay, you're coming with us, if we have to carry you," said John.

"Think of that plate of steak on the table?" said Robert. He and John hauled Hamish to his feet. Hamish put an arm round each of their shoulders. They paused a moment to steady themselves. The three brothers came out of the cave into bright sunlight. Bruce and Andy followed, talking about their homes and families, glad to be putting the battlefields and their gruesome memories behind them.

Later that day, having left the others to go their separate ways, John strode down the last hill, his homestead in view. Below, there was Annie in the yard, carrying pails of milk into the house. He shouted, and she looked up. She put the pails down, lifted her skirts and ran up the hill to meet him. Coming closer, she looked at the state of him with horror, and kissed him anyway.

In the yard, under the pump, John stripped off his clothes and washed away a month of battle grime, blood and dust, and the grief of seeing brothers and fellow Covenanters slaughtered. Indoors, Annie stoked up the fire, hotted up a tankard of ale, found some clean clothes for him, and was cooking the meal he had dreamed of on his journey home. He grabbed the warm towels she had put out, and wrapped them round his naked body. He sat by the fire for a while, sipping the ale, and gazed into the flames as he allowed himself to relax at last.

His attention wandered to Annie, his beloved wife. Her fresh, bright face was surrounded by brown hair with a hint of copper. It fell around her shoulders as she leaned forward over the table to put a steaming dish of food there for him. She faced away from him, her curvaceous figure aroused neglected feelings. His heart stirred. He stood up and let the towels fall to the floor as he went over to her. He put his arms round her waist from behind. She straightened and he rested his head on her shoulder. Emotions surged to the surface.

She turned and said, "Whisht now." She tenderly caressed his naked body, and held him close, gently swaying. "Get some food doon thee, bonny lad." Then, noticing his rising manhood, said, "There'll be time enough for that later." She gently disentangled herself, and he went to put on his clean clothes, while she disappeared out of the room. She re-appeared with the sheep shears, waving them at him.

"Let's be rid o' some of this thatch," she said, and started towards him. He dodged to the other side of the table. She chased him, laughing, until he succumbed, and pretended to struggle while the dark matted locks fell to the floor and were thrown on the fire. His beard was the next to go, and soon he was looking at her with his deep brown eyes.

"Now I can see thy face!" she cried.

He laughed and added, "And I can find ma mouth to put this food doon me."

They sat at the table.

"Tell me aboot thy brothers. Are they all safe?" Annie asked as he tucked into the meal.

"Rob and I came from the battlefield thegither, with Andy and Bruce. We had to help Hamish. He took an axe wound in his leg."

"Were ye beaten?" asked Annie.

John nodded. "The Royalists outnumbered us, led by that fiery de'il frae Ireland, Colkitto. He joined forces with the traitor Montrose, and they gathered a great following of Catholic Highlanders. The Irish fired a single shot with their muskets, then reversed them and used them as clubs. We were massacred."

"I've heard of the blood feud between Colkitto and the Campbells. He had two reasons for fighting," said Annie. "How did ye get away?"

"We were all scattered. I saw ma brother Ronald go doon... He was bludgeoned to death." John paused, and drew a breath, to hide his pain. "There was no way we could beat them, so to save masell I ran for cover. I watched..." His face showed the horror he felt. "Two or three others had the same idea. I saw Robert running, and called him over. Then Hamish went doon, and we lay low until the worst passed. When we crept over to Hamish, he was feigning death, and was mighty glad to see us. We dragged him away frae the field, and lay low until darkness came. The de'il knows what's happened to the rest of our company, if there be any alive."

John finished his meal and they sat by the fire together, quietly enjoying their companionship. Isabel, the kitchen maid, came to clear the table. She burst into tears to see her master home safe and sound.

Later, John led his lover up the stairs to their chamber, and they undressed slowly, feasting their eyes on each other's young bodies. John noticed that Annie's shape had changed. He went over to her and put his hand on the small mound, where it had been slim and flat.

"My, my, what have we here?" he whispered, his heart leaping for joy.

"'Tis thy bairn that's growing there, ma love," Annie said. He lifted her gently onto the bed, their limbs entwined and their kisses passionate...

Sleep came to them at last. John would turn his attention to his homestead and his animals in the morning.

≈ ≈ ≈

James Grant, 7th Laird of Freuchie, rode away from the battlefield at Blair Atholl and the devastating losses of the Covenanters, hoping that there was some of his clan left alive to fight another day. This conflict was not yet over, and at present he was on the losing side. Half an hour ago, he was in the thick of it, feeling more and more hopeless as he saw his men falling. He caught the eye of his leader, Archibald Campbell, the Earl of Argyll, and head of the Covenanters, who beckoned him over.

"We're hopelessly outnumbered, Grant!" he shouted above the din of screaming men and the shouts of their attackers. "There's no chance of us gaining anything. Take what's left of your company and run for your lives. We'll take stock another day."

James turned, hailed his men and waved them off the field. They seemed to be well scattered, and there were many lying slain. Those on horses joined him, and a motley band of followers marched behind, some wounded and needing assistance. James was dispirited, wondering when this fruitless conflict would end. There had been much bloodshed in the last few years. He had led his clan proudly to support the Covenanters under the Earls of Argyll and Montrose. But allegiances changed. Argyll demanded that King Charles be deposed, and Montrose, whose heart was really on the side of the king, had attempted to unseat Argyll. He was thrown into jail.

Now there was civil war in England, and a large Scottish army had marched south to support the Parliamentarians at the battle of Marston Moor. In the meantime, Montrose had been freed, and now, firmly on the side of the Royalists, had joined forces with Alistair McDonald, 'Colkitto', from County Antrim. James had just come away from the ensuing blood bath. What happened next was unpredictable. The first thing he must do was to make his family safe.

It started to rain as they approached Elchies, his home in Speyside. His hunting hounds came barking to greet him. His followers limped away to their homesteads and crofts. He shed his battle dress and weapons in the yard, and the groom took his horse to be fed and watered. James shouted to his servants, "Pack bags for your mistress. Get the horses and an escort prepared to take the Lady Mary and the children to Ballachastell." He strode up the stairs to his wife's living quarters and opened the door.

The room was in turmoil. The two babies were screaming, and that Italian charlatan, Bellini, whom his wife had engaged, was prancing around with his pricking instruments. The nursemaid was holding the toddler Mary down while Bellini administered his 'cure'. The baby Jane was covered in inflamed and weeping sores. Lady Mary was lying on the couch with her smelling salts, while her maid mopped her brow.

James roared above the noise, "Get out of this room, all of ye! I wish to speak to my wife." The children were swept away by the nursemaids, and Bellini hurriedly packed his instruments into their case and left the room, bowing as he went.

James glowered at his wife from under his jutting eyebrows. "What is that scoundrel doing here? I thought I'd left orders for him to be dismissed."

Lady Mary sat up. Her hand shook as she held the smelling salts to her nose. "Our bairns are still possessed with witches, Husband. Bellini is the only doctor who knows how to rid them," she protested tearfully.

"Balderdash! How many of our children have died under his hands? It is you who is possessed. I will allow him to prick them no more. Begone with him!"

Lady Mary was sobbing now, and James knew that he would have to be kinder in giving her the next piece of news, or he would have a scene on his hands.

"The conflict is getting closer to us here. You're to go to Ballachastell with the children, where it's more secure. The castle is well fortified, and I'll leave a garrison with you should you need it."

She looked up at him with horror. "We cannot travel in this weather. The children will die of cold. It's warm here. The castle is cold and bleak," she wailed.

"Hush Madam, you will do as I say, and you will leave at once," he said quietly. "I will follow with the servants." He left the room.

Chapter 2   1644
Conflicting loyalties

In the Grant's Castle of Ballachastell, a few miles up the valley from Elchies, the stone floor of the Great Hall rang with his footsteps as James paced up and down, his hands behind his back, his head bowed. He had summoned his clan leaders and neighbouring lairds to a council meeting, and he was waiting for their arrival. The wind hurled rain at the windows and the candles guttered on the long table as his tall figure passed. His rugged brows knotted over his eyes, deep in their sockets. He recalled the day, six years ago, when he and the Clan Grant signed the Covenant and swore the oath in Greyfriars Kirkyard in Edinburgh, along with large numbers of Scotsmen. The atmosphere was charged with religious fervour. The ceremony was led by Lord Worriston, a Presbyterian, who preached that only Jesus was King, and that faithful members of the Scottish Kirk were God's Chosen People. The Covenant renounced Catholicism and was a pledge to defend Scotland's countrymen as citizens, not subjects, who had the human right to follow their own religious beliefs. The Earls of Montrose and Argyll were the first to sign.

To sign the National Covenant was the only way to preserve all that his nation stood for in the face of this king, who was attempting to destroy the very foundations of the Kirk. He remembered the proud moment when he joined forces with Montrose and Argyll, the troops and their leaders, all wearing blue ribbons round their necks, as they marched off to take Aberdeen in the first Bishop's war This all happened years ago.

Now everything was different. Montrose had changed sides, and the Covenanters were weakening. The Marquis of Huntley ransacked and took Perth and Aberdeen for the Royalists. Montrose proposed that James, together with other Highland Lairds, should join him before he went south to support the king. James needed to discuss this proposal with his colleagues.

The door opened and the company entered, shaking their cloaks and hats and stamping their feet. The hall now echoed with the voices of Highland Lairds and their cadet leaders as they found their places. The Grant Cadets were also there, including John Grant and the leaders of Clan Ciaran. James called them to order.

"We're here to decide whether we should join forces with the Royalists under the Earl of Montrose, or continue supporting the Covenanters. McIntosh, d'you wish to speak?"

The Laird McIntosh stood up. "The Covenanters are splitting. Some are supporting King Charles against the English Parliament, who are attempting to overthrow the Crown, and rule the land themselves."

"Ay, the conflict is not about the Scottish Kirk now, but defending the Crown," commented the Earl of Strathspey. "King Charles is a Stuart, and of Scottish origin," he reminded them.

"But we all swore the oath to support the Covenant. To support the king would be treason against the Scottish Kirk," Laird MacPherson insisted.

"D'ye wish to be ruled by this upstart Cromwell?" challenged the Laird McIntosh. "We'd be under the English Puritans if they defeat King Charles. I say we support the Royalists, to give them a better chance of defeating Cromwell."

The debate continued. Voices and fists were raised. There was stamping of feet, and thumping of the table as they argued among themselves.

James Grant's deep voice boomed out. "Aberdeen has been taken for the Royalists, defeating a large company of Covenanters. Montrose is heading this way, gathering the clans for support before going south to England, where he'll be joining the king's army against Cromwell. Should we fight him or join him?"

"We'd be outnumbered if we opposed him," said Strathspey.

Fraser agreed. "It would be another massacre like the last."

They put the decision to the vote, and, to James' relief, most of those present agreed that they should join the Earl of Montrose and the Royalists. He was sorry to see that his friend and neighbour MacPherson chose to remain a Covenanter.

There was hammering at the door and a messenger was shown in, dripping wet and out of breath. "Laird, the Clan Cameron is raiding our lands in the west. They've already taken a herd of cattle."

James turned to his clan leaders. "It seems we have other business to attend to, gentlemen. Thank you for your support. We must gather the Clan Grant and defend our livestock now." They all rose, clasped each others' left forearms in salute, and left the hall, leaving

James to face another challenge. The next battle would be fought on Cameron land, at Inverlochy.

≈ ≈ ≈

They left the castle and went to collect their horses. As he mounted, John Grant heard a voice at his side. He looked round.

"So you voted to stay with the Covenanters, John," said the Laird MacPherson. "You realise that ye'll be fighting against your Laird." He mounted his horse and rode alongside.

John was angry. "I did, Sir, and I believe ma brothers in Clan Ciaran also voted against him." Their cadet branch was descended from the second Laird, and had inherited their homesteads and the land around them generations ago. They were loyal supporters of their Laird, or had been up to now. But the debate in the Great Hall had not gone the way they expected.

"How can we break our oaths to the Covenant by supporting the Royalists?" asked Robert. The others declared their agreement as they gathered round.

"Our Laird is a traitor," said John, reining in his horse to talk to MacPherson.

"We're against alliance with Montrose," cried Hamish, who had gone a little way ahead. "We must find the Earl of Argyll and the Covenanters."

"I too will be joining the Earl of Argyll, gentlemen," said MacPherson. "We might meet again!" He urged his horse into a gallop and rode away.

"But we'll help to drive the Camerons off Grant land first, "said John to his brothers, as they rode on. "We canna leave our homesteads at the mercy of those cattle thieves. They'll have suffered losses of their livestock in the conflict, and are replenishing their stock."

"We'll gather our families and support our Laird against the Camerons, then join the Covenanters," suggested Robert.

"Agreed," said the other two, and they clasped hands on it before going their separate ways home.

≈ ≈ ≈

A week later, in the Castle of Ballachastell, the Lady Mary Grant was mourning the death of the last of her children and had taken to her bed. This was the third child who had died. Blood poisoning, the doctor said. James was beginning to think he would never have heirs, and would have to pass his position as Laird on to one of his six brothers. He ate his meal that evening alone, staring into the fire. The flames of the burning logs in the hearth sent their tongues licking far up the cavernous black chimney, and the embers glowed red with a roar, a draft following the flames.

He was preparing to join the Royalists, and did not know if or when he would be returning. His relationship with Mary had been strained lately, due to his disposal of the services of her doctor, the pricker. She was not comfortable in the castle, and would rather be nestled in her room at Elchies, but James knew that she might not be safe there while he was away. He was sad at the loss of another child, and felt a strong desire to share this with his wife.

He went up to her bedchamber. She lay back on the pillows, looking distraught and vulnerable, her auburn

17

hair surrounding her pale face. She looked up at him with her brown, sorrowful eyes as he came in, and his heart melted. He went and sat on the side of the bed, not knowing what to say, but wanting to comfort her. He held her hand, and she lifted his and kissed it, and held it against her cheek.

"You're going to battle again, Husband?" she asked.

"Ay. It must be done. You'll be safe here."

Tears ran down her face. "I'm sorry, my dear. Our children are all gone," she said. They sat together and he held her in his arms for a while. Then he rose and slowly undressed. She watched him and knew that tonight she would not be alone. He climbed into her bed. They gently loved each other until their passions were aroused. They came together in harmony, and slept.

Chapter 3   1646
Covenanters on the Rampage

Spring was beginning to show through. The sap was rising. The air was full of energy and expectation. In the glen, John Grant was preparing to leave his family to join the Covenanters. He tied blue ribbons on the entrance to the farmstead. He did not want it to be mistaken for Royalist property. Annie stood in the doorway with young Jamie in her arms, waving goodbye. He heard what sounded like a large troop of horsemen galloping towards him through the glen. A company of Covenanters, who were intent on wreaking havoc on Grant land while the Laird was away on Royalist business, had caught up with the Grant brothers who joined them.

Fired up with anger at their Laird's changed loyalties, the brothers of Clan Ciaran were set on revenge. Having got clear of their own land, the company descended into the valley towards the river. They sang and shouted the Grant war cry *"Stand fast"*, as they approached the mansion and farm at Elchies. The fresh wind ruffled their hair, and sent grey and white clouds flying across the sky.

It was quiet in the grey stone courtyard, except for the snuffling of horses in the stables. The company approached the door with caution, in case a trap had been set. The door opened, and a maid in a mop cap and white apron stared at them in astonishment. She screamed to see the sun glinting on unsheathed dirks, turned and went back into the house, slamming the door shut, and bolting it behind her.

The intruders spread out, and searched round the outside of the house. One of them found a stable lad hiding in the barn. In a moment his throat was cut and he lay bleeding in the straw. John and his brothers forced the back door open and they and their companions entered the house, looking in each room for inhabitants. Apart from the maid, the place was deserted. They turned their attention to the fine furnishings and tableware. One of them took a sheaf of papers in his hand, reached into the fire, and was about to set light to the place.

"Stop, wait, what's the rush?" shouted their leader. "We've travelled a long way for this. We need food, and beds for the night. Let's enjoy it while we have the chance." They all cheered, and one of them brought the maid out of her hiding place.

"Can you cook, wench?"

"Ay, Sir," she whimpered.

"Dinner for twenty. Donal, go and kill one o' the pigs. Take someone with you to help with the butchering. Now, one o' ye pour me a dram." He made himself comfortable on the cushioned sofa.

The others were raiding the house for treasures, jewellery and stores of coins. They found the Laird's clothes cupboard, and availed themselves of clean shirts and new boots. After a few drinks they were enjoying a sociable evening, joking, laughing and teasing.

"Where are ye frae?" John asked the man sitting next to him.

"We came frae Inverness," was the reply. "We've had a few skirmishes on the way, but there are few Royalists around, only crofters."

"They're all with Montrose's forces marching to England," said John. "Our Laird changed sides because he'd had so many casualties, I reckon. The traitor!" and he spat on the rich carpet. The drink had gone to his head, intensifying his anger.

The maid produced a feast of pork for the intruders, and they spent the rest of the night revelling, some taking it in turns to have their way with the girl. This left a bad taste in John's mouth. He thought of Annie at home, and knew they would have done the same with her, if the blue ribbons had not been hanging there.

He woke with a start the next morning. The others were stirring from the positions into which they fell in their drunken stupor a few hours ago. They must hurry away before they were caught red-handed. The place was wrecked, curtains torn down, fine crockery smashed and furniture broken. This would hit his traitor Laird where it hurt, he thought. His pulses were racing, his breath came short and he felt no shame, only anger.

"Clear oot, this place is doomed!" he cried. "Take what ye want." He picked up a chair leg and placed it in the embers of the fire, leaving it there until it was alight. The others snatched trinkets and ornaments, before making their way outside. One of them despatched the maid by cutting her throat to prevent her raising the alarm. With a last triumphal shout, John tossed the flaming chair leg onto the soft furnishings and ran out of the house.

In the yard, men were taking their pick of the horses stabled there, fine breeding stallions and their mares. John picked out an Arab stallion, which was the latest breed to be used to be coupled with the tough highland horses. Then they torched the outbuildings, along with the grain store, and the company left. John felt elated by the wildness of the moment. He turned and watched as smoke poured from the windows of the house.

"Come away!" shouted Robert. "They'll no' be long in raising the alarm." They galloped along the stony road to catch up with their friends and the next opportunity to wreak havoc and revenge.

≈ ≈ ≈

Later that year, when the leaves were turning, James Grant and his Highland compatriots trudged wearily back to Speyside, having retreated from the battlefield once again. They had followed Montrose to support the King at Naseby, but were ambushed on the way. The combination of Sir Thomas Fairfax and his new Model Army of Roundheads from London and Oliver Cromwell's forces from the east finally proved too much for the Royalists, whose expected re-enforcements were slow in coming. The King advised Montrose to flee for his life, and the scattered Highlanders did likewise. James had contributed three hundred men to the Royalist cause, to no avail. Thoroughly dispirited, he turned his thoughts to spending some time with Mary at Elchies in comfort. She would be glad to get away from Balachastell.

At last his castle was in sight. He dismissed his remaining troops and they took their various ways to their homes. The evening sun shone through the trees as he rode up the long drive. He saw Mary at the window, watching for him. The grooms and servants gathered round him as he entered the yard, where he dismounted and made his way into the house. Mary emerged from their living quarters. She looked well, but had tears in her eyes as they embraced.

"What took you so long, Husband?" she asked. Not waiting for a reply, she kissed him again.

"Did you miss me?" James took her hand and she led him into the quiet comfort of her parlour. It was evident that she had spent time and effort in transforming the large, cold room into a luxurious refuge. The fire blazed in the hearth and the sun shone through the windows to light up the rich colours of the tapestries covering the stone walls. Deerskins lay on the floor, reducing the harsh sound of footsteps on stone. A servant appeared and took James' sword and outer garments.

"Come and sit beside me," Mary said. James went to sit on a comfortable chair for the first time for many months. "I heard news of your defeat. I feared for your life and am mightily glad to see you home again."

"There was much slaughter," said James. "King Charles doesn't have reliable forces behind him. I wonder what will become of him. Cromwell and the Roundheads have the advantage, and Montrose has fled."

"I also have bad news, Husband. Our house at Elchies is destroyed." Tears rolled down her delicate cheeks as she looked at him.

He stared at her, not wanting to believe her. She had a tendency to exaggerate bad news. "Nay, how can that be?" he said.

"It was soon after you left. They looted our home, killed the servants and set fire to the buildings. The horses are gone and there is little left that can be saved." Mary collapsed into sobbing grief.

James hated to see her in this state. His frayed and exhausted nerves could take no more. "Cease your wailing, woman. Tell me who discovered this. Did anyone see the marauders?"

Mary mopped her tears, and took some shuddering breaths. "One of the crofters saw the smoke and caught sight of the men as they rode away. It seems they were Covenanters." She blew her nose, covered her face with her hands and began rocking backwards and forwards in her chair.

James got up and paced the floor, simmering with anger. He was tired and it was too late to do anything now. He needed a good meal and to rest. He would go with his grieve in the morning to see the damage. He rang the bell to summon his servant, who appeared almost immediately.

"Bring the whisky, Dougal." James went and sat down again. He turned away from Mary towards the fire to avoid seeing her in her anguish.

Chapter 4   1650
Cromwell Rules

It was the end of winter at Balachastell. Spring bulbs were poking through under the trees and the days were lengthening at last. James was enjoying a brief respite from months of battle and bloodshed. He sat with Mary in the living room, each side of the fire. Mary rocked their new-born son in his crib.

"'Tis over a year since they killed the King," said James. "After all our efforts to protect Scotland from Cromwell, with more Scottish leaders joining the Royalists, it looks as if it has come to naught." He stared wearily into the fire.

"I heard Edinburgh was recaptured by the Roundheads," commented Mary. "What will happen to Scotland now?"

James shrugged his shoulders despondently. "Perhaps Prince Charles will come back and lead us to victory. We must not give up hope." He looked fondly at his son. "We'll call him Ludovick," he said.

Mary nodded. "A fine Scottish name. He's a healthy baby, Husband."

"I want no pricking doctors near him." James looked at his wife with authority.

There came a knocking at the door and the servant Dougal came in with a message. He walked across the floor and bowed. James rose and took the message.

"There is no call for a reply, Sir." Dougal bowed again and left the room.

James opened the message and read. He was pensive as he tore it up and threw it into the flames, where it curled into grey ash. He turned to face Mary, his back to the hearth.

"You're called away again, James," Mary said with tears in her eyes.

"Our prayers are answered. Prince Charles has come from Holland," announced James. "The Royalist Covenanters met him and he has been taken to Scone to be crowned King of the Scots. I will be needed." He stood for a while, looking down at his son with pride. "The rebuilding of Elchies is well under way, Wife," he said. "I've instructed my surveyor to consult you on matters of décor and furnishings. There'll be plenty to occupy you." He smiled, held her shoulders in both hands and bent to kiss her on the top of her head.

Mary dabbed her eyes with her handkerchief and stood up. "Go safely, Husband," she said. He drew her into his arms and they embraced. Now he must drag himself away from his family once again. He strode out of the room to prepare for more battles.

It was summer before James was able to return. He went with his surveyor to Elchies, to take a look at the progress of the building work. James was impressed with his new house as they approached. It was finished, and a great improvement on the old one. The outbuildings were still in progress; builders and joiners were sawing timber and knocking it together with dowels to form the framework for the stables, paviors were laying cobbles in the yard, cartloads of materials were arriving to replenish the dwindling supplies. The two men picked their way through the mud and went inside the house. People were hanging curtains at the windows, and some of the walls were decorated with patterned wallpaper.

"We'll be wanting to move into the house, Alain," James said. "General Monck proposes to put an English garrison in Balachastell."

"The work inside will be finished within the week, Laird," said Alain. "I've decorated it and furnished it according to your Lady wife's wishes."

"Some of the furnishings we can bring with us," said James. "We don't want to leave them to be ruined by English soldiers."

"'Twas a sad day the King was murthered, sir. None of us relishes being governed by a dictator. The Lord Protector, he calls hissell." Alain made disapproving noises into his beard.

"There was hope that the King's son would take his place," said James. "I sent a regiment of Grants to support him at the battle of Worcester, after his coronation, to no avail."

"Cromwell defeated them, Sir, didn't he? I heard that the young King went into hiding to save hissell."

"Let's hope that he'll be able to return in due course," said James. "I do believe the Cavaliers will beat the Roundheads. 'Tis only a matter of time."

27

Chapter 5 1655
Rumours

In his homestead in the glen, John Grant stood with his back to the parlour fire, enjoying the prospect of a civilised meal with his wife and son. He was tired of battlefields and living rough. He had survived with his brothers and most of Clan Ciaran through the blood bath that followed the taking of Edinburgh by Argyll and his Covenanters. The English troops under General Monck were now in control in Scotland. John hoped for a period of comparative peace.

Annie stood at the table where she dished up beef stew. The aroma reached into John's stomach. She handed a dish to Jamie, who took it and went to sit at the table.

"Will you be going into battle again soon, Faether?"

"Nay, son. I'll be staying here awhile. I'll be taking thee to round up the cattle. You can ride well, thy mother tells me. We've much work to do on our lands and I'll need thy help." It was time he got to know his young son and to teach him how to be a man in these uncertain times.

"Will you teach me how to fight, so that I can join you in battle?"

Annie glanced at John. "Hold thy tongue now, laddie. Thy faether dinna want to think of battle. He's had enough o' that, God knows." She sat down at the table and indicated to John to do the same. They started eating before she said, "That new stable boy, Duggan. I dinna trust him, John. He canna look me in the eye."

"He does his work, does he no'?" asked John.

Annie nodded. "Dinna have his heart in it, though. Finishes as soon as starts, and cuts corners. I've scolded him a couple of times, and made him do it properly."

"I'll keep an eye on him now I'm back. 'Tis hard finding gude labourers. All the men have been fighting. Some hav'na come home and their sons have no training."

The next day John took Jamie out to take stock of his herd of cattle. They began to build up a relationship that was long overdue.

When they returned home in the evening they found Robert waiting for them.

"This is thy Uncle Robert, Jamie," said John as he went to greet his brother.

Jamie followed his father. "Pleased to meet you, Sir," he said.

"What brings thee here, Rob? Come into the house and take a dram wi' me."

Duggan came out of the barn and took the reins of their horses. The brothers and Jamie entered the house. Annie came into the parlour from the kitchen, her hair in wisps round her flushed face. She wiped her hands on her apron.

"Welcome, Robert, we've no seen thee for a while. How's Effie and the bairns?"

Robert smiled and nodded and said that his family were well enough, thank you. He looked at John and said in a low voice, "We need to talk."

"Jamie, goo and fetch some logs in for the fire." John went to pour their drinks. Annie disappeared into the kitchen.

John brought the whisky over and indicated a chair near the fire to Robert. They both sat down. Robert took a sip and said, "There's talk going round the crofters aboot the fire at Elchies, John. Someone saw us with the company frae Inverness."

"But that was years agoo. The Laird has rebuilt Elchies now."

"Remember the stable lad and the maid who were kilt that day? The families are talking aboot revenge."

John was silent for a few moments. He took a sip of the peppery liquid and let it slide slowly down his throat, enjoying the tingling sensation it left in his mouth. He looked up. "We'll have to watch our backs. There's some who think we did wrong to side with the Covenanters instead of following our Laird. Hast spoke with Hamish?"

"Ay. He said the same as thee. Is there a man thou canst trust, that thou could leave to guard Annie and the lad when thou art away?"

John considered. "I've been away so long. Ma most trusted men have perished in battle. The crofters left at home have watched over the cattle, and the stable boy's here every day. But Annie says he canna be trusted."

Robert got up to go. John said to him, "It'll be fine. You ay were a worrier, Rob."

They passed the kitchen door and Robert called goodbye to Annie. She called back, and the brothers went out into the yard.

31

John asked, lowering his voice. "Dost know who 'twas who saw us at Elchies that day, Rob?"

"Nay, I've been trying to find oot, but mouths are tight shut."

Duggan appeared from the stable, leading Robert's horse. Robert mounted, and gave John a wave before he trotted out of the yard and down the road. Duggan took a sideways look at John, who said, "That'll be all for theday thank you, Duggan." The young man nodded and slouched away, dragging his feet on the cobbled yard.

≈ ≈ ≈

It was quiet down by the river Spey, blissfully quiet. There were hints that the summer was drawing to a close. The sun was low and casting long shadows. Gnats danced over the surface of the water and the yellowing leaves of the silver birch rustled in a light breeze. James sat on the bank and watched the brown, eddying river flow steadily past him. It seemed to be the only reliable thing in his life. He gently twitched his fishing rod, tempting his quarry with the bait on his hook. His gillie, MacDuff, scouted the bank for better positions, and kept an eye open for intruders. There were English soldiers everywhere.

During the last eight years James had little time to look after his estates. He trusted his grieve, Murdoch, to hold things together, but now there was a period of comparative peace to turn his attention to home affairs, and enjoy a few leisure activities. He was still struggling with the huge debts left by his father, and there were homesteads and crofts without their menfolk. It would take time to support the bereaved.

MacDuff came trudging along the bank towards him, his bonnet at a jaunty angle, and his cape swinging. There was pleasure on his weathered face as he approached. He had missed these days away with his master. "Methinks you're in the best place, Sir. Have you had any luck?"

"Nay, but I'm content to sit here awhile," James said with a smile. MacDuff sat down beside him.

"'Tis gude to see you installed at Elchies again, Maister. I'll warrant your Lady's happier living in comfort."

"You're right there, MacDuff, and it's a better place to raise our son."

"There's talk among the crofters, Sir that the Clan Ciaran brothers were with the bunch that looted and burnt Elchies."

James took time to absorb this information. He watched the end of his line where it entered the water.

"How do you know that? Did someone see them?"

"That I dinna ken, Sir. 'Tis what I've heard."

They both stared at the river running smoothly down the valley. Little bubbles popped on the surface. Fallen leaves and twigs were carried along. The line gave a jerk. James was distracted from his thoughts. He reeled in his line and MacDuff stood ready with the keep net. They successfully bagged a fine trout, and left it hanging in the water. It would be a good thing if he could catch another.

Later, James paced up and down in his hall at Elchies, waiting for Murdoch to arrive. He looked after his subjects well. He was their leader and defender. He constantly took up their cause when they were wronged by neighbouring clans, and, if they were the aggressors, arranged for compensation to prevent the spread of blood feuds. He arranged for the sending and protection of their droves of cattle to the market towns in the lowlands. And in times of scarcity he imported seed corn and food for the relief of his people. He did more than many Highland chiefs to support his clan and hold them together. Why, then had they turned against him? The Clan Ciaran had always been rebellious. They were now on the opposing side of the battle to save Scotland. He could not continue to support them as Clan members if they were his enemies.

A knock on the door announced the arrival of his grieve. James indicated a seat, and sat down himself.

"My gillie tells me there's talk among the crofters. They're saying that Clan Ciaran were with the company who destroyed Elchies. Can you find any proof in these rumours?"

"As it happens, Laird, I have just come frae a meeting with a young man who reported seeing the raiders as they left the buildings burning. He's unco bitter, Sir. Says that the lassie he was courting was kilt in the fire. He wants revenge, Sir."

"And can he swear that it was the Clan Ciaran brothers who were there?"

"Indeed, Sir. He's working for one of them as a stable boy. He's sure 'twas them. He's heard them talking."

"Summon the brothers, together with this stable lad. I'll think of a just punishment that will revenge both the lad and myself, for the loss of Elchies." Then he added, "Nay, summon *all* the leaders of Clan Grant to a meeting with Clan Ciaran and the stable lad. They should all hear what is said."

"Ay, Sir. Will next week be suitable?"

"Yes, Murdoch. Now go. I have work to do."

Murdoch left the room, and James resumed his pacing. His anger raged within his breast, pulsing in his ears and sticking in his throat.

Chapter 6
Who are the Traitors?

In the glen, John's corn was all gathered and threshed. It had been a productive year, and John and Jamie stood watching the last load being delivered into the great corn store at their homestead.

"That'll be bread for us and the crofters for the next year, laddie, and seed for next year's sowing."

"We've yet to shift the straw into the barn, Faether."

"Ay. 'Twill be the next task when it's dry. Let's hope the weather holds." John went to talk to Fraser who had unhitched the cart and was about to lead the horse away.

"Fraser, will thy wife be available to come and help Annie in the house? Her time's nigh and she'll need a midwife."

"That should be fine, Sir. Morag will be right glad to bring another child of yours into the world." Fraser tipped his bonnet and led the carthorse away. John and Jamie pulled the cart into the barn and shut the doors. They went into the house to find Annie sitting by the fire sewing baby clothes. She looked up and smiled to see her two men so comfortable together. John went and kissed his wife, while Jamie put another log on the fire.

"The Laird's summoned all the clan and cadet leaders to a meeting at Elchies, Annie. We'll be away over there themorrow. I've arranged for Fraser's wife Morag to attend thee. 'Tis time thou hadst some help round here and thou wilt need her at the birthing."

Annie nodded. 'Twill no' be long now. What's the purpose of this meeting, John?"

"I dinna ken. There might be some news of the new king." John sat down. "How's Isabel managing in the kitchen withoot thy help? She's no' such a cook as thee!"

"She's fine. We won't starve! Thank gudeness Jamie's feeding the beasts."

"He's shaping up well. We'll make a farmer oot of him yet."

≈ ≈ ≈

Next day, the hall at Elchies resounded with the voices of Grant leaders, discussing among themselves the reason for this meeting. Some of them had heard rumours that a cadet branch had fallen out of favour with their Laird, but which one? And what was that crofter doing here? The one standing by Murdoch.

James Grant stood before them and raised his hand for silence.

"There are traitors among us," he said. "As you all know, the house here at Elchies was ravaged while I was away supporting the Royalists. It has come to light that members of the Clan Ciaran were among the perpetrators. Stand forward, John Grant, and the brothers of Clan Ciaran."

John and his brothers moved away from the company around them.

"And stand forward the man Duggan." Duggan looked overwhelmed in the presence of these formidable leaders. He shuffled forward with the help of Murdoch's hand on his shoulder.

"Duggan," said James, "Did you see who fired my house?"

Duggan looked grim and straightened himself. "Ay, Sir, with ma Lorna inside. She was burnt to death."

"Can you see any of these men here in the hall?"

"Ay, Sir! Those are they! Murtherers!" He pointed to John and his brothers.

James addressed the brothers. "Are you the traitors who destroyed my home here when I was away fighting for the King?"

John stepped forward, his eyes blazing. He raised his fist.

"As you did sign the Covenant, so did we. It was you who changed sides, Laird. Who is the traitor?"

A great roar rose up from the company gathered there. It was unknown for anyone to challenge their Laird.

"Grants stay together, and I am Laird. Follow me with the Royalists or lose your inheritance and be gone from Grant land!" shouted James.

There was a shocked silence.

"Jesus be King. There is no King but Jesus!" cried the unrepentant John. He turned and left the hall with his brothers.

The leaders of Clan Ciaran mounted their horses in the stable yard.

John said, "We must talk. But not here."

"Ay, ay," murmured the others.

They rode away together in grim silence. They came to a grassy hollow some distance from Elchies. John reined in his horse and turned to face his followers.

"The Laird has no right to banish us," he said. "We're under English rule now. I suggest we go to speak with Captain Hill at Ballachastell. What d'ye think?"

The majority of the company nodded and said, "Ay."

Hamish said, "'Tis hard living among enemies. Some of ma crofters are loyal to the Laird, and I've no control over them. I'd thought of leaving anyway."

"I've heard there's a better life to be had over the ocean," said another.

"We must not give in," John asserted. "Remember the Grant cry: *Stand fast.*"

"I'll come with thee to Captain Hill," said Robert. "Ye others must do as ye think is right."

They all murmured assent, grasped each other's left arms in friendship, and rode away to their homesteads. Robert stayed with John. They rode on together.

"Dost really believe the Laird will listen to Captain Hill, *if* he agrees to intervene?"

John smiled. "'Tis worth a try, brother. I canna leave now. Annie will give birth soon. I'll no' budge until I'm forced." John spat on the ground. "Come away, Rob."

They agreed to call on Captain Hill as soon as possible. In the meantime, John would not tell Annie the bad news.

Chapter 7
Plea for Mercy

Early in the morning a few days later, John was suddenly wide awake. Today the future of his little family lay in the balance.

Annie stirred and clutched his arm. "John, I think ma time's come."

John sat up and looked at her in the dim light. "Stay there, love. I'll send Jamie for Morag." He got out of bed and groped for his trews, pulled them on and hastened to Jamie's chamber. He shook the lad awake.

"Come, Son. Thy mother's in labour. Goo and fetch Morag, quick as thou canst."

Jamie quickly dressed and ran out of the house to get his horse. John finished dressing and went downstairs. He found Isabel in the kitchen preparing crowdies for their breakfast.

"I'll do that, Isabel. Mistress Annie's time's come. You goo up and sit with her while Jamie brings Morag. I have to goo away when ma brother gets here. I'll be back as soon as I can, but might take all day."

Isabel curtseyed and went to get a drink for Annie before disappearing upstairs.

John stood in the kitchen absently stirring the contents of the pan over the fire. A sound startled him. He turned and saw Robert at the door. He went to show him into the parlour.

"Gude day Robert. Come in. The babe will be born soon. Jamie's gone to fetch the woman. I canna leave until they get here." The smell of burning came from the kitchen. "Dammit the crowdie's ruined!" He ran to save the pan, but the contents were a black and brown bubbling mess. He took it off the heat and plunged it into a pale of water nearby.

The sound of horses' hooves in the yard announced the arrival of Jamie and Morag. John went out to meet them. Jamie dismounted and lifted Morag down.

"We've urgent business to do this morning," John said. "Morag, the mistress is in her chamber. Isabel will do whatever you say. Jamie, I'm leaving thee in charge. Duggan will no' be coming again. If he does, send him away. I'll no' have him round this place. So there'll be some mucking oot to do, Son. Take care of thy mother. I'll be back as soon as I can. We're away to Balachastell."

By this time Morag had gone into the house. Jamie stood holding his horse's reins. He looked bewildered. "Ay, Faether. We'll see you later, then." He led his horse to its stable. Robert mounted and waited for John to saddle up. John fumbled with the straps, surprised that his hands were shaking. He tightened the girth with a determined tug, and mounted. It felt better sitting astride his sturdy beast. He gave Jamie a wave and the brothers rode away to an unknown future. This was harder than going into battle.

It was the season of wild storms and rainbows. The wind and rain lashed into their faces as they rode along the valley, soaking their plaids and bonnets. As John and Robert approached the entrance to Ballachastell, a guard came out of the gatehouse, wearing a heavy cape. He signalled to them to dismount.

"Who are ye, and what is your business?" he challenged.

"We are of the Clan Grant, come to seek the advice of Captain Hill," said John in the strongest voice he could produce.

"Charlie, take these men to Captain Hill," called the guard.

Charlie emerged from the gatehouse, buttoning his heavy buff coat against the Scottish weather. He beckoned to the brothers and walked up the long drive. They followed, leading their horses until they reached the stable yard. A group of English soldiers lounged around, armed with swords and all dressed in the same coats. One of them came and took the horses. John and Robert submitted themselves to a thorough search for weapons, and were relieved of their dirks. John felt a lump come to his throat. Charlie handed them both over to another guard standing at the door of the castle.

"Request to speak to Captain Hill," Charlie announced. He turned and went back down the drive.

The guard banged on the great oak door which was opened by another soldier.

"Request to speak to Captain Hill," repeated the guard.

The brothers were led through a labyrinth of passages and stairs, lit by flickering candles mounted on the walls. Their feet echoed on the stone floors. They arrived at a door. Their attendant knocked and another soldier appeared. A few words were exchanged and the soldier went back into the room, closing the door behind him. John and Robert waited with their attendant, feeling like prisoners about to be led into court.

At last the door opened again and the brothers were shown into a warmer room, sparsely furnished, with a fire blazing in the hearth. They found themselves standing before a large table, behind which sat a heavily bearded, bulky man of uncertain age. His beady black eyes peered at them under bushy eyebrows. A voice issued from somewhere among the hairs on his face.

"Identify yourselves."

John cleared his throat and spoke. "I'm John Grant, and this is ma brother Robert." Before he could say anything else, the Captain interrupted.

"You're related to the Laird Grant, who is a Royalist."

"Ay, we're of the Clan Grant, but are no' Royalists," John said, raising his voice. "We're frae the cadet branch, Clan Ciaran. When our Laird defected to the Royalist side we remained loyal to the Covenanters, as we had sworn."

"So, what d'you want with me, John Grant?" snapped the Captain.

"Our Laird has threatened to banish us frae our lands and livelihoods if we dinna follow him with the Royalists. Ma wife is with child. We canna move oot." John was feeling angry again. He clasped his hands behind his back to stop them shaking.

Captain Hill studied the brothers. "Hm," he said. "What d'you want me to do about it?"

Robert shifted his weight onto the other foot, and looked at John. John nodded, and Robert coughed before he spoke. "If you consider we've been unfairly treated, Sir, we'd be obliged if you would intercede for us, and persuade our Laird to withdraw his orders, Sir."

The Captain sighed and tilted himself back on his chair. He stared at the brothers again for a few minutes, which increased their discomfort.

"I would not normally interfere in a clan's affairs, but I believe you have a right to choose which side to support. I'll make some enquiries and speak with your Laird. You'll be sent for in due course." He rose from his seat behind the table and came round to face the brothers. John was taken aback at his great stature. Hill continued, "In the meantime I wish you well, John, for the birth of your child." He offered his right hand to John, who reacted by reaching for his absent dirk. In the moment he realised that this was the English way, and reached forward to grasp the Captain's cold hand with both of his. Robert did the same.

"Thank you, Sir," they both said in unison.

Captain Hill turned away and went towards the fire, rubbing his hands together.   John and Robert were shown out.

The rain had stopped. A flurry of little golden leaves surrounded the two riders and danced across their path to rest in the ditch with their fellows. Rose-hips and haws shone red as jewels in the hedgerows. The sombre crags held the brothers in a protective embrace.

"I canna think what it would be like to leave this place," said Robert. "How can the Laird tear us up frae our roots?"

John's thoughts were elsewhere. "It might yet no' come to that, brother. Come, make haste. I'm anxious to get back to Annie." He nudged his horse into a trot and Robert followed.

All was quiet as they approached John's homestead.

"Wilt come in for a dram, Rob?

"Ay, maybe the bairn's arrived." They dismounted and Jamie appeared in the doorway, smiling.

"'Tis a son for thee, Faether. He's so tiny. I never thought there could be anything so bonny." He took their horses, and the men went indoors. John strode up the stairs leaving Robert warming himself by the fire. The chamber door was slightly open.

Annie lay in the bed, her face flushed, her eyes sparkling. "Come and welcome thy wee son, John." He went over to her and kissed her cheek. Then he pulled back the sheet which covered the bundle in her arms. A small head of black hair was revealed. Tiny hands curled into fists under a pink face, eyes and mouth tightly shut. John felt tears coming into his eyes.

He looked at Annie. "This day be a blessed one, thanks be."

"He's a fine wee laddie, surely. How was thy day, John?"

"I believe we've made progress. I'll explain later. Rob's here. Shall I send him up? Then we'll drink a dram to gude fortune."

"Ay, I'll be pleased to see Robert," she said.

Chapter 8
Winter

James rode home to Elchies after a day's hunting with his friends. Alex MacPherson was coming with him. Their friendship had not been spoilt by James joining the Royalists.

"I've heard that Clan Ciaran is out of favour, James," said Alex.

"Ay, they've gone too far this time. I cannot continue to support them on my land. I've disinherited them."

"'Tis a drastic step to take. This is their home. They know no other life. Did you know that John's wife has recently birthed a second child? You cannot turn them out of their homes with winter approaching, surely?"

James rode on, deep in thought. After a while, he said, "They destroyed my house at Elchies, Alex. How could they do that?"

"'Twas in revenge for you going against the Covenanters, James. They are loyal and true men at heart, but fired up with anger. To repay revenge with more will only fuel the fire, you know that."

"Ay, ay," James replied irritably. He knew he had been harsh, acting in anger as Clan Ciaran had done. There was silence between the two men as they reached Elchies and dismounted. They handed the horses to the stable lad and went indoors.

"'Twill be grand to get a whisky doon me," said James. "Will you stay for dinner, Alex? Mary will welcome your company, and you can meet our new son, Ludovick"

"I'll be glad to stay, James," said Alex.

They unbuckled their belts and discarded their heavy plaids, giving them to Dougal, who was hovering nearby. It would be warmer in their living quarters. The new Elchies had been built with glass in the windows and the fire would be blazing.

≈ ≈ ≈

The first snow fell in the night and Jamie was out in the yard at the homestead, clearing it away. If it froze on the ground it would be treacherous. John was in the parlour giving Annie a last kiss before going out.

"We'll be bringing the cattle doon to the fields theday, love. 'Twill take all day," he said.

"Isabel's packed ye a bag of food. Ye'll no forget to eat it, mind."

"Jamie will remember," he assured her. He went over to the crib to find baby Thomas examining his fingers and gurgling.

Jamie came in. "Faether, there's a soldier oot in the yard. Wants a word with thee."

This must be news from Captain Hill. John went outside.

"John Grant?" the soldier enquired.

"Ay, 'tis I." replied John.

"Captain Hill has summoned you and your brother Robert. He wants to see you tomorrow morning."

John looked up at the sky, which was grey and cold. "We'll be there if we can. But if more snow falls our journey might be impossible. How was it coming through the valley theday?"

"'Twas not difficult," the soldier said. "But I'll tell Captain Hill that you might be prevented."

"I'd be obliged," said John. The soldier saluted and turned his horse to retrace his journey back to Ballachastell.

John went into the house. "We have to call on Robert before going up to get the cattle," he said to Jamie. "Let's hope we don't get caught up there with more snow. 'Twill be difficult herding in this weather." Jamie collected their snacks from the kitchen and they went to saddle up their horses.

As they rode to Robert's homestead, Jamie said, "What did the soldier want, Faether?"

John considered for a moment. "Robert and I have business with Captain Hill at Ballachastell, son. Clan Ciaran's in trouble with our Laird, and we're hoping Captain Hill can speak for us. I dinna wish to worry thy mother. Dinna mention it to her. I'll explain everything when we know the outcome of this meeting."

"Will you have to go into battle again, Faether?"

"Nay, 'tis nothing like that. Dinna fash thysel'. Come, we've much to do theday." John urged his horse on, and Jamie followed.

The snow was deeper on the hills, and the icy wind was picking up. The cattle were huddled in groups under the scrubby trees, where the snow had left bare patches. They scratched at the ground, finding what little they could to eat.

It was hard going, riding through the drifts, not knowing how far the ground was underneath, and where the rocky outcrops were waiting to make the horses stumble. John felt proud of his young son as he faced the elements bravely.

It was getting dark by the time they had rounded up all the cattle and started to herd them down the hill. Little white flakes drifted from a heavily laden sky, brushing their faces and settling on their shoulders. They would not be going to see Captain Hill tomorrow, or for a few weeks, if John's instincts were right. As they drew nearer to the lights of the homestead where the snow lay thinner, the cattle started to run, their hooves throwing up muddy white clods behind them. At last they were all safely enclosed in the field.

John and his son rode into the yard and left their horses to munch a welcome bag of hay, while they went to fetch the cart. They loaded it up with hay from the barn, hitched up to the carthorse and took it to the hungry cattle. The flakes were thicker now, and the two were grateful to shake them off their plaids and bonnets and go indoors to a warm parlour with food on the table. It was only then that John realised they had not eaten the food they had taken with them.

The snow lay thick until after Christmas, preventing all travel and restricting farming activities. The beasts had to be fed and the cows milked. There were enough stores of salted beef and grain; the family did not starve. John was glad to have the time to play with his growing son. They went out into the yard and John taught Jamie how to defend himself with his dirk, and how to use a sword in battle. They had archery competitions, and John found that Jamie had a natural eye for the target. John unearthed his pipes and played while Annie and

Jamie, and sometimes Isabel, danced reels and jigs, to the delight of the baby. They brought the backgammon board out of the cupboard and spent long evenings challenging each other. John taught Jamie how to whittle wood and they made a whistle and a rattle for Thomas, and a catapult, which Jamie took out and practised aiming at the pigeons as they sheltered in the barn. They regularly had pigeon pie for dinner.

There was no way their Laird could enforce their banishment as long as the snow lasted. John was glad of this respite. But he was afraid Captain Hill would forget his promise after all this time.

Chapter 9   1657
Conference

James Grant rode towards Ballachastell, picking his way through the remnants of snow drifts with his two attendants. It was January and they knew that this lull in the wintry weather was only temporary. They were in the widening valley, having followed the river from Elchies where it was warmer. On the surrounding hills the snow still lay thick. Birds and animals came down to seek shelter and food by the flowing water and the swampy ground. Shrieking his alarm, a blackbird flew up in front of James' horse, which shied nervously. Soon they reached a track more frequently used and the going was easier. This was James' territory, his home ground, and he resented the invasion of the English garrison. He wondered why he had been summoned to meet Captain Hill, and felt apprehensive about entering his castle while it was occupied by strangers.

As they came into the stable yard, the guard who had accompanied them from the gatehouse saluted and left James and his servants in the charge of the next guard. James dismounted and ordered his men to remain with the horses. He allowed himself to be relieved of his sword and dirk, and was shown through the back entrance. He was led along familiar passageways to the door of the living room, which Mary had made so comfortable. The guard knocked and James was shown into the bare bones of the room he knew so well. He looked round and saw Alex MacPherson standing with two of the Clan Ciaran brothers. He realised that he would soon be under pressure to withdraw his judgement on his wayward subjects.

Captain Hill rose from his chair behind the table and came to meet James. He stood as tall as James, but more bulky in stature. He held out his right hand.

"Sir, thank you for coming."

James hesitated before shaking the Captain's outstretched hand. To him, this was a strange way of greeting.

"Take your seats, gentlemen." Captain Hill indicated four chairs, which had been positioned round the table, facing his own. He waited until his visitors were seated before sitting himself. A soldier hovered in the background. James felt awkward; he would rather argue his case standing.

Captain Hill addressed him, "Grant," he said, "these two men from Clan Ciaran are your kin, I believe."

James nodded.

"They've come to me hoping that I would intercede for them." He looked at John and Robert.

They both said, "Ay, Sir."

Captain Hill leaned forward on his forearms towards James. "They tell me that you've dispossessed them because they refuse to follow you with the Royalists."

James affirmed this with another nod. He felt reprimanded, as a child by his father.

"And yet they have, in the past, been loyal subjects to you in your clan."

James nodded again. "Ay," he said.

"Do they not have a right to choose their religion? They are loyal to the Scottish Kirk, as they have always been. They see you as having joined the Catholic Royalists."

James was reluctant to start a confrontation with a Puritan on the subject of religion. This was no business of the Captain's, who did not understand the ways of Highland Clans. But here James was on English territory, however temporary. He was tongue-tied.

Alex MacPherson spoke. "Captain Hill, I believe John and Robert Grant would like to say something to their Laird."

Hill nodded and indicated to the brothers to speak. He sat back in his chair to watch the proceedings.

John stirred, and looked his Laird in the eye. "Laird, we of Clan Ciaran will follow you anywhere in battle, but not against Covenanters. We came with you to defend Grant land from the Camerons, and would do so again if need be. But we are Scots, of the Scottish Kirk, and will remain so." He stood up, and supported himself on the table, craning towards his Laird. His voice rose. "To banish us frae our homes and livelihoods is cruel. We have families to care for. How would we survive in this harsh weather?" He paused before sitting down heavily.

James cleared his throat. "How can I fight against my own clan in battle? I believe that Scotland needs a king, and that the Royalists are not yet crushed." He looked at Captain Hill. "Pardon me, Sir."

Hill pushed his chair back and crossed his legs. "It seems to me that you are both loyal to Scotland, whatever your beliefs."

James said, "Of course. But I am also loyal to the Royal Family. King Charles was a Stuart, of Scottish stock, as is his son. Both England and Scotland need a king as well as a parliament."

"But you swore an oath!" shouted John. "As we did. Whoever rules Scotland should abide by the Covenant."

James stood up. "You had no right to destroy my property, Covenant or no. If you were true Grants you would have been protecting it."

"Gentlemen, please," drawled Captain Hill without moving. "I didn't bring you all here to have a family squabble. The question is, Laird Grant, can you really bring yourself to throw your subjects out of their homesteads into the snow, wives, children and all?"

MacPherson spoke again. "I propose, Grant, that you withdraw your punishment on these your subjects. They act in all honesty. The punishment is harsh. Besides, we are not at war now, but under English rule. We should listen to Captain Hill."

James thumped the table. He was not going to be told what he should do. "I am Laird. My clans should follow me in all things. How am I to rely on them if they are disloyal?" He stood up and strode over to MacPherson. "They destroyed my house at Elchies. They killed my servants. For these things they must be punished, otherwise I will have no authority over any of my people."

MacPherson remained calm. "Is there not another way to punish them, James? You are angry about their actions which they carried out in anger because they felt you had betrayed them. An eye for an eye achieves nothing but resentment."

"The Grants of Clan Ciaran have always been rebellious," said James, pacing the floor. "They have

56

often gone their own way and got themselves into trouble with other clans." He approached John and Robert and spoke directly to them. "There have been many times when I've had to come between you and your enemies before a battle between clans is sparked off in order to resolve your differences peacefully. At least if you were no longer part of Clan Grant, you would no longer be a thorn in my side."

Robert scraped his chair back as he stood to face James. "We'll aye be Grants, no matter where we go, Laird. That's our inheritance, and we're proud of it. Perhaps it is better that we leave your lands, as you feel so strongly against us. Life is hard enough in these Highlands wi'oot being oot of favour with our Laird."

James observed his two subjects. He saw a grim determination behind their eyes, and a pride that he had often seen in Grant faces. They were strong men and brave to stand up to their Laird in this manner. He needed strong men behind him when fighting his enemies among other clans. He went and sat down, and looked at his restless hands. After a few minutes, he said, "Ay, ay. I will withdraw." He sighed and looked across at the brothers. Their faces lit up.

Captain Hill sat forward and said, "Well done, well done. I believe this is right. I propose that my clerk draws up an agreement for you to sign, Grant, vowing that Clan Ciaran will never be disinherited from Clan Grant." He beckoned his soldier who approached the table and bent his head towards the Captain. They conferred and the soldier left the room.

Captain Hill stood up and went round to the four men. They stood and shook his hand in turn. "The whisky is on its way, gentlemen. I believe we should drink to this agreement while it is being prepared."

The soldier returned, carrying a tray with glasses and a bottle of James' best whisky. James wondered how much was left in his cellar.

"Let bygones be bygones," proposed Captain Hill as he raised his glass.

"Ay", "Ay", "Ay", declared MacPherson, John and Robert and, finally, James. He was relieved that his ordeal was over, and curiously happy that his quarrel with Clan Ciaran was dispelled, if not resolved. He realised that he had a soft spot for these rebels in his family. They all raised their glasses and grasped their left arms in friendship, the Grant way.

There was a knock on the door and the clerk entered with two copies of the document and quill and ink. Captain Hill read it carefully and handed it to James. James read it, showed it to his friend, Alex, and signed both copies. Alex signed them as a witness, and slapped James on the shoulder. "Good man," he said.

Captain Hill handed a copy of the signed agreement to John, and the other to James.

Chapter 10
Snow

John and Robert raced each other down the glen, shouting with laughter as their horses carried them home. When they arrived at John's homestead, Robert reined in and said, "I'll goo straight home. Effie will be waiting."

"Wilt spread the word to the Clan, Rob? We'll go hunting and have a feast to celebrate."

"As long as this weather holds," said Robert, looking at the grey sky. Winter was only just beginning.

The brothers punched the air in triumph as they said farewell. John led his horse into its stall, where Jamie was filling the hay bags.

"Come indoors, Son. I've news to tell thee," said John.

The family sat round the fire. Thomas in his crib had just woken and was playing with his rattle and blowing bubbles.

John went and poured whisky for each. He came to sit down again, raised his glass and said, "*Stand fast.*"

Jamie and Annie raised their glasses and sat forward in their chairs, looking at John in anticipation.

John took a sip and began. He told them of his escapade with the Covenanters and the burning of Elchies. He told them how, years later, when their Laird returned from battle, word had got out that some of Clan Ciaran were among the marauders, and how their Laird had called a meeting of all Grant leaders. He recalled how Duggan said he had been a witness, and pointed at John as the culprit.

"He lost his sweetheart in the fire, and for that I am right sorry," said John. He paused, seeing in his mind's eye the barbarous treatment the maid received from his fellow raiders before they slit her throat.

Then he told them of the Laird's judgement, that Clan Ciaran was to forfeit their inheritance and be gone from Grant land. At this Annie and Jamie gasped. Annie said, "Och, no," and put her hand to her face.

"Dinna fash thysel' Annie, love. Robert and I sought the help of Captain Hill at Ballachastell. Theday, our Laird was persuaded to withdraw his judgement. He signed a document to say that Clan Ciaran would never be banished from Grant land. All is well, we can stay!" He brought out the document from his pocket and waved it in front of them. Then he drained his glass and got up from his chair, going over to embrace Annie, who was laughing and crying at the same time.

Jamie leaned his elbows on his knees and sat contemplating all that he had heard.

He looked up and said, "You kept that frae us a long time, Faether."

"I didna want to worry thee, Son, and it's all turned oot right." John went to sit beside Jamie again.

Jamie sat up. "Duggan'll no' be pleased. He craved revenge."

Snow descended on the Highlands once again. It was impossible to consider hunting deer until the warmer April sunshine revealed a green and luscious countryside to replace the stark grey and white of winter. As soon as the members of Clan Ciaran could reach each other's homesteads, they spread the word, and one day they rose at dawn as planned. They crept out armed with dirks and longbows, and loaded quivers, to meet at the top of the glen. Jamie accompanied his father. This was his first hunting expedition. He had practised his archery all through the winter and could now look forward to proving his skill.

The hunting party clambered up the boggy slope by the crystal spring water, which tumbled down towards the valley. There were pockets of snow clinging in places. The men kept close to the low cover afforded by hawthorn bushes, which grew in the path of the water. There were those among the company who knew the likely places to find their quarry at this time of the year. The going became steeper. Rocks appeared above the grassy slopes. When they reached the brow of the hill the signal came to spread out and lie low. Peering over the top, John saw what they must all be looking at: four does with their stag, wandering quietly along a lower slope, at the edge of a wood, grazing the fresh new turf, which had been inaccessible for months. There was more cover down there. The hunters must skirt round the herd, up-wind, to be closer.

Scrambling and slithering, they descended to within reach of the deer without attracting their attention. The men spread out again, and, finding what cover they could, they each prepared to shoot. A twig snapped. The stag raised his head and looked in the direction of the hunters. He would be off in a trice. The twang of a bowstring sent an arrow hissing to its target. The deer sprang into action and headed away. But one of the does was injured, and shook her head. An arrow had pierced her shoulder. John took aim, fired his arrow, and the doe went down. Other arrows fell short. John looked at Jamie, who was staring in disbelief.

"I hit it, Faether!" He leapt up and bounded down the hillside to collect his prize, shouting in triumph.

The hunters stood around the young animal. Jamie bent down and stroked her smooth coat. He removed the arrow and backed away. John remembered his first kill and knew that the lad was almost regretting the death of such a beautiful beast.

"Come, Son. We have to find a branch to carry her home."

The seasoned hunters were slapping Jamie on the back in congratulation.

Angus said, "Some of us will stay and slay another. The day's no' over yet."

"We'll carry this to thy homestead," said John.

Five men made their way to Angus's place, taking it in turns to carry the deer, strung from a pole by its feet. They hung it in Angus's courtyard to allow the blood to drain out before roasting. The other party was not far behind with another doe. They all took a glass of whisky to toast the future of Clan Ciaran, before going home to their families.

Angus had the best facilities for feasting. A few days later the men gathered there to set up the spits and prepare the carcasses, working in two teams. Jamie joined in, helping to strip the skin off the beast carefully and set it aside for curing. They slit the belly open and removed the slithery innards, tipping them into a pail. John pointed out the heart, liver and kidneys, all of which would be used by the women in stews. Jamie did not appear to be upset by this gory process.

They had almost finished, except for some clearing up and preparing the fires. It was going to get dark soon. John called to his son.

"Jamie, I want thee to goo home now and feed the beasts before thy mother starts doing it by hersel'."

"Ay, Faether. I'll goo now. Will you be following soon?"

"Ay, I'll just finish this. I'll be on ma way." John watched his son galloping down the glen. His chest swelled with pride, and a little tear crept out of the corner of his eye. He wiped it away and continued building the fire under the spit.

Later, John cantered home in the twilight with a smile on his face, his mind reflecting on the day. There would be feasting and music, dancing and laughter tomorrow. Clan Ciaran had been saved.

He approached the homestead but the lights were not lit. There was not enough wind to have blown the candle in the lantern out. He urged his horse into a gallop. As he approached he heard screams coming from the yard. Terrible screams. A dark shadow spilled out of the entrance and disappeared round the corner of the barn.

John jerked his horse's head sideways to follow the shadow. The screams persisted. It was too dark to see who was there. He leapt off his horse and followed the route the intruder might take to make a getaway. A sound alerted him. He lunged towards it, and found a foot. He took hold of it with both hands and pulled. The shoe came off. He heard the owner scramble up the bank and gave up the chase.

Annie was in distress.

John ran back round the side of the barn and stumbled into the yard. It was nearly dark, but he could see a group of figures. Annie's white shawl revealed her crouching over someone lying on the ground. Her screams had turned to sobs. John threw the shoe down and ran over to Annie.

"John, John! Our son is dead!"

"Jamie?" John bent over the recumbent form. He put his hand to the pulse in Jamie's neck. It was warm and sticky. John cradled his son's shoulders and lifted him to kiss his face.

"Jamie, ma son," he sobbed.

Jamie's head moved slightly. John heard a faint whisper.

"Faether, are Mother and Thomas safe?"

Oh, God! John thought, *He's going…* "Safe and sound, Son. Ye did well." Jamie's head flopped and he relaxed into his father's arms.

Chapter 11
Revenge

"Mama, Mama!" Little Thomas aroused them from their grieving. Annie held the child to her and kissed the top of his head. She clambered to her feet, stiff after crouching so long. She picked up her only son and carried him into the house, calling, "Isabel!"

John laid Jamie's head down gently, sat back on his heels and heaved a deep shuddering breath. The moon had risen and cast a cold silver light on the scene. John could see Jamie now. Blood seeped out of his stomach just below the ribs, soaking his plaid. His bloody dirk lay by his right hand. Jamie had fought back bravely.

John heard the thud of approaching horse's hooves. He stood and turned to see Robert galloping into the yard.

"John, Ellie was attacked. Duggan was after revenge. He came this way…" Robert's voice trailed off as he saw the corpse on the ground.

"'Tis too late, Rob. Jamie's dead. Help me carry him into the house."

Robert dismounted and they lifted the young body and took it upstairs to his chamber. Annie had prepared the bed. They covered Jamie's body and face with a blanket and left a candle flickering on the shelf to ward off evil spirits.

Back in the parlour, Annie sat by the fire, rocking Thomas in her arms. Isabel was lighting the lamps. Her hand was shaking. The men sat down. Robert started to tell his story.

"One o' ma crofters was mending the roof of the barn. He saw Duggan come by, not expecting anyone to be there. He snooped around the cow stalls and stables. Then Ellie came oot of the house and Duggan threatened her with his dirk, swearing vengeance for his dead sweetheart. Ma crofter jumped from the roof and surprised him. Ellie ran indoors and Duggan was chased away. I came home later to find Ellie and the bairns still hiding in the house, dreadfully afeared."

Annie had been listening. Robert's voice seemed to have calmed her.

"I was going to feed the beasts," she said. "Someone grabbed me frae behind and stuck a dirk under ma chin. He said he wanted revenge for his murthered lassie. Thomas was screaming and clinging to ma leg. Isabel came oot of the house, then went in again and shut the door. We didn't hear Jamie coming. He must have seen what was happening and crept in withoot Duggan knowing. Duggan was shouting at the bairn and lashing oot with his foot. Suddenly he let go of me. Jamie had come up behind him. They fought. Duggan was injured. Jamie fell, and we heard thee coming, John. Duggan..." She collapsed into tears again.

John stared into the fire in horror.

The next morning John struggled to bring himself back to practicalities. There were the animals to attend to, the stables to muck out and he must go and find a crofter to help him take the cattle into the hills. The two women went about their work mechanically. Thomas caught the subdued atmosphere and was quiet. Robert had said he would arrange a wake for Jamie. There would be no feasting for John and Annie today.

In the afternoon John climbed the hill at the back of the barn where he had caught Duggan's foot. He examined the place, and found blood on the flattened grass. There was a trail up the slope, as if something had been dragged. John followed, realising that Duggan might still be close by and injured. John reached the top of the first level, where a track ran along the side of the hill, gradually making its way to the second level. He stood and looked around him. There was a trail of blood along the upward slope of the track. He followed it and came to a thicket of thorn bushes. A shoe lay discarded.

John crept into the thicket. There were few paths and he had to crawl as the bushes were low. Rabbits had built a warren there; the ground was uneven with holes and mounds of excavated earth. It was not a sensible place to be in the dark, and John could not imagine Duggan being able to make any progress. He was about to turn round and give up the search when he saw a bare foot, then a leg. A body was lying prone among the bushes. John crept closer. Duggan's hands and face were deeply scratched and it appeared that he had stumbled and fallen forward. John felt his pulse. The body was cold and lifeless. He turned it over with difficulty and found the source of the blood. Duggan had bled to death from a wound in his right armpit. Jamie had fought well.

John dragged the body out of the thicket and slung it over his shoulder. It was heavy, but he was determined to get Duggan back to his family. He trudged over the hills to the huddle of crofters' turf cottages where Fraser and Morag lived. As he approached, two crofters came out and stood watching. John laid the body down in front of them. An old woman appeared from a third cottage. With the aid of a stick, she limped towards the body on the ground.

She looked down at Duggan, and spoke in Gaelic, "He came to nae gude. 'Is Faether foretold it." She looked up at John.

"He kilt ma son before he died," said John. "Seeking revenge only makes things worse."

It was the day of the burial. The horse and cart stood ready in the yard. John and Robbie carried Jamie in his coffin down the narrow stairs and out into the bright sunshine. It was just such a day as this, long ago, John thought, that he and Robert had set off with other Covenanters to ransack the Laird's house at Elchies. That was the beginning of all their troubles.

Music sounded in the distance and soon a procession of mourners appeared along the track. The whole of Clan Ciaran had turned out, carrying lanterns. Jamie in his coffin was waiting on the cart. The wail of pipes and the sombre beat of drums surrounded it as the horse led them towards the Kirk. John lifted Annie onto his horse and sat little Thomas in front of her. He led the horse, walking along with their brothers and sisters, cousins and fathers and mothers. The women moaned with the dirges, the men stony-faced and silent.

John and Robert lifted the coffin into the grave. The men removed their bonnets in respect. The people took handfuls of earth and threw them onto the coffin. Everyone stood close around the grave while the piper played a last lament. Robert turned the cart around and one by one the mourners walked away, leaving John, Annie and little Thomas standing alone. John picked up the toddler and sat him on his hip, putting the other arm round Annie's waist.

"He was a brave boy. We must give thanks for the joy he gave us, and his courage in protecting thee and the bairn," John said.

Annie was sobbing. She nodded. "He would have wanted us to celebrate. His spirit will be with us."

They walked to where the horse was tethered. John helped Annie mount and handed her the child. John led them down the track to the homestead, and they dismounted and climbed onto the cart where Robert had left it. John drove to Angus's homestead, where the feast was being prepared. An aroma of roasting venison met them as they approached. The gathering was subdued, quietly going through the rituals of food preparation. Robbie and Ellie came forward to greet the little family. Others came and said words of comfort. Ale and spirits began to flow liberally, and gradually John and Annie were swept into the warmth of the occasion.

How lucky they were, John thought, to be part of such a family. He raised his tankard. "To Clan Ciaran and the future!" he shouted.

There were cheers and shouts of *"Stand fast!"* and the music started.

Chapter 12 1662
Summons

Five years later James Grant and his family sat round the dining table at Elchies, eating their dinner. The only sounds that could be heard were the blazing of the fire and the clatter of cutlery on china. Twelve-year-old Ludovick, a tall boy for his age, with fair, curly hair, sat opposite his brother, seven-year-old Patrick, who took after his father in looks and temperament. Patrick was a quiet, well-mannered boy, who amused himself and did as he was told. But if his person or belongings were threatened, he defended himself fiercely. He was more accomplished than his older brother in everything he did, even at this early age. Ludovick had been pampered by his mother from the moment he left the womb. She lavished him with affection and answered to his every call for attention. When his brother arrived on the scene, Ludovick's security was threatened, and he treated his baby brother with contempt, sometimes cruelly. There were constant fights in which Patrick was usually the winner. But he was invariably blamed for any consequential damage.

Ludovick was suffering from the bruises he had received in a quarrel with Patrick that morning. Patrick was suffering from the beating his father had given him. James had found Patrick boxing his brother's ears for interfering with the battle scene of his model soldiers.

James' health had been troubling him lately. He was forty years old, but felt older. He looked at his wife, who was eating her dinner with no pleasure. Mary was

71

not well either. The doctor attended them both, and could give them no diagnosis. He treated them each by bleeding, to no avail, and said that there was nothing more he could do. As if that was not enough to worry about, James was talking to his neighbouring friends today. They all confessed the same fears: the leaders who had fought against Charles I, including the original Covenanters, were being sought out by the new King Charles, now that he was on the throne of England. They were being charged with treason. Although James had joined the Royalists subsequently, he had started as a Covenanter. He was unwilling to talk about this with Mary, as she would no doubt react with a fit of the vapours and take to her bed for days. So he kept his worries to himself, and the meal passed in silence.

All plates were cleared, except for Ludovick's, who had eaten only a little of his meal.

"Ludo, dear," said Mary, "Can you not eat your dinner? What ails you?"

Ludovick turned soulful eyes to his mother. "I cannot eat, Mother. My jaw aches where Patrick hit me."

Mary looked at Patrick, then at James.

James said hastily, "He has been punished, Wife. Leave him be." He rang the bell which was standing on the table by his place and Dougal came into the room. "Clear the table, Dougal. Wife, you may retire with the children." James left the table and went to pour himself a dram. He filled his pipe with the new tobacco and lit it. He walked over to a chair by the fire.

He was so tired. His head hurt and his bones ached. If he had been ten years younger he could have risen above all this. He took a long draw on his pipe. An exotic aroma filled the room and carried him to a more comfortable place.

There was a knock on the door and Dougal came in with a letter.

"A messenger brought this, Laird. 'Tis late and he's in strange country. Shall I offer him shelter for thenight?"

James took the letter and nodded. "Ay, give the man a meal, too."

Dougal bowed and left the room.

James broke the seal of the letter and started reading. It was the worst possible news. His heart started thumping. He leaned forward and put his head in his hands.

A week later, the carriage was waiting in the stable yard. It was a damp summer's day.

James was giving his staff, headed by Murdoch, his grieve, some last minute instructions before leaving them in charge of Elchies.

"I am unsure how long we will be gone. Maintain the house and lands as usual, and keep them ready for our return."

"Ay, Laird," said Murdoch.

James nodded and called for his horse. He had told no-one the reason for his journey to Edinburgh. He had written his will in the presence of a lawyer and two witnesses, giving instructions for the care and education of the two boys. His brother, Colonel Patrick Grant, was to take over this task, and also, with other curators, the responsibilities of Laird, until Ludovick became of age. He had bequeathed to his wife, Mary, the use of Elchies as her home for as long as she should live. Ballachastell was in the charge of a small staff, although the place was barely habitable since Captain Hill and his soldiers left.

Mary and the two boys appeared in the doorway, followed by a maid and Dougal, who carried the luggage. The coachman helped them into their seats and ensured that the luggage was strapped on securely. The maid and Dougal were to ride outside. James mounted his horse and proceeded down the drive, followed by the carriage. They had a long journey ahead of them, during which James would be alone with his thoughts.

He had told Mary that he had business to attend to, and that they all needed a change of scene. The boys were looking forward to a new adventure and their first experience of a large town. There had been fewer arguments between them lately. Mary did not like adventures. She preferred to stay in the familiarity and comfort of her own home, but James ignored her protestations. He needed all his family close to him. He knew there was a possibility that he would never see his home again. He had spent a day fishing with his gillie, perhaps for the last time. It had been a good day, but, try as he might, it was not a relaxing one. MacDuff had noticed there was something amiss, and did all he could to raise his master's spirits. James thought fondly of his gillie. He was the only person to whom he could confide his private concerns, but this time he was unable to talk about what was on his mind.

It took three days to reach the capital, staying at country inns on the way, where the horses were changed for fresh ones. At last the Castle on its hill came into view. The boys were enthralled. They drove through the gates in the high city walls and were plunged into the hurly burly of city life: carriages and horses on cobbles, street traders shouting their wares, ladies carried in sedan chairs by lavishly laced footmen, people milling about gossiping and gentlemen striding along the roads on business. Maids wearing mop caps threw slops from the windows onto the streets below, and stray dogs hung around in dark alleys. There was a smell of horse dung and other unidentifiable rotting refuse. The coachman drove into the yard of a large inn, and James followed. He knew this place as the only accommodation that would suit Mary. He dismounted and handed his horse over to a waiting groom. He went indoors to announce their arrival and to confirm that the messenger he had sent ahead of them had engaged rooms for them. All was well, and he went to escort Mary and the boys indoors, while the servants dealt with the luggage.

It was still early afternoon, and, after refreshing themselves and exploring their suite of rooms, they had a late dinner. The boys were eager to go sightseeing with their father. Mary would rest until supper. They bade her goodbye and emerged from the comparative peace of the inn into the busy town. They climbed the hill to see the Castle. There were soldiers in uniforms, the like of which the boys had never seen. James took them to look at the grand shop fronts displaying their wares: cloth merchants, clock makers, silver smiths, coffee and tea rooms. Many of these luxuries came from foreign lands. They walked along the Leith Water, which was a rushing torrent in a gulley flowing to the port of Leith, where merchant vessels brought their goods to be sold in the shops. On the opposite bank of the Leith Water mills were producing flour for the town's bread. They went to see the Tolbooth, a forbidding place, now a prison. A human skull perched on one of the spikes of the tower. Ludovick asked whose head it was.

"That's the head of James Graham, Marquis of Montrose. It's been there since his execution, ten years ago," James said.

"What did he do wrong, Father?" asked Patrick.

"He was the leader of the Royalists when we were defending Scotland from Oliver Cromwell and the Parliamentarians. If he had been spared then, he would have been rewarded now for his loyalty to the King."

James and his sons stared at the macabre sight. The flesh had been pecked off by the birds long ago, but a mane of grey hair still clung on, blowing in the wind. James was acutely aware that his own head could be up there if his defence did not convince the Attorney General of his innocence. He led the boys away, winding back to the inn through narrow streets between tall buildings, seven or eight stories high.

Chapter 13
Indictment

The family ate their supper together. The boys told their mother all that they had seen, and James sat quietly watching them. At least, now, he had heirs to take over when he was gone, although Ludovick would need rigorous training if he was ever to be effective as Laird.

"Tomorrow," James said, when there was a lull in the conversation, "I will leave early and do my business. It will probably take all day. You boys will attend your mother at all times, and if you wish to go out you must take at least one of the servants, preferably a groom."

"Yes, Father," replied the two boys.

"You may now leave me and go to your chambers. Goodnight, Wife." James got up from the table and went to Mary. He gave her an affectionate kiss on the cheek.

She looked surprised, and a shadow crossed her face. She waited until the boys had left the room, then said, "Shall I not see thee in my bed tonight, Husband? You have serious business tomorrow, that I can tell. Will you not speak to me about it?"

"'Tis best if you don't know. It will all be plain, soon enough." He kissed her again, and she rose and left the room with a rustle of skirts.

James rang for Dougal, who came at once. "Pour me a dram, Dougal," he said.

Dougal went over to the dresser and poured the honey-coloured liquid into a glass. He presented it to his master on a tray.

James took the glass and put it to his lips, savouring the hot taste before swallowing. "Stay, Dougal," he said, "I must give you instructions for tomorrow."

Dougal returned the tray to its place, and came to stand by his Laird.

"Dougal, I trust you above all of my servants. You have served me honestly and faithfully. I am going to tell you the true purpose of our visit here. No-one else knows, and you must not breathe a word of it to anyone until I give you permission."

James paused and took another sip of his whisky. "Owing to my past association with the Covenanters, and my involvement in battle against the Royalists, the Lord Advocate has accused me of treason, as instructed by King Charles. I have come here to plead my case. As you know, I became loyal to the Royalists under Montrose, to the end. Montrose was executed by Cromwell, so can no longer speak for me. Archibald Campbell, the Marquis of Argyll, has been indicted, and is at present awaiting execution here in Edinburgh. That fate is likely to come to all those accused of treason."

Dougal stood with his hands clasped behind his back, listening intently to all his Laird had to say, his face showing no emotion. But his jaw dropped slightly at this last revelation, his forehead puckered, and his eyes now showed deep concern. He drew a breath and pushed his shoulders back, saying nothing.

James continued. "Tomorrow I will rise early and go to the Law Courts, where I am to be interviewed. I hope to persuade them there that I am innocent, and am a loyal subject to the King. If they are not convinced and they detain me I will send a message to you here, with a letter to my Lady Mary. I wish you to be ready to attend to her needs as you think fit, and to explain to my sons what is happening. It may be that they release me after conferring with the Lord Advocate, so my incarceration need not signify the worst. Keep the family in Edinburgh until the matter is resolved, one way or another."

Dougal waited until he was sure James had finished, then he spoke. "May I offer you ma sincere gude wishes, Sir, and hope for your safe return to the family. I will do all that you have asked, to the best of ma ability. It has aye been a pleasure, serving you, Laird. You are a kind maister."

His features softened and he looked down at the floor.

"Thank you, Dougal," said James. "That will be all."

Dougal took a bow and walked out.

The next day, James dressed carefully and had a hearty breakfast. He left the inn and strode down the road. A misty rain filled the air, the kind that would later give way to the warmth of the sun. He felt confident that he would be cleared of all charges of treason. He had come prepared with documents to prove that he had served the Royalists well. The Law courts were in Parliament House, an imposing building, and he hesitated before approaching the great door. A footman demanded to know his business. He was shown into a room with chairs arranged around the walls, and told to wait.

During the next few hours other gentlemen were shown in. No-one spoke. James half expected to see someone he knew. They each avoided catching the others' eyes. The air became stale, and the ticking of the clock grew louder with each waiting moment. At last a clerk entered the room.

"James Grant," he said. "Come with me."

James was led up several flights of stairs. Clerks holding bundles of papers passed them going up and down. The clerk stopped on a small landing and opened the door into a spacious room. Seven men dressed in dark robes were sitting at one side of a table facing the door. An empty chair waited on the other side, facing the lawyers. The clerk indicated this chair, and James sat down. It was disconcerting not to be in charge; to be at the mercy of men more powerful than himself.

The man in the centre spoke. "You are James Grant, 7th Laird of Freuchie, Strathspey?"

"I am," said James.

"We have orders to indict you for treason, having led Covenanter armies against King Charles. Do you have anything to say?"

James sat erect, his hands on his lap. He breathed deeply before he spoke, determined to stay calm. "I did indeed support the Covenanters until after the battle at Inverlochy. When the purpose of the conflict changed from the defence of our Scottish Kirk against the King, to defending the throne against Parliament, I joined the Royalists under the Earl of Montrose, with other Highland Lairds. I subsequently supplied 300 men to the Royalist cause. I raised a troop of infantry to oppose Cromwell's invasion of Scotland, and I sent a regiment to the Battle of Worcester with our present king, as King of the Scots. I have documents here providing the names of witnesses." He handed the papers over to the spokesman. A clerk had been making notes of James' defence. The lawyers conferred, nodding and shaking their heads as they discussed what they had heard.

When they had finished, the spokesman said, "James Grant, we have listened to your defence. We must consult with the Attorney General before we can make a decision. Please be aware that your future is at present uncertain. You will be kept here in Edinburgh until a verdict can be reached."

James' heart sank. "My lords, I have a wife and family waiting for me here in Edinburgh. May I go and stay with them in the meantime? You have my word that I will not leave before you summon me again." He naïvely thought that they would take his word for it, bearing in mind his station in life.

After conferring again, the spokesman said, "You will be imprisoned until a decision has been made. You may write a letter to your wife, which will be delivered today."

He took a bell from the table and rang it.

Two men entered the room.

"Take this man to the Tollbooth. You may allow him paper and quill with which to write to his wife, informing her of his whereabouts."

The gaolers took James roughly by the arms and jostled him through the door and down the stairs.

Chapter 14
Haunted

Down in the Spey valley, a herd of shiny black cattle stood in the pound, restless and braying, unused to being enclosed in this way. John said goodbye to Annie, who stood at the door with seven-year-old Thomas. It would be a two day trip to the tryst at Pitmain and back.

"Ye've gude weather for it," said Annie.

John lifted his son and kissed him on the forehead. "'Twill soon be time to take thee with me," he said.

Fraser was waiting by the pound. The two men opened the gates and drove the steers down the track and along the river towards Pitmain. John was glad of this opportunity to get away from the homestead; there were images of Jamie everywhere there. Even when he was with Annie and Thomas, he was aware of Jamie's absence. It was as if the memory was coming between John and his family, pushing them away.

And he could not get the picture of the maid at Elchies out of his head; Duggan's sweetheart. He could have tried to stop his fellow raiders treating her so cruelly. He might have been able to help her escape before they slit her throat. If he had, Jamie would still be alive. John lay awake at night going through the same scene repeatedly, working out ways he could have prevented her death. But it always came to the same conclusion; he remembered that he was fired up with anger like the rest of them, and that he had been drinking heavily.

Once the cattle became accustomed to the idea that this was a journey, they sauntered along easily, one or two stopping now and again to munch a choice shoot from the hedgerow. The sun shone strongly through the quivering leaves of the birches along the river and John was glad he was wearing a wide-brimmed hat. The cattle waved their tails in rhythm to keep off the flies which swarmed round them.

Fraser was about twenty years older than John. He never talked much, and John thought he was becoming more dour in his latter years. It would soon be time to find a replacement for his faithful worker. If Jamie had still been alive…

John had to stop himself thinking. "How is Morag, Fraser? Is she keeping well?"

"Ay, she's well."

"Dost have grandchildren?"

"Ay, ay. Weans, like your Thomas."

"I expect Morag is busy minding them."

"Ay, she is that."

A fox trotted across the road in front of them, with only a glance in their direction. Over the next few miles John managed to squeeze out of Fraser a trickle of information about his family. His two sons worked for the Laird and both their wives laboured in the crofters' fields and gardens, as most wives did. There were three grandchildren under four years old, and Morag helped with their care.

They were nearing the town and the road became busier. They could hear the roaring of many cattle, and the bleating of sheep as they drew near to the common where the tryst was held. They were there in their many thousands. Mounted drovers shouted to each other, their dogs barking, and the buzzing of clouds of flies added to the mayhem. The drovers were a rough breed of men, with their long hair and swarthy faces, who lived their dangerous lives in the open air. They wore tartan plaids and blue bonnets, and carried snuff mulls. Their collie dogs were always by their side. The drovers bought their cattle and sheep from the farmers at these trysts, and drove herds of several hundred over rough terrain to be sold in England and the south. They lived on nothing but oatmeal mixed with water, and sometimes black pudding made with the blood of their cattle.

John and Fraser drove their herd into the melée, and stood around waiting to catch the eye of a drover who was not busy with other tradesmen. They saw horsemen of status going around on the lookout for new stock to build up their herds. There were new breeds of cattle being introduced to mix with the hardy black shorthorns, making heavier and more lucrative stock. John noticed that some of the cattle at this year's tryst were brown with longer horns and thicker hair.

"The Laird Grant will no' be here," remarked Fraser. "He's away to Edinburgh, I've heard, with his family. I dinna ken the reason."

"It must be urgent business," said John. "He'd no' miss the tryst otherwise."

A great bear of a man pushed through the crowds towards them. He looked at the cattle they had brought and offered a price. John tried to persuade him they were worth more, but there was no bargaining to be had. He accepted the price, and the money was handed over. John gave Fraser enough for a meal and a bed for the night, and they walked into the town, relieved of their burden.

John found an alehouse where he sat enjoying a hearty meal and a tankard of the landlord's best ale. The girl behind the bar was flirting and giggling with the customers. John watched her pretty face under the mop cap, surrounded by brown curls. Her cheeks were flushed and she had a dimple in her chin. The bar was becoming more crowded as other farmers came for refreshments after days driving their cattle. The atmosphere was hot and stuffy.

John got up to buy a refill of his tankard. While he was waiting to be served, one of the men standing next to him made a grab at the barmaid intending to snatch a kiss. John was back at Elchies. This time he would protect her. He swung his arm and punched the man in the face, felling him to the ground. Instantly, he was attacked from all sides. He fought back, but had no chance, and found himself on the floor next to the man he had punched. The barmaid was screaming. The landlord came, and with help from his customers, dragged the two out into the street.

John sat up and looked around him. It was dark. There were still crowds of people milling around. Some had had their fill of ale and were staggering in merry huddles, leaning on each other for a tenuous stability. John could not go back into the alehouse to claim his accommodation. He struggled to his feet and felt the effects of his beating. He forced himself into a steady walk towards another possible bed for the night. But all the rooms were taken by now, and his face must be bruised; he'd had some wary looks from the people he asked. The only answer was to search the back streets for an empty barn, hopefully with straw in it.

It was a long time before John fell asleep. When he did, he dreamed that Annie was being raped by three or four men, all looking like Duggan. He watched, powerless to save her. Then they set about her with their dirks, and he woke in a panic. Sweat poured off his face and his body was shaking. He needed a wash before the day began. It was painful getting up; his limbs were stiff and sore. Slowly he rose to standing and brushed the straw off his clothes. He went off in search of a stream or a well, where he could refresh himself.

His dreams had followed him. There was no escape. He summoned his strength and went to look for a trinket or ribbon for Annie and a toy for Thomas. He was missing them, and vowed to be more attentive when he returned home.

Chapter 15
The Toll Booth

It was dark and dank in the cell. Never had James been in such an unpleasant, uncomfortable place. The rough shelters they made themselves on the battlefields were better than this. There was a stench of stale urine, and drips of cold water fell from the ceiling. He could see nothing through the slit in the thick stone walls, which were covered in green slime, except a thin shaft of sunlight. He was to cherish that sliver of light when the dark of the night gave way to dawn. He could hear the noises of the busy town outside. He could picture the place next to the Tollbooth, where the scaffold would be erected, for those indicted for treason, and the block where heads would roll. He thought of Mary and the boys. They would have the letter by now. He had written that he did not want them to worry; that it was only a matter of time before he would be reprieved. But Dougal would have a hard task dealing with Mary's highly-strung reaction to the news.

James' eyes were getting used to the dark, and he noticed a pile of something light coloured along one wall. He groped his way over to it, and found a bench covered with straw. At least it seemed clean. He sat down and leaned forward, head in his hands.

Several hours later, the door of the cell rattled. He heard keys in the lock, and sat up. The door opened, and a bowed old man wearing a bonnet and cloak came in, carrying a bowl of what might be food and a candle.

"The Laird Grant, ain't it? 'Tis no' what you'll be accustomed to in here, Sir. Sup this, 'tis hot at least. I'll leave you the light." He placed the candle on the floor, handed James the bowl, and shuffled out, closing and locking the door behind him.

James wrapped his hands round the bowl. He shook with cold and fear. The bowl was full of a hot, watery gruel. It was better than nothing, and might help to warm him. He sipped it slowly until the last drop was gone. The bowl no longer warmed his hands. He lay down on the straw and spent the next long hours in extreme discomfort, staring at the ceiling, watching the drips, which were the only sound to be heard. The candle burned out, and he was left in complete darkness. Exhaustion overtook the pain. He dozed until morning.

He could not remember how long he had been locked in the stinking cell. Was it three days, or four? He was cold to the bone, his clothes were damp, and his stomach had long ago given up its expectation of a good, nourishing meal, though his mind kept going back to thoughts of steaks and beef stews. He passed the time pacing the small space available, listening to shouts and screams coming from the other prisoners, and praying to God to have mercy on his soul. His whole life marched through his memory, causing him to question everything he had done, every decision he had made. Still, he could not see any reason why he should be punished like this.

One day, he heard crowds of people outside. They were jeering and shouting, *"Traitor!"* Suddenly there was silence, except for the occasional shout of abuse. He heard a resounding thud. A roar arose from the crowd, followed by more screams and shouts. Gradually the noise subsided as the crowds dispersed, and James was left with his thoughts and fears once more.

A noise at the door alerted him. He stood up, expecting a visitor. Was it the daily bowl of gruel being delivered? It was the wrong time, it must be someone else. The door opened and he heard voices. James held his breath.

"James Grant?" The voice came from one of the shadowy figures who had entered.

"Ay, that is my name," he croaked. His voice failed him after days of silence.

The figures became more distinct, as James' eyes accustomed themselves to the harsh light coming through the door. These men were more respectably dressed than the servant who brought him his broth.

"James Grant, I have orders to release you. I have a letter here from the Attorney General. You are pardoned."

James had to sit down on the bench which had been his bed for so long. He could hardly believe what he had just heard. He felt afraid of leaving his now familiar and secure surroundings, to face bright light, warmth and people.

"Come now, Sir. I will assist you," said a kind voice.

James rose. His legs did not belong to him. An arm took his, and led him out into the light. His deliverers spoke to each other in lowered tones. They assisted James through passages and up stone stairs. The light became brighter as they progressed. They entered a room with windows. Sunlight streamed in, dazzling James. He was shown to a chair and told to be seated.

"I believe it will be necessary for you to be escorted to your inn, Sir. Wait here and I will arrange it. In the meantime, perhaps this will help to revive you." The man passed James a flask, from which he had removed the stopper.

James took it with a shaking hand, and poured the brandy into his mouth. The effect was almost painful, but so warming. His eyes watered as he handed the flask back.

"Thank you kindly, Sir." James was regaining his dignity, slowly but surely, and beginning to think for himself. "Would it be possible, Sir, for a message to be taken to my servant, Dougal, at The Bull? He will arrange some means of transport and escort me back."

"Of course. That will be done at once." The man handed the letter from the Attorney General to James, and left the room with his companion.

James sat back in his chair and closed his eyes. The brandy had gone to his head, his stomach having nothing in it to keep it company. He relaxed, allowed the stress of the last few days to melt away, and anticipated his reunion with his family.

A little while later, Dougal stood in the doorway, a wide smile on his face. "You'll be wanting to be oot of here, Sir," he said.

James stood up and wavered a little before walking towards Dougal. "'Tis good to see a friendly face, Dougal. Have you brought transport? I'm a little weak."

"A sedan chair awaits you, Sir." He offered James his arm, and assisted him out of the nightmare of the last few days.

"How long was I in that hell-hole, Dougal?" he asked as he sat gratefully on the chair. The two porters lifted the chair and started moving away.

"Four days, Sir. I canna tell you how worried we all were."

They came away from the Tollbooth into the town. James looked back, and saw that there was a new head in the place of the skull of Montrose. Archibald Campbell, Marquis of Argyll, now stared down at him from the spike on the turret. James shivered, and turned towards the sun and his family.

Chapter 16
The Journey Home

Lady Mary Grant was not well. The shock and worry over her husband's imprisonment had taken its toll. On James' release and return to the family she rallied, but she was concerned to see him in such a debilitated state. The doctor who had been attending her examined James and re-assured the family that there was nothing that a few good meals and some sleep would not cure.

During the next week, Dougal took the two boys under his wing and they explored the town. James spent the time resting by his wife's bed, and began to feel better. One day he was woken from a light doze by Mary's plaintive voice.

"James, are you there?"

He rose from his chair and went to the bedside. "Yes, Mary. I'm close by."

There was no colour in her face and her eyes were sunken in dark hollows. She stretched a limp hand towards him. "James, I would like to go home."

"Are you not comfortable here, my dear? The journey would be a great strain on your health."

She looked at him with liquid eyes. "I'll not get well here, Husband. I need to be in my own home. I don't want to die here."

"You're not dying, Wife. But I'll ask the doctor's advice." He also had a longing to return to Elchies, and the boys needed to get back to their schooling.

A week later the family were on their way home. The doctor considered that if Lady Mary was in her home environment, her health might improve. She must travel in a sedan chair, and Dr McBain would travel in attendance. He was a burly man, always dressed in Puritan black. His florid face was decorated with a wide moustache, which perched on his upper lip as if about to take flight. On the journey James discovered that the doctor enjoyed his food and drink, sometimes to excess.

James and the doctor rode by Mary's side, the two boys and Dougal and the maid in the carriage. The going was slow and the resting stops frequent. They could only go as fast as the porters could walk with the sedan chair in one day. James sent a messenger to the next resting place each day they travelled, and arranged replacements for the porters as well as the carriage horses. Mary was comfortable reclining in her chair, surrounded by soft cushions and covered with a deerskin. The summer sunshine and fresh air brought a glow to her cheeks and the anticipation of returning to home surroundings lifted her spirits. Sometimes Ludovick would come and walk by her side, pointing out landmarks and views of lochs and mountains. Patrick ran on ahead, exploring as he went, until he tired and retreated to the shelter of the carriage.

The inns they stayed at varied greatly in comfort and standard of cooking, as did the demeanour of the hosts. Sometimes they stayed two or three days as Lady Mary took a turn for the worse. Doctor McBain and his attentions revived her, and they were on their way again. The weather also delayed them. For three days it poured with thundery rain. The road became a mud bath and no travel was possible until it had dried up. This time they were in good company, and were entertained by the local customers and the other travellers. Their host brought his fiddle out, and after supper the company danced jigs and reels and sang Highland songs into the night. The other travellers amused the boys and they learned to play backgammon and chess. James was pleased to see his sons learning some social graces and skills which they rarely came across at home.

Mary, though, was failing again. The long journey had lost its novelty, and was becoming tedious. They set off again when the weather and condition of the road allowed. But the travelling was slower as Mary needed medical attention more frequently.

At last Elchies was in sight. The boys asked if they could walk the remainder of the journey, and their father agreed. They ran on ahead, shouting with excitement. When the carriage and sedan chair finally entered the courtyard, Dougal and the coachman carried Mary into her chamber, where Doctor McBain and her maid assisted her with settling in.

James went to see his staff, who greeted him warmly. Then he retired to his drawing room, poured himself a dram and went to sit by the fire, alone in his own comfortable surroundings at last. He took out his pipe and filled it with his favourite tobacco, lit it with a taper from the fire, and sucked the cool smoke into his mouth. He blew it out to surround himself in a rich blue aroma, which lightened his head. A sip of whisky completed the feeling of wellbeing and he relaxed back in his chair and closed his eyes. He could now release all the stress of the last few months. Everything would be all right. Mary's health would improve, and the boys would settle down to their studies, all the better for their enlightening adventure. He would go fishing tomorrow.

Doctor McBain stayed with them and did the best he could, bleeding and administering potions. Mary started going into violent fits, which were frightening for everybody, and lasted longer and longer each time. Each time James was called, as she was not expected to survive. Each time she came round exhausted and more fragile. James became afraid to leave the house in case the end was near. The boys were subdued, and found it hard to settle to their studies.

One morning James woke early and went to his wife's chamber. Doctor McBain looked up and shook his head as James entered the room, and James hurried to the bed. Mary appeared to be sleeping. He took hold of her hand, which was lying outside the covers. She opened her eyes and smiled.

"I'll not be here long, now, Husband," she murmured. "I know you'll take care of the boys."

"D'you wish them here?"

"I would like to see them, yes."

Mary's maid was close by. James nodded to her and she left the room.

Mary rested until the boys entered, rubbing the sleep out of their eyes. They approached the bed, one on each side, and their mother stirred. She offered a hand to each. "Kiss me, children," she said. They leaned over and kissed her on the cheeks. "I'm going to sleep for a very long time. Thy father will care for you and teach you to how become fine, brave men. Heed him well. Ludo, you will be Laird one day. Be good to your subjects and keep the peace. God bless ye all. Now, please leave me." She closed her eyes.

The boys stood rooted to the spot. Ludovick's face was pale and drawn. Patrick's was crumpled, but he did not cry.

"Go now, children. I'll come to ye shortly." James nodded to his sons and they turned away from their mother and left the room. James bent to kiss his wife on the forehead, and sat on a chair by the bed. Soon Mary's breathing became shallower, and Doctor McBain came to check her pulse. She had drifted away quietly. James stayed for a while, feeling lonely and tired. The suffering was over. He stood up and went to find his boys.

Chapter 17
Recognition

A year later, James stood looking out of the parlour window. He could see the rugged Highlands stretching into the distance, with patches of snow nestling in the hollows. He drew his gaze closer and saw flowers in the garden which was sheltered from northerly winds and caught the best of the sun. Mary had designed this tranquil place and he remembered her sitting among the roses in high summer, wearing a wide-brimmed hat secured by a broad ribbon which was tied in a bow under her chin.

He missed having her beside him. She had been taken from him so suddenly at a time when he needed her most. He was feeling insulted by the way he had been treated in Edinburgh after all he had done for the king. He suspected that his brother George had something to do with the accusation of treason. George was next in line for the position as head of Clan Grant after Ludovick. The Lord Advocate should have got his facts straight before he brought out the indictment. James' imprisonment and the subsequent loss of Mary had severely affected his health.

A door banged in a distant part of the house. The boys' voices reached him. They had been released from the classroom, and it was time for their afternoon ride. James listened as they raced to the back door and out into the yard. They were growing up and needed more formal schooling. Ludovick was becoming pompous and cocky. He would benefit from some healthy competition.

A knock at the door brought him out of his reverie. Dougal entered.

"A letter has arrived for you, Sir," he said, as he handed a sealed paper to James.

"Thank you, Dougal. Does the messenger need an answer?"

"No, Sir." He bowed and left the room.

James opened the message and read it with surprise and gratification. At last his services to the king had been recognised. He was to be elevated and given the titles of Earl of Strathspey and Lord Grant of Freuchies and Urquart. He had been called to Edinburgh to receive the honour. He read the letter again, and started to plan the journey. He would take Ludovick with him. It would be a good experience for him to be present at a civil ceremony, and would encourage a sense of pride when he eventually inherited his father's titles.

A sharp pain took him unawares, and he staggered to a chair to sit down. An iron fist gripped him in his chest, and he cried out. Gradually the cramp loosened its hold and he was able to breathe freely. He leaned back, feeling utterly exhausted. The letter fell to the floor.

The journey to Edinburgh was tedious as James was not well and needed frequent stops to rest. He had chosen to ride, as this method of travel should take less time, but he began to wish they had come by chaise. Ludovick became impatient to be at their destination. Dougal was also with them, faithfully attending to his master's needs. After several days they arrived at The Bull in

102

Edinburgh, with its painful memories of the previous visit. James rested a day and Doctor McBain was called for.

"Your heart is in poor shape, Sir," he said, after he had examined the patient. "I'm afraid to say that every time you have one of your attacks, it will weaken. It will not last much longer. Rest is the only recommendation I can give."

James was angry. Rest was not in his nature. He wrote a letter to the patent authorities, announcing his arrival in Edinburgh. He received a reply saying that the patent was not yet complete. Ludovick was bored and bad tempered. James spent time explaining to his son the titles he was about to receive, and that he would then have a seat in Parliament. He tried to impress on the boy what a responsibility this was, and that he would inherit this from his father.

Ludovick showed little interest, and made a quick getaway to seek his friends, the two sons of another resident. They were older than himself, and James did not approve of their unruly behaviour.

One afternoon, Ludovick came to his father in the private lounge they had as part of their suite. James looked up from the newspaper he was reading.

"Father, will you loan me some money? William and Richard are taking me to the gaming tables."

James stared in astonishment at his son. "How dare you ask me for money, young man!" he shouted.

"I'll let you have it back. They say it's easy winnings." Ludovick brazenly stood his ground.

James stood up. He strode over to where his son was standing. "Did I give you permission to go to the gaming tables? That is no place for the well-bred son of a laird…

You young upstart…!" He began to feel unsteady, and that pain in his chest returned. He could not breathe. The pain was overpowering. The iron fist crushed him to death. His body fell to the floor.

Ludovick became the eighth Laird of Freuchie at the age of thirteen, too young to inherit his father's new title. His Uncle, Colonel Patrick Grant, sent him to school in Elgin and then to University at St Andrew's. Curators were appointed to run the estate. Careful accounts were kept and the debts were paid off before Ludovick came of age in 1671.

Chapter 18   1665
The Shadows take Control

"Where is that boy?" John shouted as he came into the homestead yard. "Thomas, dost hear? These stables haven't been cleaned properly for a couple of days."

Annie came out of the house. "Thomas is away up to Fraser and Morag. He'll no' be back 'til dinner time. He fed the beasts afore he went."

"He's never here when I want him. What does he get up to with the crofters?" John knocked the mud off his boots before removing them and going indoors.

Annie followed him. "He finds them better company than thee, John. He's learning to grow vegetables with Fraser and his grandchildren. They get on well thegither."

John went to the dresser and poured himself a dram. "'Tis time he started taking an interest in the farm. I could do with another pair of hands."

Annie stood in the doorway, watching her husband knock back the whisky. "'Tis a bit early to be taking the drink, John. Hast finished for theday?"

"No, I've to go and brand some more cattle." He refilled his glass.

Annie said, "I was thinking, 'tis time Thomas was riding his own horse. He might be more use to thee then. And if you need his help, you must show him what you want him to do." She turned and went into the kitchen.

John drained his second glass and went out into the warm sunshine, welcome after a long period of rain. But he hardly noticed the warmth on his face. He was finding it difficult to relate to his son, Thomas, who was growing more like Jamie every time John looked at him. But he was not Jamie. He was a boy who went his own way. He did his duty feeding the animals and mucking out the stables as quickly as possible. He had to be told to bring the wood in for the fire, and carry heavy things for his mother. He could not wait to be roaming in the hills with his catapult, the one he had found that had belonged to Jamie. He brought rabbits home sometimes. Annie showed him how to skin and gut them and prepare them for the pot. Thomas loved his mother above all else, as Jamie had done. He made very little attempt to communicate with his father.

The cattle were some distance away and John decided to go on horseback. He put the branding irons into his saddlebag, and went to get his horse from the pasture, Annie's words echoing in his ears. If he let Thomas have his own horse, John would have to teach him how to ride and to look after it. Then Thomas would wander further afield, and they would never see him at home.

John reached the enclosure where he had put the cattle to be branded. He dismounted, tethered the horse and lifted the saddlebag down. He knew he should not be doing this job on his own, but he had done it so many times before it was second nature. He lit the fire and collected more wood to build it up, then laid the irons in the hot ashes. The cattle were bunched in the corner of the enclosure, too far away. He must get them closer to the fire. There were some hurdles left over and he re-arranged them to form a small pen, so that he could deal with the beasts one by one.

When the irons were glowing red, John went and threw a rope round the neck of one of the steers. He gently led him into the pen, within reach of the fire. Holding the rope with his left hand, he reached for the hot iron with his right, and pressed it onto the flank of the steer. The animal snorted and bucked. John let the rope out and put the iron back into the fire. He led the branded steer out of the pen and went to collect another.

It was all going well, except that John's eyes were not focussing properly, and some of the marks were not in the right place. He tripped over the rope and fell onto the grass. He had to let go. He scrambled to his feet and went after the end of the rope, which was being dragged along by the escaping steer. He retrieved the rope and led the steer back into the pen. His hands were shaking. He paused to steady himself. He took the hot iron out of the fire, and aimed for the rump of the beast. But the steer bucked and knocked the iron out of John's hand. It flew through the air. The hot end landed on his other hand. It rested there before falling to the ground. John yelled with pain and let go of the rope. The steer made off to the other end of the enclosure.

The pain was excruciating. John knelt on the grass, hugging his injured hand. Tears came to his eyes. Anger and grief seethed in his breast. He lifted his head and screamed, "No...o...o...o...!" He collapsed on the ground and cried like a baby.

After several minutes, John struggled to his senses. He sat on the grass and tore his left sleeve off his shirt to make a rough bandage. The hand was still burning with pain. He wrapped the sleeve round it as best he could, and struggled to his feet. It was impossible to continue his task. He went and released the last steer from the rope, and walked over to the fire. There was one iron still red hot. He took it out of the fire. The other lay on the grass where it had fallen. It was now cold enough to handle. John picked it up and used it to spread the burning ashes around and push the logs away. He staggered as he picked up the saddlebag to put the irons into it. He was feeling faint. He must somehow mount his horse and make his way home.

John was in Hell. He was being punished for his evil deeds, burning in everlasting fire. Voices gabbled all round him, screaming and whimpering. There was Jamie above him, looking down from a great height, surrounded in golden light. He was smiling, grinning, laughing cruelly. The face became that of an ugly beast, eyes ablaze. It was Duggan who shouted and screamed at John, shaking his fist. He poured hot liquid from a cauldron, which burned John's mouth and throat. His left arm and hand were on fire. He tried to scream. No sound came. He was in agonising pain. His whole body was scorched by the heat.

Everything went dark. There was no pain, no voices, nothing but blackness. He felt nothing.

He heard a sound; the rustling of someone moving. He turned his head.

Someone said, *"Faether?"*

He opened his eyes and saw a young face surrounded by a mop of dark hair. "Jamie?" he said.

The face disappeared. *"Mother, Faether's awake!"* a young voice shouted.

Another voice, a long way off, called, *"Coming."*

John closed his eyes. This was not Hell. He was in bed at home. It appeared to be daylight. He should be out working by now. He had those cattle to brand today. He opened his eyes and moved as if to sit up. But what was wrong with his left arm? He felt it with his right hand, and pulled the covers back. This was not his arm. It was covered in bandages. He tried to move his left hand and felt searing pain. He looked more closely. There was no hand…

Chapter 19
Lessons to be Learnt

Annie stood by the bed, her face pale. There was no tenderness in her eyes.

"You would have died if the hand had been left to fester." Her voice had a hard ring. "Robert's been a godsend. He employed a gude crofter to do the work, and Thomas is doing more, helping Colin with the cattle. He's riding now."

"I thought I saw Jamie when I woke," said John, and then regretted it as a dark shadow passed over Annie's face.

"That was Thomas," she snapped. "And the sooner you recognise your only son and get Jamie oot of your head the better. You'll be wanting to eat, now you've come back to us."

John nodded and his wife left the room. He lifted his left arm and looked at it. He was useless as a husband and a father now. No wonder Annie was upset. It would have been better to have died. He would only be a burden, not able to work to keep the farm going. He lay back on the pillows and tears filled his eyes. He tried to remember what had happened to cause the injury to his hand. The last thing he recalled was riding up to the cattle enclosure, feeling angry about something that Annie had said.

Annie came back into the chamber, carrying a bowl and a spoon. She sat on the edge of the bed. "Sit up and eat, John. I'll help thee." There was kindness in her voice. John leaned on his right arm and lifted himself awkwardly, pushing with his feet. He would have to learn everything all over again. Annie filled the spoon and lifted it to John's lips. He took the food into his mouth and savoured the comforting tastes. But this would not do. He could not have Annie feed him. He leaned back on the pillow and took the spoon from her. She held the bowl for him while he finished his meal. He put the spoon back into the bowl and looked at her.

"I surely am sorry, Annie. I'm useless to thee now. What'll we do?"

Annie's face softened. "John, we've been through bad times before. Thou art far frae useless. I need thy support, and Thomas needs thy love. We'll find a way if we work at it all thegither." She stood up and leaned over to kiss his forehead before leaving the room.

It was several days before John felt fit enough to dress himself and come downstairs to be part of the family again. In the meantime he found ways of doing things with only one hand. His self-pity subsided, and anger fuelled his determination to succeed. He saw Thomas briefly when he brought meals up to his father. The boy looked at him sideways, and was gone before John had a chance to say anything.

He felt better downstairs. He pottered about doing small things; putting logs on the fire, and carrying empty plates out into the kitchen after meals. One day he was sitting in his fireside chair when Thomas came in after a day out with Colin.

"Come and talk to me, Son. Thee and me need to get to know each other if I'm ever to be a proper faether to thee."

Thomas looked warily at his father and sat down opposite him.

"Tell me what you've been doing theday. I miss being oot on the hills with the beasts. Tell me how the farm's doing. Hast taken any steers to market?"

"'Twill soon be time for harvesting, Faether. We went to look at the grain theday. Colin says, in a week or two, 'twill be ready."

"Ye'll need more labourers for harvest," said John. They sat in silence for a few moments. Then he said, "I hear thou art riding now. Which horse didst choose?"

"Mother chose for me, and taught me how to ride. I've got the black pony with the shaggy mane. His name's Prince." Thomas became animated. He evidently enjoyed his new companion.

John saw that his son was wearing a dirk, and thought that he was too young for weapons. "Has anyone taught thee how to use thy dirk? They can be dangerous if used as a plaything."

Thomas put his hand to his dirk. "I use it for skinning rabbits, sharpening stakes and cutting ropes. No-one taught me."

John said, "I can teach thee how to defend thysel', and whittle with it, and keep it sharp."

An insolent look came over his young son's face. "I know how to whittle and look after ma dirk. Gran'faether Fraser and Colin have taught me." He looked at his father's bandaged arm and laughed. "How're you going to teach me anything with only one hand?" he sneered.

"Dinna speak to thy Faether in that tone, Thomas." Annie had come into the room. Her eyes were blazing.

113

"He'll find ways of doing all manner of things, you wait and see. It'll no' help to mock him." She banged the pot of stew down onto the table. "Come and sit at the table, thy dinner's here."

John shook with fear, anger and humiliation. He pushed himself out of his chair and went over to where the whisky bottle stood on the dresser, with a glass beside it. He picked up the bottle and put it to his mouth. He drew the cork out with his teeth and poured himself a dram, put the bottle down and replaced the cork. He lifted the glass to his lips, which calmed him. When he sat at the table and glanced at Annie, she had the vestige of a smile on her face.

He looked at Thomas, who was watching him across the table. "I'll find a way, but I'll need thy help, Son."

Thomas looked down at his plate and started eating.

The next day, John went out to the stable after breakfast. He had to work out how to saddle up his horse. He lifted the saddle down from its peg and placed it with difficulty on the back of his horse and adjusted its position. He had forgotten how heavy it was. He groped under the animal for the straps, and heard a sound behind him. Thomas was there, watching.

"D'you need help with that, Faether?" They looked each other in the eyes.

"Theday, Son, I'd be glad of thy help. But I'll have to work oot how to do it masell."

While Thomas was tightening the girth, he said, "Were you thinking of going far theday, Faether?

"I have to visit the saddler. This bandage is a mess, and the stump's painful. I'm going to get him to fashion me a leather boot for it that I can strap on masell."

Thomas said, "Does Mother know?"

"I didna like to bother her."

Thomas gave his father a hitch up onto his horse and went indoors.

John set off down the lane, slowly at first, enjoying the gentle motion of the horse beneath him, and adjusting himself to the rhythm, and to handling the reins with one hand. He thought about the design of the leather boot he wanted, and realised that it would be useful to have a metal hook fixed on the end that he could attach when needed. He heard a horse trotting up behind him.

"Mother said I should come with you, Faether."

John resisted the idea. He wanted to do this on his own. But he must give the lad a chance.

"I'll be glad of thy company, Son," he said.

It was a balmy July day. There was little wind, and the atmosphere was hazy. The bees were buzzing in the hedgerows where wild flowers were growing. The hills rose up all round them and mountains filled the distant view. John absorbed all this hungrily, taking deep breaths of fresh air into his lungs. He noticed that Thomas looked good on a horse.

"You ride well, Thomas," he said.

"I like to ride," said Thomas. "It feels grand up here, off the ground. I feel equal to a man. No-one looks doon on me."

They rode along companionably, then John said, "I've no' been a gude faether to thee, Thomas. I'm sorry. All that's changed. I'm willing for us to be friends if thou art."

Thomas rode in silence for a while. "You thought I was Jamie," he burst out. "I dinna ken who Jamie was. I canna remember ma brother. You want me to be like him. How can I?"

John was shocked. How could the boy not remember Jamie? He looked around him. There were tears in his eyes. He wanted Thomas to know what happened. He started talking. He told his son about the deer hunt and how Jamie killed his first deer, and how they were going to celebrate the reprieve of Clan Ciaran. Then he told how he had sent Jamie home and how Jamie had saved their mother from Duggan. And he told Thomas how, as a baby, he had watched it all, before John arrived home to find Jamie dying. Tears ran down his cheeks, and he stopped his horse and looked at Thomas.

"Jamie is dead, Thomas. I will aye love him and cherish his memory. But thou art alive, ma only son, and I love thee equally." John reached out and touched Thomas' shoulder. "We will do great things thegither, Son."

Thomas looked John in the eyes and nodded. "We'd best be riding on, Faether, or we'll no' be back by sundoon."

Thomas was his own man already. At ten years old, he had had to grow up very quickly.

Chapter 20   1675
Ten Years Later

Thomas Grant had grown strong and tall, with a rugged, swarthy complexion. He heaved the last log onto the pile in the wood store, ready for winter use, anxious to finish this task quickly. There was a girl in town, who had attracted his attention last market day. There would be time to go and seek her out if he left now. His father unhitched the horse from the cart and took him to pasture. Thomas hauled the cart into the barn and shut the door. He would be glad to get away for the evening. His father's handicap was an irritation to both of them. It was amazing the way he had worked out how to achieve most tasks, with the hook on the end of his arm. But it was the little things he found difficult, like tying knots.

Thomas went into the house shedding his boots at the door. He found his mother in the kitchen preparing vegetables. He went and kissed the top of her head.

"I'll no' be wanting a meal, Mother. I'm gooing into town."

Annie turned her head. "You'll need to eat, Son. Take some siller frae the pot over the fire. And dinna drink too much." She smiled.

Thomas went to his chamber and found some clean clothes and a fresh plaid. He dressed carefully and brushed the mat of dark brown hair into a semblance of tidiness. He looked closely into the mirror at the beginnings of a beard, and rubbed his chin vigorously to fluff it up. His deep brown eyes matched his hair, and he looked critically at the somewhat bulbous nose he had inherited from the Grants.

John came into the house as Thomas was leaving.

"You'll be away to town, I see. Didst feed the beasts?"

"Ay, Faether," called Thomas, going quickly into the stable before his father could think of any more tasks for him. He saddled his horse and rode away.

"I'll have thee to masell this evening," said John, as he put his arm round Annie's waist and hugged her to him.

"Ay." She looked up into his eyes. The sparkle had gone from her face long ago. She was looking older. John supposed that he also had aged in the last few years.

"Dost want help with anything?" Always conscious that he might be a burden, he wanted to make up for it by doing things for her. Isabel was no longer with them, and Annie rarely had time to sit and rest.

"Take a look at the fire and see if it needs another log," she said. "And pour us both a dram."

Something was troubling Annie. She very rarely drank whisky. He went into the parlour and attended to the fire. The level in the whisky bottle was going down. He would have to buy some more. He went to look in the pot over the fire. He was sure there was more in there last time he looked. He could feel his temper rising and took a mouthful from his glass. Annie came in, wiping her hands on her apron.

"Where's our savings for the drink?" he demanded.

Annie went to sit in her chair by the fire. "Didst pour me one?" she asked.

John went over and fetched her glass and gave it to her. "There's no' enough in the pot for another bottle. Has that boy taken it?"

Annie sighed. "I said he could take some for a meal in town. He's no' eaten theday."

"He's no right to ma whisky money. If he wants to go gallivanting he can goo withoot his supper." John knocked back the rest of his drink. He looked at the empty glass and threw it into the fireplace, where it shattered into a thousand pieces. There was a silence between husband and wife, while they stared at the fresh log catching fire, sending sparks up the chimney.

"Did that make thee feel better?" asked Annie, looking up at John. "Sit thee doon, I have a letter here for thee to read." She searched in her apron pocket and brought out a letter sealed with red wax. She handed it to John.

John sat down, took the letter and looked at it. "Who brought this?"

"A messenger frae the Laird, this morning," said Annie. She looked concerned. "I'm afeared, John. I've heard that the new Laird is making changes in his clans and he dinna like the Covenanters."

This brought John's anger back to the surface. He held the letter on his knee with his left stump and tore it open with his right hand. He saw that it was indeed from the Laird Ludovick. John read the letter, looked at Annie and shouted, "The young upstart! He'll goo against his faether's agreement, will he? We'll see aboot that!"

He lurched out of his chair and went over to the dresser. He looked at the nearly empty whisky bottle,

119

hesitated, then opened the drawer. He fished around for a few minutes before he found what he was looking for. He took a paper out and carried it to his chair.

Annie sat waiting for an explanation. She took a sip of her whisky.

"Tell me, John, what is it?"

John read the signed agreement he had received from Captain Hill, years ago. He was not mistaken. This was a promise that Clan Ciaran would never be dispossessed. So what did young Ludovick think he was doing?

"The letter says that all Covenanters must leave Grant land. We'll protest. I have to goo and gather the Clan Ciaran." John stood up and went towards the door.

"Dost have to goo now? At this hour? 'Twill be dark soon and you've had no supper, John. Can it no' wait until morning? We're surely no' aboot to be dragged frae our beds and turned oot into the night. What else does the letter say?"

Annie came to where John stood at the door. She snatched the letter out of his hand and waved it in front of him.

"How does the Laird propose to banish us? This is just a letter."

John snatched the letter back from Annie. He read it again. "It says we must be gone before Michaelmas, leaving all our livestock, as that and our homesteads now belong to the Laird." He shook his fist with the letter in it and shouted, "This is ootrageous!"

"John, John! Calm thysel'. Save thy rage for the Laird. Come and sit doon. We must make plans." She went to the dresser, took out another glass, and emptied the bottle into it. She took it to the fireplace and sat down again, watching John get a hold of himself.

She was right, of course. No amount of shouting at Annie was going to help. He went and slumped back into his chair, accepting the glass that Annie was offering. He took a grateful mouthful, savouring the warming effect that it had.

The leaders of Clan Ciaran met the next morning. They had all received the same letter, and were ready to go and protest at the judgement against them. John had the agreement close to his chest as they rode to Ballachastell. The new Laird had had the castle restored and made comfortable, and he was now installed with his new bride. He kept a small company of militia there as security.

John, Robert and their brothers rode along the valley and approached the castle. They were escorted up the drive by an armed guard and were met in the courtyard by more soldiers. They were told to dismount, were relieved of their dirks, and asked the purpose of their visit.

John said, "We are the leaders of Clan Ciaran, come to protest against the judgement we've received. We wish to see the Laird."

One of the soldiers disappeared into the castle.

The brothers stood around in the courtyard. There was a cold wind blowing up here on the exposed slope of the hill. They stamped their feet and muttered to each other. John's temper was rising.

121

Robert looked at him and said, "'Twill no help to get angry, brother. Try and keep calm."

"The man is playing with us, Rob. I dinna trust him." John wrapped his plaid round him, keeping his left arm covered.

The door opened and a man John did not recognise stepped out into the courtyard.

"I am Alain McDonald, the Laird's grieve. What is your business?"

"We've received this letter frae the Laird." John handed his letter to the grieve, who waved it away.

"I ken what is in the letter. Ye must all be gone frae this land by Michaelmas. The Laird's instructions are final."

John took his late Laird's agreement out and showed it to the grieve. "His faether signed this. He has no right to banish us."

McDonald took the paper and cast his eyes over it briefly. "Wait here," he said, and went indoors.

There was another long wait. John's blood was boiling by the time the grieve re-appeared. He had a satisfied smirk on his face. His eyes glittered menacingly.

"The matter stands. The Laird's instructions are the same. If they are not obeyed ye will be forcibly removed."

A great roar came from the leaders of Clan Ciaran. They shouted and waved their fists. The soldiers around them closed in to contain them. The grieve stood his ground.

Robert shouted, "What aboot his faether's agreement? He swore that Clan Ciaran would never be dispossessed."

McDonald pursed his lips. "There is no agreement. Go and prepare to leave. Any further protest and ye will be forced to leave immediately." He turned away and retreated into the Castle. The door slammed behind him.

The soldiers in the courtyard raised their guns and aimed them at John and his clan while their dirks were returned to them. The men of Clan Ciaran mounted their horses and, still protesting and shaking their fists, proceeded down the long drive and out through the gate.

John's mind was racing as they rode back through the valley. There was nothing they could do it seemed, to change the Laird's mind. But if they had to go, they would take as much with them as possible. The rest of the company were riding in a stunned silence. No longer a clan, they must go their separate ways and rely on their own resources. They had four weeks in which to prepare to leave their ancestral homes for ever.

Chapter 21
Feasting and Farewells

Clan Ciaran went on their last hunting expedition the next day. They all vowed to take as much away with them as they could. This included venison to sustain them on their journeys. No-one knew how long it would take to get away from an angry Laird and his militia, for indeed he would be angry when he saw what they had left behind. This was to be their last act of vengeance.

The hunting party aimed to take home two deer for their farewell feast, and enough to butcher and share round. John and Thomas set off with their bows and quivers. John had fashioned a glove to hold his bow with his left arm. He was not as good a shot as he had been, but he could certainly take part as a useful hunter. Thomas proved to be as good a shot as his brother had proved to be.

A light drizzly rain accompanied them as they scrambled over craggy heather-clad hills. The visibility was poor and it took them a long time to track down their first quarry. Two young does were killed and taken to Angus's homestead. By midday the drizzle had cleared, and they spotted a stag with a large herd around him on the edge of a wood.

The hunters spread out, some aiming to shoot the stag. The others would aim at the does. All prepared their bows and watched for Angus's signal. Angus's hand went down and a chorus of twanging bowstrings filled the air, followed by a shower of arrows hissing to their targets. The herd scattered in panic. The stag sprang forward with a bunch of arrows piercing his neck. He went down after a few yards, and the bowmen ran to claim their prize. Angus dispatched the animal by slitting its throat with his dirk, and the blood flowed. Three does lay dead or dying. The rest had disappeared into the trees. The hunters set about tying the corpses onto carrying poles, and trudged home singing Highland songs.

The feasting was noisy and the drink flowed liberally. If they could not take it with them, they would consume it before they went. Annie had to load her two ale-sodden men into the cart with their share of the venison, in order to carry them home.

Preparations for a long journey were soon under way. John had heard that the drovers were passing through the valley, buying small herds of cattle from farmers on the way to the tryst. He and Thomas rounded up all the unmarked cattle and took them to the meeting place to sell them to the drovers.

"I dinna want to be seen at the tryst, where Laird Ludovick will be strutting around in his tartan trews with his grieve," he told Annie.

The money they had from the beasts would have to last them until they were able to work for a living. The cattle that were branded to keep and breed from John released from their winter pasture to roam the hills and forage for food. The Laird would have to find them if he wanted them. John picked out the two best cart horses and a horse each for himself and Thomas to ride. The breeding mares and the stallion were released with the rest of the horses, to fend for themselves. They killed a pig and Annie salted it down with some beef for supplies on the journey. The other pigs they would set free before they left.

John and his son took the cart out of the barn and discussed how they would convert it into a travelling vehicle.

Thomas said, "How will we fit sleeping places in among all the supplies?"

"We could make a false floor and stow all the goods and apparel underneath," John said. "We need planks of wood." He stroked his beard and looked around for inspiration.

"Why dinna we dismantle the barn, and use the wood frae that?" suggested Thomas.

"Gude idea." John was beginning to enjoy the challenge.

"We'll need a roof to keep the rain off." Thomas was warming to the idea of a journey into the unknown.

Over the next few days, the cart became a travellers' caravan. John and Thomas took fence posts from the pasture and lashed them to the corners to support a roof, the framework of which came from the barn. Hides covered the roof, and more hides would line the floor of the cart to protect the supplies from wet from the road. The ladders used to make it into a hay wain were fixed in place to protect the contents of the cart.

John slapped his son on the back as they went into the house after a day's work.

"'Tis shaping up nicely," he said.

Annie had been baking all day, preparing bread, oatcakes and pies to take with them. She had made butter and cheese, wrapping each in muslin before putting them into crocks. She had sown bags to carry supplies of wheat and oats, and would be taking her quern to grind the wheat when needed.

The family sat round the table for their dinner. "We'll aim to set off themorrow night," said John, between mouthfuls.

"Dost ken where we'll be heading?" asked Annie.

"We'll go south, to Edinburgh first. But I want to get oot o' Scotland entirely. We'll find a place to settle right away frae here."

"The road will take us past Ballachastell. Will the laird's soldiers no' be on the lookoot, and take our horses and anything else they think is his?" said Thomas.

"Not if we goo at night. They'll no' see what we've left behind until the next day, when we'll be clear of Grant land."

There was a pause in the conversation. They all had mixed feelings about the forthcoming journey. John was relieved in some ways that he would be leaving. There were so many unpleasant memories here. He was ready to turn away from the grief and anger. He would be more comfortable as his own master, not beholden to his Laird. But he dreaded leaving behind his brothers and the clan. At least he had the support of a son who was strong and healthy. John was beginning to feel the effects of ageing. His eyesight was not as good as it had been, and his limbs were stiff first thing in the morning. He looked at Annie. She was worried about the future. She would have to spend the next weeks and maybe months in a man's world. Women were vulnerable away from their home territory.

"Annie," he said. She looked up at him, her forehead wrinkled. "Dost think thou could cut off some of that bonny hair and dress as a man for our journey?"

She stopped eating. She thought for a few moments, holding her spoon poised in the air. "Ay," she said. "I canna grow a beard, though." Her eyes twinkled with her old humour.

John smiled. "You'll be driving the cart some of the time, and going into town for provisions. You'd be in less danger of being molested if you looked like a boy."

Annie nodded and took another mouthful. Thomas was staring at them both.

"I still have some of ma old trews that I grew oot of," he said. "They should fit you perfectly, Mother. You'll be more comfortable riding a horse in breeches."

They continued to eat.

John put his spoon down on an empty plate. "We'll pack the provisions in the cart first thing themorn. I want all the deerskins ye can find in the house frae the floor and the walls. We can use them to cover us at night. Before we go to bed I want everything we need to take put in the kitchen. Then we can decide what we dinna have room for. Bedding will be the last to goo in."

The family rose at first light and had a good breakfast. They were busy packing the cart when Robert and Ellie and their son and daughter came into the yard.

"Ye'll be leaving soon," said Robert, looking at the cart and its contents.

"Ay," said John. "What aboot thee?"

129

"We'll goo to Inverness and find a ship sailing for America. They say there's land a-plenty there, and fine farming country."

"We're heading south thenight," said John. He looked at his brother and offered his left arm. Robbie grasped it with his left, and their right arms went around each other's shoulders in a long embrace. There were tears in their eyes when they released their hold.

"Goo safely," said Robert.

"God speed," said John.

They each went to embrace the women and the sons. Robert wiped his eyes with the back of his hand and led his family back down the lane. John, Annie and Thomas looked after them for a while, then turned to continue their work.

At midday the packing was almost done.

"I'll be going up the hill to say farewell to the crofters," said Thomas.

"Ay," said his father. "Take any provisions they could use."

Thomas went to the corn store and filled a sack. Then he went to the hog pound and picked up one of the young pigs and put it squealing into another sack. He slung both sacks over his shoulders and set off up the hill.

John looked round the house checking for things forgotten. He found his beloved bagpipes and touched them in farewell. He was unable to play them now and there was no space for them. But they would need music on the way. He picked up the pipe Jamie had carved from a piece of elder and slipped it into the money pouch which hung on a strap over his shoulder.

The sun was going down as John went round his homestead making sure that there was no livestock in the buildings, and that they had left nothing that they needed. He filled as many hay bags as he could find and hung them round the sides of the cart. Then he went up the hill a short distance and sat looking down at the home he was about to leave for ever. Presently there was a movement behind him, and Thomas was there. He sat down next to his father. They stayed still and quiet, each with their own thoughts.

Thomas stirred and looked at John. "We'll be fine, Faether," he said, and grasped John's shoulder in friendship. Then he got to his feet and went down to the house. An inviting aroma of cooked food wafted up to John, and he followed his son to have the last meal.

Annie was serving up the dinner, dressed in a shirt and breeches. Her hair was shoulder length. Thomas went and kissed the top of her head.

"You make a fine wee brother," he said. They both chuckled, and the family sat down to eat.

It was time to go. They dressed themselves in their plaids and bonnets, took a last look round the house, and went to saddle up the horses. John had chosen two of his best breeding stock, the grey mare, Clover, for Thomas or Annie to ride, and Shadow, a black stallion. They were both descended from the Arab stallion he had stolen from Elchies. Thomas brought the cart horses and hitched them to the cart.

John helped Annie into the driver's seat and said, "I want thee and Thomas to goo down the road away from here. Keep going. I'll follow and catch up with ye. On

131

no account stop or look back. Now goo." He slapped the rump of one of the cart horses and they started off down the lane towards the river. John did not want Annie to see what he was going to do next.

When Thomas on his horse and the cart had disappeared into the dark, John went back into the house, carrying a torch which he had prepared. He lit it in the embers of the still smouldering fire and set light to the soft furnishings in the parlour, recalling the day he did the same thing at Elchies, years ago. He went out into the yard and set light to the straw in the stables, what was left of the barn, and the corn store. He flung the still burning torch into the wood store, then mounted Shadow and galloped away until it was safe to stop and look back. The leaders of Clan Ciaran had agreed to set fire to their homesteads before leaving tonight. There would be a chain of fires through the glen, leaving nothing for Laird Ludovick to claim. John could see the flames sending sparks into the night sky, and lighting up the surrounding land. He caught sight of two shadowy figures, his old mare and stallion, on the hill. They stood staring at the flames, then lifted their heads and galloped away.

John turned his horse's head and made his way forward to join his family, leaving his shadows behind him.

Part 2

The Long Journey

Chapter 22
Flight into the Unknown

The fugitives were surrounded by a sea of pink and mauve heather. There were few trees up here on the moor, which was bleak and exposed. They had been travelling for nearly twenty four hours, with a few short breaks to refresh themselves and the horses. They could go no further without rest.

"Thomas!" John called to his son, who was riding in front of the cart.

Thomas stopped and waited for John to catch up.

"Canst ride ahead and find a place to rest for thenight, Son?"

"Ay, Faether." Thomas spurred his horse on, and trotted away.

John came up level with the cart. Annie was holding the reins, but had a glazed look in her eyes. "We'll stop as soon as we find a place, Annie."

She looked at him and nodded, shook her shoulders, took a deep breath and sat upright. There was a dip in the road in front. Thomas appeared and waved. He trotted up to them.

"There's water doon there and a wee patch of grass by the road."

They continued down the hill, stopped at some trees and dismounted. Two streams tumbled down from the hills and met each other in a deep pool, before continuing as a small river. Thomas and John unhitched the horses and led them to drink. Annie went and bathed her face in the cool water. They tethered the horses to the trees and allowed them to graze on the grassy banks. Thomas collected an armful of dry heather and lit a fire under the trivet they had brought with them. Annie found a pot of stew she had prepared the day before.

The family were soon sitting round the fire with their bowls and spoons, enjoying the hot food. The sun was sinking as they finished their meal. John found a bottle of whisky and they all took a draught. Little was said as they washed the dishes in the pool, gave the horses a bag of hay and relieved themselves in the heather. John and Annie climbed into the cart and lay together in the moonlight.

Thomas took a couple of skins and made himself comfortable in the heather. He lay looking at the stars, thinking about the journey. They had ridden through Pitmain in the early morning, too early for anyone to be about. It was the week of the Michaelmas Tryst, and they heard the cattle waking up, snorting and roaring as they passed the common. By the time that they had travelled a few miles past the town and found the drove road over the moors, they were safe from the Laird Grant's scouts and could rest awhile. His mother found oat biscuits and milk among the stores. Soon they would have finished the prepared food they had brought, and would need to start cooking. This would slow their progress. That would be a relief. The last few hours had been hard. He wondered how long his mother would be able to keep on travelling. She was not used to the outdoor life.

Dawn woke him from a deep sleep. He sat up and looked around him. The weather remained calm and clear. There was no movement in the cart and Thomas fancied a bowl of crowdies this morning. He collected some heather and started a fire, which crackled and hissed. His father's head emerged from the cart.

"Faether, canst find milk, oats and eggs? I'll make thy breakfast."

John's head disappeared. Minutes later, he climbed down from the cart with the required ingredients. "There's no end to thy talents, Son. I didna ken thou couldst cook, too."

"I've watched Mother often enough. It canna be difficult."

Annie climbed down from the cart. "Mmmm! Smells like food. That's ma boy." She yawned and stretched, her hair tousled and the warmth of sleep still on her cheeks.

John said, "I hope to get to Edinburgh theday. Are you willing to drive the cart, Annie, or shall Thomas take over?"

"I can do it for the morn," said Annie, coming to sit by the fire.

They were washing the dishes and hitching up the cart horses, when a great rumbling came towards them along the road. The family stood and watched. Clouds of dust surrounded hundreds of cattle as they were driven south. Collie dogs ran round the leading cattle, keeping them in check. Four or five mounted drovers surrounded the herd behind. The shouts, whistles and barks faded as the herd thundered away.

"Thanks be we were no' on the road when they passed!" remarked John, as they prepared to follow.

John had misjudged the distance. It took them three days to reach the outskirts of Edinburgh. They kept clear of towns, feeling more comfortable on drove roads through countryside and villages. A few travellers passed them; walkers, horsemen and two coaches with their passengers.

"We'll find an inn for the night," John said to Thomas when they stopped at midday. "We'll buy a cooked meal there, and thy mother can have a good night's sleep in a bed. Wilt sleep in the cart and keep an eye on the horses? I dinna want to find them gone themorn."

"Ay, that'll be fine, Faether."

It was not long before an inn came in sight. Annie was still dressed as a boy and John asked if they could have a room to share. The innkeeper, who had watched them drive in with a laden cart, looked them up and down warily and nodded.

"You've travelled far?" he asked.

"Frae Inverness," John lied. He did not want too many questions asked. They were shown a room with one bed. John said the lad could sleep on the floor. They were left alone. John put his arms round Annie and held her there. She relaxed, and he picked her up and laid her on the bed, then sat beside her.

"Rest while I go and help Thomas with the horses." He hesitated before he said, "I'm proud of thee, Annie." He left the room, his emotions floating to the surface.

He found Thomas with the cart in a quiet corner of the yard. He had declined the help of the ostler and tethered the horses nearby with bags of hay. They would have to buy some more soon. John took a few things from the cart, which he didn't want stolen, and covered the rest with deerskins. They walked into the inn together.

They left their plaids and bonnets in their room and came down to the bar in their shirts and trews. John bought three mugs of ale. They sat at a table in a dark corner, feeling vulnerable in these unfamiliar surroundings. John ordered three meals and they sat quietly eating, grateful for the warmth and comfort. John listened to the conversations of some locals, who had come in for a drink.

Their host was saying, "...did you see the militia in town, Angus?"

"Nay, they were going along the road to Dalkeith," said Angus.

Another man joined in. "I heard they've been sent by the Laird Grant in the Highlands. They have orders to seek oot Covenanters who might be lurking aboot in the Lowlands."

A newcomer said, "Ay, there are wee companies of them all over. I dinna ken what'll become of those they find."

John gulped down his mouthful and looked at Thomas. "Didst hear that?" he muttered.

Thomas nodded and went on eating, watching the man at the bar. No more was said on the subject. The innkeeper glanced in their direction and went to serve another customer.

John spent the night wondering how they could avoid Ludovick's militia. He woke early and crept downstairs, hoping that the door to the yard would be unlocked. He wanted to talk to Thomas.

A voice startled him.

"I dinna ken who ye are, or where ye're frae, and I dinna wish to. If ye'll take ma advice ye'll no' be wearing the Highland dress." The landlord spoke in a low voice. "To keep oot of the way o' the militia ye'd best be travelling east along this road 'til ye meet a farm track into the hills." He gestured to his right and upwards. "That brings ye to a drove road which leads to the border." He unlocked the door to the yard. "I'll have breakfast ready in a wee while." He disappeared along the dark passage.

John entered the yard, quietly shutting the door behind him. He climbed into the cart and shook Thomas to wake him. He repeated what the innkeeper had said, and they both went back into the house to wake Annie and have their breakfast.

"I'm obliged to you, landlord," said John as he paid what he owed. The man nodded and they shook hands.

Chapter 23
Hunted

The family were on the road again. Darkness gave way to a grey dawn. A few spots of rain touched their faces. It was cold without their plaids and bonnets, but John knew that their Highland dress would attract attention. They would have to buy jackets and hats. Winter was on its way.

At last John saw a track leading off to the right and up into the hills. It was steep and stony. The carthorses stumbled and the cart swayed and shuddered. The rain came down heavily. Their clothes were soaked. Annie was partly sheltered by the roof of the cart. She was finding it hard to stay in her seat and keep the horses going. Thomas dismounted, left his horse with his father, and went to lead the carthorses.

"Goo under the roof and keep dry, Mother," he shouted above the noise of the rain. Annie crept under cover.

Thomas slipped and slid with the horses on the muddy uneven surface which led steeply uphill. They passed a farmhouse with a light glowing in one of the windows. After this the track levelled out. They trudged on until they met a road crossing their path. Thomas halted the horses and John dismounted. The rain continued to hammer down. John could hardly see for the water pouring off his face. The track they were following appeared to go uphill. He walked a little way along the road to the right. This felt like a drovers' road. He thought they should be going in the other direction, so turned round and followed the road to the left of the cart. This, he reckoned, was east. The road became wider and turned south-east and slightly uphill. That felt better. He walked back to the cart.

"I believe that way is best," he said to Thomas.

Annie appeared from her hiding place. "I can drive again now, if it's level."

"'Tis better than it was," said John. They looked at each other's faces with water running down from their sodden hair, and laughed.

Annie said, "The roof's holding up well. All's dry inside.

John's spirits rose as they set off again. The soldiers would not want to be out in this. The rain was as good a cover as any.

For hours they followed the drove road in the pouring rain. It seemed there was no end to it. The road was becoming muddier, with little rivulets crossing the surface, from the hills above. It was time they stopped and had something to eat. John signed to Thomas and dismounted. There was grass at the side of the road for the horses to graze. They pulled the cart over and unhitched the carthorses.

John said to Annie, "Canst find food for us, love?"

She disappeared into the cart and brought out the last of the meat pies. They washed them down with a flagon of ale from the keg they had brought with them. Thomas found a bag of oats and took a handful to each of the horses. As they were all eating, the rain eased up. They began to see their surroundings. Thomas wandered along the road and disappeared round a

142

corner. John saw some rocks and beckoned to Annie to come and sit down. They sat in silence for a while.

Annie looked up and asked, "Where are we going, John?"

John did not answer at first. He was not sure himself. All he knew was that they must get away from Scotland as soon as they could. He knew nothing about England and the people who lived there. He did not even know if they spoke the same language.

"As soon as we cross the border, we'll look for a place to stop for a few days. We want to find oot aboot the people and what they do. We need to buy supplies and winter clothes. We might have to live in the open until we can find work."

He paused, looked at Annie and said, "I dinna ken where we're going, Annie."

Thomas made his way along the drove road. The hill dropped steeply down to the left. The road followed the ridge, winding downhill. On his right, the land rose up to higher levels, hidden in the mist. There were rocks along the edge of the ridge, as if to hold the road in place. He sat on one of them and gazed at the view over the valley. As the rain cleared, green pastures appeared below. Trees in their autumn clothing revealed themselves. There were little farmsteads nestling in the lower hills, with tracks leading from them to a wider road, which ran along the valley. Beyond, the land was relatively level. On the distant horizon a grey haze merged with the grey sky. But what was that? A shaft of sunlight beamed from a break in the clouds, and lit up what looked like water. As he watched, a strip of shining gold spread across the horizon. That must be the ocean! Thomas gazed in astonishment at so much water! His gaze was drawn back to the land as he noticed movement on the road. A group of horsemen was travelling south. He looked more carefully and saw that they were all dressed the same. The militia! It appeared that their paths would cross, if this drove road continued downhill.

John stood up and went to meet Thomas as he ran towards him. "Faether! Faether! there's soldiers doon there, riding along the road."

"Are they coming this way?"

"No. It's a long way off on another road. They're riding in the same direction as us." Thomas was out of breath. He sat on the stone beside his mother.

John thought for a moment. "We'll keep going," he said. "We might miss them."

"I saw the ocean, Faether!"

"That's gude news," said John. "We're going the right way."

They set off again. Thomas pointed out the road where he had seen the soldiers. The route took them downhill, steep and winding. The brakes were not sufficient to hold the cart back, and John and Thomas had to dismount and strap themselves to the rear, leaning back to stop it running away. The landscape became more wooded, with streams cascading through rocky gulleys. They found themselves entering a small town and proceeded cautiously, watching out for any sign of militia.

The town was busy with a cattle market. The drovers were there and the farmers, buying and selling cattle. No-one noticed a covered cart being driven by a boy with two men on fine horses following. Their clothes were almost dry. John looked for somewhere to leave the cart out of sight. They were coming out of the centre of town when he saw an alleyway leading to open fields. They took the cart up the alley and came to a large yard behind a house. Nobody was about except a farm cat. John and Thomas dismounted and Annie climbed stiffly down from the cart.

"I'll stay here in case someone comes," said John. "Thomas, take thy mother into town and find oot if ye can buy fresh food, and hay for the horses, and anything else we need. Here's siller." He handed Annie some money out of his purse, and watched them walking away.

He strolled round the yard, peering into the wooden buildings and cow stalls. They were all empty, and gave the impression of being abandoned. The cat came and rubbed against his legs, calling for attention. John bent down and stroked it. He wondered if there was anything that he could eat while he was waiting. He climbed up into the cart and rummaged round. He found the crock that had contained oat biscuits. It was empty. He remembered the bottle of whisky. It would not hurt to have a drop to keep his spirits up. He found the bottle. They'd used nearly half of that, too. He uncorked it with his teeth and put the cork down while he took a mouthful. That felt good. He took another.

The sound of footsteps nearby stopped him drinking. He replaced the cork and peered out from under the covers. No-one in sight. He checked the other side. Still no-one. He sat still and listened. Footsteps approached. John's hand went to his dirk. Someone was there, trying to see what was inside the cart. The footsteps went over to where the horses were tethered. There was a pause, then the sound of hooves on the cobbled yard. John leapt from the cart, dirk in hand, and faced the intruder.

"Where d'you think you're gooing with ma horse?" he demanded.

The man, raggedly dressed in jacket, breeches and a wide-brimmed hat, stopped and regarded John who was standing in his way.

"Give me those reins and be on your way, or I'll call for help." John hoped he would not have to. He really did not want to attract attention.

The man realised his game was up, and handed the reins to John. He sidled off into the fields.

As John was tethering the horse, Annie and Thomas came up the alleyway, their arms full of provisions and smiles on their faces.

"There's hay for sale, but we had no bags to put it in," said Annie. "And there's a stall selling working clothes, but we'd no' enough siller." She handed the change to John.

"Did ye see any soldiers?" asked John.

"No," said Thomas. "And no-one looked at us queer."

"I'll go and get hay and the jackets, and find oot how to get to the border. Watch oot, there was a man attempting to take ma horse." John walked down the alley with the empty hay bags.

It was good to be among the bustle of a town. John found a tavern where he could buy another bottle of whisky. He walked through the open door into the gloom. Standing at the bar were five soldiers. To walk out again would arouse suspicion. He went up to the bar. The soldiers were laughing and joking between themselves and were unaware of John and his Highland trews and leather stump. John caught the landlord's eye and asked for ale. He stood leaning on the bar with his back turned and sipped the drink carefully. It was not what he wanted after the whisky. The soldiers were talking.

"Well, there dinna seem to be Covenanters in these parts. Have you seen strangers in town, landlord?"

"No, they've probably all taken to the hills when they heard ye war seekin' 'em. The most likely place ye'll find 'em is on the drove roads, up on the moor. Is that not so, Jock?" he addressed John, who nodded.

"Ay. I reckon."

The soldiers conferred. "We'll mebbe goo back that way," one of them said. They drained their glasses and walked out into the sunshine.

The landlord winked at John. "Can I get you another, Sir?"

"No, but I'd be obliged if you'd sell me a bottle of whisky," John replied. He paid the landlord and left, slipping the whisky inside his shirt.

He found a stall selling clothes, and bought three farmer's jackets and hats. He dressed himself in one set, and draped the others over his left arm. As he was paying, he said to the vendor, "Can ye tell me the best way to the border. I've business in England."

"There's a road over there between those two dwellings. That will take thee to the river Tweed, which is the border. There's a ferry over the river there."

"Will the ferry take a laden cart and horses?"

"Ay," the man said.

"Thank you kindly, Sir," John said, tipping the brim of his hat as he had seen other men do. On the other side of the road there was a farmer with a hay wain, selling bait for horses. John went across and filled as many bags as he could carry over his shoulder, paid the farmer and thanked him. It was laborious carrying his purchases back to the cart, and he was grateful to see Thomas coming towards him down the alley. He handed over part of his load and they walked back together.

"Is all well?" John asked.

"Ay. A farm hand came and questioned me. Mother hid in the cart. I said we only stopped to buy hay for the horses, and would be on our way presently. That seemed to satisfy him."

John handed over the jackets, and Annie and Thomas dressed themselves in their new disguise. He told them of his brush with the soldiers. They agreed it would be best to make a move before they were hunted down. They hitched up the horses and Thomas took over driving the cart. John helped Annie onto Thomas' mare and they headed out of town on the road indicated by the clothes vendor.

Chapter 24
Pursuit

The day was drawing to a close, and it was time they had a meal. They came to a wooded area and John rode ahead. He found a path between the trees leading to a clearing. He could hear running water. He rode back to the road and signalled to Thomas. They found a level place for the cart and prepared to stay there for the night.

"There's venison here," said Annie, as she rummaged among the stores under the false floor of the cart. "I can cook us a nice stew if ye can find water."

Thomas and John brought water and collected wood to make a fire. They were soon sitting round drinking ale and talking about the day while the stew pot bubbled. They were glad of their jackets in the October evening.

"We'll no' be long in Scotland," said John. "I reckon we'll be crossing the border themorrow."

After the meal they took off their new jackets and wrapped themselves in their plaids before settling down all together in the cart. Annie lay between the two men. Thomas felt cramped and could not sleep. He crept out of the cart quietly and went to sit by the embers of the fire, keeping his plaid round him.

A twig snapped.

Thomas slipped under the cart. It might be an animal, but it was more likely that they had an intruder. He waited. He heard voices. Two shapes came out of the darkness of the wood, and walked towards the horses. Thomas crawled out from under the cart and followed. The two men started untying the tethers.

Thomas said loudly, so that his father could hear, "Stop right there!" He put his arm round the shoulders of the nearest man and his dirk to the man's throat."

The other man turned round, his dirk at the ready.

"Any trouble and your friend will be finished," Thomas said. "Get away frae here and I'll let him go."

But he had relaxed his hold on his captive, who turned quickly and knocked Thomas to the ground.

"Quick! Cut the tethers and we'll ride away!" the thief shouted to his accomplice.

"Hold it!" John's voice caused the thieves to freeze. "The first one to move gets a bullet in the knee."

Thomas staggered to his feet, retrieved his dirk, and went to secure the horses.

"Here's rope, Thomas," John called. He held out the rope, which was hanging on the hook of his left stump, while he kept pointing the gun at the thieves. "Tie their wrists and take them away. I'll follow."

Thomas tied the men and led them away. John found a mature tree some distance away from the cart. He and Thomas threw the free ends of the rope over an overhanging branch, pulling the men's arms up above their heads and securing the ropes. They were now hanging with their feet barely touching the ground.

"Sleep well!" called Thomas as he walked back to the cart with his father.

"Get some rest, Son," said John as he climbed back onto the cart. "We might have a long day ahead of us."

As they were having breakfast Thomas said, "It was likely the same man who tried to take the horse in town. I reckon they followed us."

John grinned as he finished his mouthful. "There were no bullets in the gun," he said. "I couldna load it quick enough in the dark wi' one hand."

Thomas laughed. "You fooled 'em, Faether. They were dreadfully afeared!"

Before leaving, John rode to where the two thieves were hanging on the tree. He cut them down and left them in a disgruntled heap. He caught up with Thomas driving the cart and Annie on horseback. Their spirits were high. Even the horses seemed refreshed. They picked up their feet and raised their heads as they trotted towards England.

The road was mostly downhill and the going was easier. It was not long before they saw the River Tweed winding its way through the valley below. Thomas shouted with excitement. Soon they could relax, with no-one in pursuit. They travelled through green country with trees in their autumn colours and crops in the fields. He marvelled at the beauty of this strange land. He thought he could see the ferry crossing the river.

There was a shout from his father behind him. John increased his pace to catch up with the cart.

"We saw militia on the road behind us, riding at speed," called John as he came level with Thomas. "We'd best make haste."

Thomas urged the horses on and John hung back to allow Annie to catch up. Thomas could see the ferry clearly now. It was on the way back after taking the last

151

passengers over to England. Thomas shouted, but the ferryman did not hear.

John galloped ahead to alert the ferryman to wait before he crossed again. Thomas could hear the soldiers' horses following them now. He looked round and saw his mother's horse stagger. He looked ahead. His father was talking to the ferryman.

Thomas turned again to check on Annie's progress. Clover was limping badly. She would never make it. He slowed the cart horses until his mother came level with the cart.

"Canst jump across to the cart, Mother?" Thomas put his hand out to help her.

Annie let go of the reins and lifted her leg over the neck of the horse. She threw herself towards Thomas and he caught her round the waist.

"What aboot Clover?" she asked.

"She might follow, but we'll have to leave her if she canna keep up," said Thomas as he urged the carthorses on again.

The soldiers were closing in on them.

"I canna wait long," said the ferryman. "There's more passengers waiting on t'other side."

John watched Annie leaping from her horse to the cart. Clover limped to the grassy verge and stopped. The soldiers were out of sight round a bend in the road. He did not want to lose a horse. He spurred Shadow into action. It would take time to load the cart and horses onto the ferry. There might be enough time to rescue Clover.

He shouted to Thomas as he passed the cart, "Get on the ferry. I'll catch ye up." He could see the soldiers now. He grabbed the mare's reins and gently encouraged her to follow.

"Come, you can do it. It's no' far" He nudged Shadow into a trot. Clover did not resist, and the limping was less severe now she had no rider. They made steady progress, and reached the ferry with only about five lengths to spare between them and their pursuers. The ferryman waited for John to encourage the horses on board, and cast off.

The soldiers reined in and shouted angrily, waving their fists.

The ferry floated out into the river. The shore was receding. The soldiers stood helpless.

Thomas asked, "How dost think they kenned we were on the road?"

"I reckon those horse thieves heard us talking in the woods yest'reen," said John. "They wanted revenge and reported us to the militia."

Chapter 25
England

The road followed the river for a mile or two before turning south. Thomas continued driving the cart and Annie sat beside him. John rode Shadow and led Clover, whose walking was improving.

John came level with Thomas and said, "We'll stop as soon as we can and have something to eat."

They kept a leisurely pace now they were no longer pursued, and were able to take in their surroundings. There were green pastures where cattle grazed, and golden fields dotted with stooks of the corn which had been cut recently. On their right were grassy hills where sheep stood and watched them as they passed. Streams cascaded down the slopes to join a river on their left. The horses splashed through water flowing over the road in places.

Thomas found a place for them to rest. The family dismounted and released the horses from the cart. They led them to a small stream and allowed them to drink their fill. Annie found a piece of salted pork in the food store and a loaf of bread she had bought the day before. She carved off slices of the meat with her dirk and put it between chunks of the bread. John found the keg of ale, which was almost empty, and poured them all a tankard full. They sat on the ground and rested.

John felt elated. He had led the family into safety. They had lost nothing on the way, and they still had food left. Some of the money he had brought remained in his purse. They were all healthy, if a little weary. He examined the leg and foot of Clover and believed that some rest would cure the minor sprain.

"We'll find somewhere to stay for a few days and find oot if there's work round here," he said. "The next town we come to we'll make enquiries. If there's nothing we'll move on."

It was dusk when they came round a corner and saw a bridge at the bottom of a hill. In front of them, towering above, was the dim outline of a magnificent castle. There was no sign of life, but to the right there were other buildings on a high bank, the lights in their windows piercing the gloom. As they came down towards the bridge they saw the river flowing beneath. John called a halt.

"There's woods at the side here. We can shelter in there for thenight."

They drove off the road and found a level area on high ground with the river running below. They set up camp and had a meal and a good night's rest.

The sun filtered through the trees, arousing the sleeping family. Thomas crept out from under the cart, looking around him as he went down to the river bank. The town on the other side was clearly visible now. Smoke came from some of the chimneys. Somewhere a dog barked. Cockerels crowed. Annie and John came to join him. They had not washed their bodies since leaving home and their clothes were bedraggled and unsavoury. They stripped off and ventured into the swift flowing river, the shock of cold water making them gasp and squeal. As they became acclimatised, it was refreshing to feel the soft water on their skin and the fishes nibbling curiously. They splashed and cavorted, washing all the travel dust and weariness away. John and Annie came out and lay on the grass, panting and laughing with delight. Thomas swam a little way upstream and crawled out to sit on the bank. He saw a kingfisher fly to the other side; a flash of blue reflected on the silver water. It perched on a branch, merging with the autumn colours. A water rat dived, then re-appeared in another place. Thomas watched until the wind gave him goose pimples and he swam back to the camp. They found clean clothes in the cart, and while Annie washed the dirty ones in the river and hung them on the roof to dry, John and Thomas went searching for firewood. Soon the fire was blazing. They spent the day taking stock of the food store. Annie and Thomas walked over the bridge to buy what they needed. They found the town busy with many tradesmen and possibilities of finding work. John stayed in the woods, rubbing the horses down and checking the ropes which held the roof on the cart.

Thomas and Annie returned towards evening. The last of the supplies which they had brought with them went down well with the remains of the ale. They sat around until the stars came out in the night sky. John brought out his pipe and contrived to play Highland tunes with one hand, while Annie sang. They slept well that night, Thomas under the cart, wrapped in plaids on a deer skin. The nights were becoming colder.

Chapter 26
Alnwick

John was on the bank of the river, surrounded by trees. The horses were quietly feeding in a grassy clearing away from the road. He could see them from where he sat. He held a makeshift rod and line in the hope of catching a fish for dinner. The autumn sunbeams slanted through the trees lighting up yellow, red and orange leaves as they floated down. Some landed on the water, to be carried away by the fast flowing river. Others lay softly on the ground. A sudden breeze swept them up and took them in a flurry to join their fellows in a nearby ditch.

John missed his home and his clan. He longed to be in familiar territory where most things were predictable and manageable. He wanted to be among the mountains and heather, to watch the buzzards circling and calling to each other high above, or to hear the curlews' cries echoing across the glen.

Thomas and Annie were spending a third day in the town. They had no luck finding work. This was not the season. Farmers had finished their harvesting and there were other migrant workers in the same position as themselves. It was hopeless for John to seek work with one hand. The money was running low. Thomas caught a few rabbits for their dinners and Annie finished off the last of their supplies making oatcakes and bannocks. She had taken some skins to sell today. There were leatherworkers of all descriptions in the town. She hoped to buy some supplies with the proceeds. They were rationing the whisky to one dram each as a nightcap.

A crackling among the trees alerted John. He turned to see a man making his way towards him, pushing branches aside and stepping high over the tangle of brambles. The stranger was dressed in a jacket and breeches which he had evidently been wearing for some years. His beard and hair were matted and his face weather-worn. John caught his breath at the stench which surrounded him. Beady eyes twinkled at John.

"Caught owt yet?" he asked.

John stared at his visitor. He did not understand this man's speech.

"Art deef, man?" the stranger asked.

"I canna tell what you're saying," said John.

It was the stranger's turn to look blank. Then he said, "Ah, you're Scottish, I'll warrant."

John heard the word Scottish and nodded, saying "Ay."

"You've travelled a lang wee." The man looked at John's fishing line and came to sit on the bank. "You'll niver catch a fish wi' that, man. I'll show you." He lay down on his front and looked closely into the water. After a while, he looked at John and put his finger to his lips. He pulled up his right sleeve and slid his hand slowly into the water. John watched, fascinated. There was a fine trout resting under the overhang of the river bank, apparently enjoying the fingers tickling its belly. All at once, the hand lifted the fish from the water and flung it onto the bank. It flopped and wriggled in protest, and was soon knocked senseless with a stone.

The two men laughed, and John got up to shake his companion by the hand.

"Thank you, ma friend," he said. "You'll stay to dinner? We'll need one or two more of them." The man seemed to catch the jist of what he said, and they went back to lie on the bank with several feet between them.

Annie and Thomas walked over the bridge. They passed the castle, which looked neglected. Thomas had been told that it belonged to the Percy family who did not live there now. He was getting to know the town and its nooks and crannies. There were many industries here, and, having tried the tannery, weavers, metalworkers, cordwainers, carpenters and butchers, he wanted to see what work he could get at one of the mills north of the river. The skilled craft workers did not want to take him on as an apprentice at his age, and he had no skills that they needed. But he could fill sacks and carry heavy loads. He and Annie agreed a meeting place for the end of the day and went their separate ways.

Walking back over the river and towards the mills, Thomas thought about his situation. His adventurous spirit was sated for the time being. He felt the need for work and the companionship of fellow workers. He liked the atmosphere of this town. There was always something going on. Everyone was busy and most people were friendly. He was getting accustomed to the strange language, realising that people said the same words, but pronounced them differently. They seemed unperturbed at his way of speech.

As he made his way along the river, he came to a large water-mill. He walked into the yard where there

161

were men loading sacks of flour onto a cart. They were covered in the white dust which was everywhere, even stuck to the outside of the building like thick mould. Thomas approached one of the men who pointed to a door into the mill.

"Yonder's Master," he said.

Thomas went and opened the door. The noise of the machinery was deafening. A man came towards him. He also was covered in flour. He signalled to Thomas to come outside.

In the yard, Thomas said, "D'you need a strong worker? I can carry sacks and drive a cart."

The man looked Thomas up and down. "Why aye, man. You're Scottish, ain't you? One of my men is off sick. I can teck you on while he gets back. Away. I'll get you a frock."

Thomas had not expected to be taken on immediately, but he was not going to turn the work down. Wearing a round frock over his shirt, he was shown to where a pile of sacks of wheat were lying. He was to carry them one by one up some rickety stairs where another man was pouring the wheat into a hopper. From here it was being slowly released through the floor to where the gigantic millstones were grinding it into flour. Thomas emptied his sack and followed the other man down the stairs. A fall from here would be fatal. A man would be mashed to pulp by the massive wheels and cogs which drove the granite millstones. It was laborious work. At the end of the day, with hardly a break, Thomas found himself receiving his first wages. He trudged wearily back to the clearing in the woods.

While his companion cleaned the fish, John collected sticks and wood for the fire.

"I'm John," he said as he laid the sticks and struck the tinder. "What shall I call you?"

"Sam," replied the vagrant. "Have you been camping here long?"

"Four days," said John. He thought carefully before saying, "Ma two sons have gone into town, looking for work. They should be back soon." He found the frying pan in the cart and held it out for the three large trout which Sam had prepared.

"We'll no' start cooking until An... they get here." To cover his confusion he said, "What town is it yonder?"

"Annick," said Sam. "I've gi'en up seekin' work," he went on. "They divent want to employ the likes of us."

"How d'you find food and shelter?" John was shocked. He and his family could end up like Sam.

"There's plenty in the fields and woods if you know where to look," said Sam. "I'll gang and find summat to cook wi' t'fish." He shambled off into the woods.

As John tended the fire Annie came into the clearing, alone. John looked at her questioningly. "Where's Thomas?"

"He might have found work," said Annie, sitting down on one of the logs they had arranged round the fire. "He was no' at the meeting place we agreed, so I came back." She sighed, took off her hat and said, "They didna give me much for the skins, but I got some cooking fat and bread. We'll have to drink water. I could no' carry ale." She looked up as Sam came back with his hands cupped. John found an empty crock and Sam unloaded berries, nuts, mushrooms and green

163

leaves from his red-stained hands. He stood looking at Annie with a twinkle in his eyes, grinning broadly.

"Good evening, Ma'am," he said, and raised his hat. "Or should I say young Sir?"

John and Annie looked at Sam with their mouths open.

"You canna fool old Sam," he said. "I knows a bonny woman when I sees yan."

Annie shrugged and John felt embarrassed. "I believed she'd be safer in the towns," he said. "There are men who would take advantage…"

"Mebbe you're right," said Sam. "What shall I call you, Ma'am? I'm Sam."

"Annie," she said with a scowl. Her eyes left Sam's face and looked towards the pan of fish, waiting to be cooked over the fire. "That looks a fine meal, John."

"Ay, Sam showed me how to catch them. I said he could stay and eat with us."

Annie produced the cooking fat she had brought with her and put the pan over the fire. "Did I see mushrooms?" she asked. She soon had the pan of fish cooking with the mushrooms. She went to examine the fruit and nuts Sam had collected and nodded approval.

"Sam lives off the land," said John, by way of explanation.

Thomas came towards them from the road, covered in flour dust.

"I've been working," he said triumphantly, and showed John his wages. They congratulated him and he went to wash in the river before having his meal. He took off his frock and shook it vigorously before stowing it under the cart, ready for the morning.

They passed the evening in jovial spirits and retired to their several sleeping places with satisfied bellies.

Sam had moved on before the dawn roused the family.

Chapter 27
Good Prospects

Now that Thomas was bringing wages back every day, John could buy more ale, and hay for the horses. Thomas had arranged for them to buy flour at the mill at a bargain price. One of the cart horses needed new shoes, so they hitched him up to the cart and left Annie to watch over the other horses and to forage for nuts and berries.

There was a cold wind blowing as John and Thomas drove into town. John wondered how long the roof of the cart would hold up in rough weather. They would all have to sleep beneath if it blew off.

The cart rattled into the mill yard just as the miller arrived. He came over and tipped his hat as Thomas climbed out.

"'Tis a hard-working lad you have there, Grant," he said smiling and holding his hand out for John to shake. John jumped down from the cart and shook the miller's hand, which was firm and strong. He was a bulky man with a well-trimmed beard and moustache of red hair. His bushy red eyebrows overhung a kindly face.

John smiled back and said, "Thank you for taking Thomas on, Master Collins. He said you would sell me flour."

"That I will. How much will you be wanting? Thomas, gang and fetch whatever you need." Thomas went into the mill. "Did ye travel from Scotland in that wagon?" asked Collins.

"Ay, we've been living in it for a wee while," John replied.

Master Collins looked shocked. "Have ye nowhere to bide, man?"

"Not yet." John felt unaccountably ashamed as he admitted, "We've no siller for rent."

Master Collins removed his hat and scratched his head through the thin covering of red hair. "Mmm..." He replaced his hat.

Thomas came out of the mill with a small sack of flour and put it in the cart.

Master Collins looked at the cart, then at John. He put his hands on his hips. "I could do wi' another carter. Can you lift sacks of flour wi' yan hand?"

John nodded.

"Would you be willing to drive and deliver flour, and collect wheat? I'll pay you."

John was dumbfounded. He slowly realised that he might have employment. "Ay. Ay, Master Collins," he said. "Thank you kindly." A wave of relief swept over him.

Master Collins was still looking pensive. "I might have a cottage available for ye to rent. But 'twill teck a few days to arrange. Ye divent want to be biding out all winter."

John and his cart were not needed until the next day. He paid for the flour and drove away to find a blacksmith. There was just enough money to pay for the shoeing of the horse, and to buy hay and ale, with a little left over. He left the horse and cart with the blacksmith and went searching for something they could have for dinner. He persuaded the butcher to let him have some scraps of beef trimmings he reckoned Annie could make into a stew, and drove back to the camp feeling that there was at last a hope of them settling into a more comfortable life.

Annie came to meet him as he drove into the clearing. "Och, John!" she cried, "Thank God you're back!"

John jumped down from the cart and she flung herself into his arms. He held her there, shaking, for a while. Slowly she relaxed and released herself. They went and sat on the logs by the ashes of the fire.

"Dinna leave me again, John," she said. "That man, Sam, he came and tried to kiss me! He put his arms round me. I struggled and found ma dirk. I had to threaten him with it before he would let go. The vile man!" She burst into fearful sobbing.

John's heart missed a beat. He took a deep breath. He could not leave Annie alone in the woods in danger. But he should go and work for Master Collins the next day.

"Dinna fash thyself, Annie," said John as he put his arm round her shoulders. "Look, I bought some provisions." He got up and went over to the cart, picked out the flour and meat and gave them to her. He unhitched the cart and gave each horse a bag of hay.

All day John's mind was in turmoil. There seemed to be no solution to the problem. He should not turn down an offer of work. This was just what they needed. He could not leave Annie alone with the horses again. And he would not leave the horses unattended after the thieves' attempt to steal them. Perhaps Master Collins would allow him to tether the horses in his yard for the day, and Annie could come with him into town. But she would be just as vulnerable there; perhaps more so.

Annie was unaware of his state of agitation. She made bannocks with the flour he had brought, prepared the meat and set it over the fire to stew. She collected mushrooms to add to the pot and more nuts and berries. Thomas came back tired and hungry after his day's work. They spent a quiet evening by the fire.

Chapter 28
Hopes Dashed

Next morning, before Annie was up, John took Thomas aside and said, "I'll no be coming to cart Master Collins' flour theday, Thomas. I canna leave thy mother alone again. When Master Collins has found us that cottage, then I can work for him. Canst explain that to him, Son?"

Thomas looked worried. "I'll try, Faether." He set off walking into town, munching one of Annie's bannocks for his breakfast.

Thomas was disappointed that his father would not be working today. It had seemed that they would be settled in Alnwick, and their worries would be over. But he felt uneasy about telling Master Collins his father's news. He had discovered that his employer had a quick temper. He walked into the mill yard.

The miller was already there, preparing sacks of flour to load onto John's cart. He looked puzzled when he saw Thomas on his own.

"Where's thy Da with the cart, Thomas?" We must load up soon. There's two or three deliveries to meck."

Thomas gulped. "Faether canna come theday, Master Collins. Mother…"

A red flush ascended from the base of the miller's neck to his hair roots. "Canna come? What am I going to do without a carter?"

Thomas had an idea. "I could go and get the cart and do the work masell, Sir."

"But I need you at the mill. I canna stop all work at the whim of an auld ne'er-do-weel."

Thomas' temper was rising now. "There's no call to insult him! He has to stay with Mother. He says when you can let us have the cottage…"

"You think I'm going to put myself out to help ye when he's let us down? How do I know he's reliable?" The miller's face became redder with each sentence and his voice grew louder. "How do I know either of you's reliable?" he shouted. "Get out of my way. I have to find another carter and someone to do thy job." He started striding out of the yard.

Thomas shouted, "You firing me?"

Master Collins turned round without stopping. "You're fired!" he yelled, waving his fist. "Get off my property. I divent want ter see you again." He disappeared round the corner.

Thomas stood watching him go. He felt utterly weary and depressed. He took off his round frock and turned towards the mill.

Jethro, the other millworker, was standing at the door shaking his head. "Tha's anither yan bites the dust," he said, apparently unmoved by the scene he had witnessed.

He took Thomas' smock, touched the brim of his hat and went into the mill, shutting the door behind him.

Thomas took his time to walk back to the camp. They would have to start all over again. They could not look for more work in Alnwick. News would spread that they were not to be trusted to keep their word.

John looked up with surprise when he saw Thomas. He had caught a fish and was carrying it to Annie, who was wearing a dress for the first time since they set off from their homestead. Thomas thought how pretty she looked.

"Not at work, Son?" John said, as he handed Annie the gutted fish, water still dripping from it.

Annie took it and put it on a plate. She looked at Thomas with a frown.

Thomas sat down on a log. "Lost the job," he said.

"Och no!" cried Annie.

"What?" yelled John.

Annie put the plate of fish down on the trivet over the ashes of the fire and came to sit by Thomas.

"Master Collins was mad when I said you could no' goo carting theday." Thomas looked up at his father. "He had all the sacks ready to load up."

Annie looked up at John. "Thou didna tell me thou hadst work." She sounded annoyed.

"No, lass. You were upset. I couldna leave thee to be mauled by that Sam again."

Thomas sprang up. "That man mauled you, Mother? By God I'll hunt him doon and..."

"But you should no' have let Master Collins doon, John." Annie's voice strengthened. "I was upset, but I defended masel'."

"For why didst lose thy job, Thomas?" John asked.

"Master Collins said he couldna trust either of us to keep our word, and he never wanted to see us again." Thomas sat down again next to his mother.

Shadow stamped his foot and snorted.

"What aboot the cottage he said he'd find for us?"

"What cottage?" Annie asked in astonishment.

"I didna want to tell thee until it was settled. He was going to find us a cottage…"

"That's no' happening either," said Thomas, leaning on his elbows and staring at the ground in front of him.

The sound of a horse's hooves distracted them, and John went to meet a barrel-chested man riding up the road from town. The visitor was wearing a brimmed black hat, black riding jacket and breeches, with a crop tucked under his arm. He rode his bay gelding into the clearing and looked down on the three refugees. Thomas got up and stood beside his father. Annie stood behind them.

The newcomer was the first to speak. "You are trespassing," he said with the voice of authority. "This is private land."

"We didna ken that, Sir. We'll be moving themorn." John said. "We've done no harm."

The man looked around at the cart and the horses, then at the plate of fish on the trivet. "I see you've been poaching fish. That's an offence. Did you steal those horses, also?"

"No, Sir." John raised his voice. "They're ma own, bred by masell in Scotland. We're seeking a place to settle in England…" His voice trailed off as the man took his crop from under his arm.

"Poaching is a criminal offence. I could have ye all put in the stocks." He paused then continued with ice in his voice, "But I will overlook one fish if ye leave here immediately. This is the property of the town burghers. If I see ye on this land again ye will be arrested." He looked at Annie. "All of ye. And your property will be

174

impounded, including the fine horses." He turned the bay and, using his crop, trotted out onto the road towards the town.

Annie silently went about tidying away the trivet and the pots and dishes left on the ground. She put the trout in an empty crock and packed it all away under the false floor of the cart, keeping the crocks with the nuts and fruit and bannocks where she could reach them. Yesterday's wind was picking up and blew John's hat off. He went to retrieve it and looked at the roof of the cart.

"Thomas, I reckon we should take the roof doon, before it blows off."

Thomas nodded and went to help his father untie the lashings round the supporting posts. They worked together without a word until all the hides and posts were stacked up in the cart. They would have to be unpacked before they could have a meal later on.

Annie climbed into the driver's seat once again. John and Thomas hitched up the cart horses, jammed their hats tightly onto their heads and saddled up Clover and Shadow. The rain started as they turned towards the south. They rode over the bridge and took the first road out of town. They did not want to see Alnwick again.

Chapter 29
Back on the Road

The road climbed up onto the moor where the storm lashed their faces. The brims of their hats down, they battled against it all afternoon. The track they were on became waterlogged and slippery. There was no shelter to be found.

They tethered the horses on the leeward side of the cart with bags of hay, and ate nuts and fruit for their evening meal. Their clothes were soaking wet, and they were chilled to the bone. They huddled together under the cart with hides over them.

Sunshine began to light up the new day. The wind had blown the clouds away. Thomas rolled out from under the cart and stood up shakily. He stretched his arms, shook his hair out of his eyes and walked onto the track which had brought them here. He looked around him. Brown moorland stretched for miles on all sides. There was no sign of human habitation. The only movement was caused by the wind in the grasses and reeds, and a solitary raptor circling high above, on the hunt for small mammals. Thomas' stomach reminded him that he had eaten little since yesterday morning. And what a day that was! Hopes raised the day before were shattered in a few moments. What was promising to be a secure future was snatched away. They had been banished like criminals, as they had in Scotland, all through his father's stubborn nature. How did he expect Thomas to co-operate when he would not share his concerns before making a decision? Thomas had submitted himself to John's authority without question. But now he wanted to make up his own mind; he wanted to buckle his girdle his own way.

He walked down the road a little way to stretch his legs and saw a rabbit bouncing away across the grass. That would make a nice meal. But it would mean unpacking all the roof supports to get at the trivet and pots. There was no wood to be seen, and if there had been, it would be too wet to burn. They must find shelter and a place to dry their clothes. He shivered as he made his way back to the cart.

His parents were struggling from their resting places. They looked around them. Annie put her hands to her face and broke down in tears. John looked at her helplessly and went over to the horses. Thomas took his mother in his arms and held her until the sobs subsided.

"You shall drive the cart theday, Thomas," said John. "The sooner we find shelter, the better."

Thomas shot a resentful glance at his father. He kept his anger to himself and went to saddle up the grey mare for Annie. He helped her up, and squeezed her arm. She looked down at him with a watery smile. John was hitching up the cart horses. Thomas climbed up into the driver's seat.

Progress was slow. None of them had the energy to pick up speed. The wind was still strong and the going was rough. The patient cart horses plodded on. Thomas wondered where his father thought he was going to find money to buy food. They could last a day or two by foraging, but the horses must be fed. An idea began to form in his mind as he drove on.

178

The track began to descend. Thomas made ready to apply the brakes to hold the cart back. They were coming up to a junction with a wider road. There was a signpost. Thomas looked at his father who had also seen the sign.

John rode up to it and read, "*Durham. 3 miles.* That must be a town, to have a signpost," he said.

They turned in the direction of Durham. The road was in better condition. Thomas spurred his horses on and his parents followed. Round the next corner he saw an inn. If he had been able to read, he would have seen it was The Travellers' Rest. He drove the cart into the yard.

An ostler came and said, "I'll teck care of the horses, Sir."

Thomas nodded. "Thank you." He climbed down from the cart.

John rode into the yard. "What dost think thou art doing, Thomas? There's no siller to pay for us to bide here."

"Leave it to me, Faether. Wait here." He walked into the inn, and found the landlord behind the bar. "Gude day, Landlord," he said, taking his hat off. "D'you have accommodation here?"

"Why aye, young man. Have you travelled far? How many of ye are there?"

"Masell and ma mother and faether. We've travelled frae Scotland, and have no siller left. We've been sleeping in the cart."

The landlord looked at Thomas more closely. "Were ye out in that storm yesterday and last night? You look travel weary. I reckon ye could do with a good rest and a decent meal. How d'you propose to pay me?"

"We've two cart horses oot there. We only need one. Can I sell you the other?"

The landlord came out from behind the bar. "Let's have a look," he said, and walked out into the yard.

John and Annie remained mounted, looking anxious. The horses were restless.

Thomas went up to John. "We might be able to sell one of the cart horses, Faether. We only need one, now we've less to carry, and there'd be one less to feed."

John's face changed from concern to approval; the knots on his forehead smoothed out and a light began to shine in his widening eyes. He dismounted and approached the landlord who was examining the carthorses with the ostler.

The landlord looked up. "Which yan were you thinking of selling?"

John indicated the horse which had not had new shoes recently.

The landlord ran his hand up and down the horse's legs and stood up. "How much d'you want for him?"

John boldly mentioned a price which Thomas thought was ambitious.

"Mm," said the landlord. He looked at Annie sitting on the grey mare. Shadow stood nearby. "Were you thinking of selling one o' them, Sir?"

"No," said John. "We need them for travelling. We're seeking somewhere to settle. But we need work, and a place to bide."

The landlord nodded. He stood back and smoothed his thinning grey hair. He was a middle aged, wiry man with a slight stoop, suggesting habitual bowing to customers. But he was anything but subservient. His face was creased with laughter lines. He put his hands on his hips and looked at John.

"I'll gi' you the money for the carthorse and I'll throw in a meal and beds for the night. Would that suit you, Sir?"

John flushed with pleasure. "Ay, ay. We're unco obliged, Sir." He shook the landlord's hand vigorously.

Thomas went to help Annie down from Clover. Relief suffused his whole body, and when Annie leaned on him he nearly toppled over. The ostler led the horses away and the landlord ushered the family into his parlour where comfortable chairs were arranged round a roaring fire.

"Away, sit thisells down," the landlord said. "Can I get ye a dram while ye're waiting for the wife ter cook ye up a fine meal?"

"That would be welcome," said John.

They sat down, mesmerised by the flames. Soon they were each holding a glass of whisky. They sipped slowly, relishing the heat soaking into their cold bones. The landlord disappeared through a door, rubbing his hands together.

The following morning, John and his family were preparing to leave The Travellers' Rest. The landlord came to say goodbye. He handed John the cash for the carthorse.

"Now then, if ye teck the road to Durham, 'tis market day today. Ye'll be able to buy supplies for you and the horses. Then ye should foller the same road south. 'Tis called the Great North Road. 'Twill teck ye three-four days to get to a town called York. There's plenty of farmers in those parts. Ye might find work there. Now, there's highwaymen and robbers alang the road that would think nowt of shooting ye all if they thought ye had summat they wanted. Teck care o' them horses, mind. I wish ye the best of good fortune." The landlord wiped his hands on his apron and shook all their hands as they left the inn.

"You've been verra kind, Landlord," said John

"'Twas a pleasure to meet ye. And no-one can say I didn't do me best for ye."

John took a turn at driving the cart to Durham. His heart was still warm with the generosity of his host. He felt that things would be better when they reached York.

Durham was hilly with narrow winding streets. A great river surrounded the town in a deep ravine and a massive church and a castle stood on top of the hill, overlooking the town. The market place brimmed with activity; animals bleated and roared and people shouted. John found an alehouse where there was space to stop the cart. Annie and Thomas dismounted and tethered the horses to the cart in case John had to drive away. He gave Annie some of the landlord's money, and she and Thomas went in search of supplies for the next few days.

John sat on the cart and looked around him, watching the people about their business. There was still a cold wind blowing, though the sun was warm on his back. This way of life was taking its toll on them all. He knew he would not have been able to do this without young

Thomas. He was now 18 years old, and developing a mind of his own. John was determined to keep going and not lose sight of their goal. The next few days might be tough if the weather broke again.

Annie and Thomas soon returned, laden with their purchases which they put in the cart, hoping it would not rain before they had time to stow it all away properly. John called the cart horse into action as soon as they had mounted, and they were on their way.

Chapter 30
The Journey to York.

The road took them over moorland, up and down steep hills. They travelled through sleepy villages where smoke came from the chimneys horizontally, caught by the ever strengthening wind. The family pulled their hats down, turned their collars up and battled on. At night they sheltered in the lee of hills, under trees if they could find them. One night they found an abandoned cottage and slept under cover. There was no sign of the highway robbers they had been warned about.

One morning Thomas woke early. A watery dawn was breaking over rough country, hilly and wooded. There were sheep on the slopes. He scrambled up a bank and walked over a hill. The view was of more rolling hills with scrubby bushes and groups of trees on the skyline. He walked on, stretching his legs, glad of the exercise. He found a path made by the sheep and followed it. It led down a steep bank with a pool at the bottom, made by a stream which tumbled down the opposite slope. Thomas could see something moving under a bush. Curious to see what it was, he crept forward, careful not to frighten it away.

A black and white face looked up at him as he approached. Fear was in the brown eyes. The collie's ears were pressed back and a growl rumbled in its throat. But it did not move from where it lay. Thomas cautiously held out a hand. The dog snarled, nose pulled up to show bared teeth. Thomas sat on the ground as close as he could without invading the animal's space. He started to talk softly.

"I'll no hurt thee. Good dog. Wilt let me see what's amiss? By the looks of thee, thou hasna eaten in days…"

Gradually he shifted closer to the dog. It continued to growl. He got up and went to the pool, cupped his hands and carried some water back. The collie stretched out its neck and sniffed. The temptation was too great to resist. It licked the water in Thomas' hands. Thomas went to get some more. After the third helping the dog was licking Thomas' fingers. He put his hand on the collie's neck and stroked it, noticing how thin and fragile it was.

Thomas sat down close to the animal and fondled its shoulder and behind its ears. The dog showed appreciation by closing its eyes and pushing its head against Thomas' leg. It relaxed and rested in the same position, rolling its eyes up to gaze into Thomas', then pushed its nose against him for more fondling. Thomas let his hand travel gently down the dog's back. The dog winced and gave a growl when he came to the right shoulder. After more fondling to reassure, he was allowed to reach underneath. Thomas lifted gently and the dog yelped. Thomas lifted again and it sat up, with only one paw supporting it in front. The other leg hung misshapen. This was the cause of the pain. Thomas encouraged the dog to stand on her back legs and reluctantly she struggled to her feet. She stood with her injured leg lifted, trembled violently, and sat down again.

"If you wants me to help thee, you'll have to let me carry thee, Floss."

She looked at him and whimpered.

He bent down and folded his arms round her middle. He supported her back end and lifted her. She was so light, Thomas was not sure that she would survive. The smell coming from beneath her was almost overpowering.

He carried her back to the cart where Annie and John were eating bread and cheese for their breakfast. John stopped eating when he saw Floss in Thomas' arms.

"I could no' leave her there to starve," Thomas said, before John could get a word in.

"We've enough trouble feeding ourselves withoot another mouth. Looks in bad shape. She'll be dead before the day's oot." John took another mouthful.

Thomas laid Floss in the cart and wished they had oats. He poured some milk into a plate and put it by her. She lapped it up. He broke up a chunk of bread into small pieces and soaked it in more milk. Floss took it delicately and licked her lips. She looked at Thomas with gratitude.

Annie came to see what was happening. "We could try mending that leg. If it's left like that she'll be so lame life willna be worth living."

Thomas laid the dog on her good side and held her firmly. Annie fingered the injured leg all over, then with a strong movement pulled it back into shape. Floss yelped, shuddered, and lay still.

"Keep her there," she said to Thomas. "John, canst find us a strong stick, and tear a strip off ma skirt to make a bandage?" she shouted over her shoulder.

187

John got up from where he was sitting and came over to see what was required. "What do we want a dog for, anyway?" he grumbled. He searched around and found a stick. He placed it on a stone and held it there with his foot, while he cut it to the right length with his dirk. He cut a tear in Annie's skirt, and ripped off a strip, dislodging some of the mud which clung to it. Annie held the splint in place while John held the foot. Floss struggled until John's hand tightened its grip. Thomas murmured gentle words to calm her as he bound the bandage and secured it.

When John let go the leg, he stroked Floss behind the ears. "Good dog," he said.

Floss lay still, and Thomas covered her with a deer skin. He went to have his breakfast. "What if we canna find work in York, Faether?"

"We'll continue travelling south doon this road until we do," said John.

The scenery became flat as they journeyed on. The hills were all behind them. There were white windmills dotted across the landscape. Their sails flailed in the wind which swept mercilessly across the plain in gusts. Swirls of dust rose from the road, depositing grit between their teeth and in their eyes. It was dark when they came to an inn by the roadside.

John said, "We've enough siller to stay here one night. We'll get a good meal and find oot aboot York."

"I'll sleep in the cart with Floss, Faether," said Thomas. "'Tisna raining."

188

"If that's what thou wants, Son." John resented taking the dog on board. They did not have the resources to look after it properly.

The shelter of the inn was a welcome relief. The meal was good and John's feelings mellowed in the warmth with a dram of whisky going down nicely. He bought Annie and Thomas a mug of ale each, and was shocked at the small size compared with the Scottish ones. He stood at the bar listening to the local banter.

"Afore I knew it t'owd sow were buttin' and rammin' at t'yat 'til it broke throw!"

The speaker's companions roared with laughter. One of them said between bursts of mirth, "I'll be danged if she didn't knock thee ower. I saw it wi' me own eyes." Tears were running down his face. "Fred went sprawlin' in t'mud and sow scarpered."

Fred grimaced. "'Twere no joke, I can tell ye."

There was more laughter.

John was having trouble understanding yet another way of speaking. As he listened, it became easier. He sipped his whisky.

"Ye're not from round 'ere. Have ye travelled far?" the landlord asked him.

"We've travelled frae Scotland. We're wanting to settle here. D'you ken any farmers wanting labourers?"

"Nay. Ye'd best gang into York when t'market's on. There'll be other labourers for hire. That's where farmers go to find 'em."

"Is York far frae here?" asked John.

"A few mile." The landlord paused. "Hey, Fred. Is it hirin' day termorrer, or was it last week?"

189

Fred had calmed down by now. "Aye, 'tis this week." He looked at John. "You lookin' for work?"

"Ma son and masel', we're seeking farm work," said John, nodding to where Thomas sat with Annie. "And a place to bide."

Fred's eyes sparkled with the recent laughter. His greying hair was tousled. The hand with which he held his beer mug had dirt under the nails. He wore a round frock and breeches and his boots had been ankle-deep in mud that day. His face was flushed with the drink and the warmth of the bar after a day working outdoors. He took a long draught of ale, and wiped his mouth on his sleeve. He looked over the room at Thomas and Annie. Then he spoke.

"Me Master's short of a labourer. There might be a cottage. Where can 'e find ye termorrer? At t'market? What name shall I give 'im?"

John pushed his excitement down. This might come to nothing. "We'll be in York themorn. We'll goo to the hiring place. The name's Grant. John and Thomas Grant." He put his hand forward in case this called for a handshake. Fred took it and John felt warmth and honest friendship under the roughness. "I'm obliged to you," he said.

"Me Master's Mr William Todd," said Fred. "'E's more likely to send 'is foreman, Jemmy Smallbone. I'll let 'em know ye were askin'." He turned back to his companions and they went and sat at one of the tables.

Chapter 31
York

Thomas spent a cold, uncomfortable night with Floss in the cart. The ostler, who looked at Thomas with disbelief, brought out a hot toddy.

"Yow didn't 'ave to sleep out 'ere," he said. "I'd 'ave looked after t'bitch."

Thomas took his time working out what the ostler had said while he sipped the hot ale. "I'm accustomed to sleeping oot now," he said gloomily.

Floss lifted her head when she heard them talking. She rested back again with one wag of her tail.

Thomas looked at her. "She's still alive at least." He told the ostler about the journey from Scotland and how he had found Floss. The man said she was probably a drover's dog, left behind because they could not look after an injured animal.

Thomas thanked the man for his toddy and took his mug into the inn. John and Annie were feasting on a good breakfast of bacon and egg with mountains of fried bread. The maid brought a plateful to Thomas.

"This'll last me a few days!" he said.

"Dinna believe it!" said Annie. "Thou wilt be starving again by dinner time!"

York was a bustling city. Annie drove the cart through narrow streets, John riding in front, Thomas behind. They stopped when they came to the Minster, a towering great stone church. It had carving round the arches and all up the spires, which reached into the heavens. Carved faces, some ugly, threatening, some beautiful, looked down on them from the corners and out of crevices. The family stared in awe, never having been so close to such a building.

Further on, the market was crowded with stalls selling bread, cloth, leather goods, meat, vegetables, fruit and other wares. Farmers and housewives, clerics and gentry, beggars and vagrants jostled with groups of people gossiping, while stray dogs scavenged and bickered under the stalls. The place rang with the cries of the vendors and the rattle of horses' hooves on the cobbles. Smells of raw meat, then fruit, leather and home-made bread mingled with the earthy tang of horse droppings and discarded kitchen waste.

John led the cart round the outside of the market place to the forecourt of a coaching inn, where there were horses tethered. He and Thomas tied theirs alongside. Nearby was the market cross where some stalls were under cover. Men and women stood there with the tools of their trades. Farm labourers wore round frocks and milkmaids held their stools.

John took the reins from Annie. "I'll sit over there with the cart and see if I can hire masell as a carter," he said. "You goo with Thomas and stand with the others."

Farmers and tradesmen came and went, some hiring, some looking. They talked to the girls and looked them up and down as if they were cattle in a market. John did not want anyone looking at Annie like that. She was older than most of the other women. She was being ignored.

A small man carrying a thumb stick came and stood to look at all the men for hire. He sucked at a clay pipe and pushed his hat back on his head, revealing a bald patch. John climbed down from the cart. He had the feeling that this was Jemmy Smallbone, the foreman.

"Mister Smallbone?" he asked.

The man looked at John blankly. Then it seemed as if he had emerged from a dream. His face became attentive. He regarded John, his weathered face, his dusty clothes, his jaded demeanour and, lastly, the leather stump of his left arm.

John said, "I'm John Grant. I believe the man Fred has spoken to you…"

The foreman removed his pipe from his mouth. "Aye," he said. "Yow seekin' labour?" His teeth were worn into a groove where his pipe had rested for years. He showed no emotion. There were no laughter lines.

"You have a son?"

"Ay." John nodded towards Thomas.

Mister Smallbone's eyes followed John's. He walked to where Thomas was being looked over by a man who, judging by his smart clothing, was a gentleman farmer.

"D'you intend hiring that young man, Squire?"

The man turned round. He said, "Good day, Smallbone. I could do with another groom. Are you interested? Thinking of filling Stonehouse's place?"

"Aye, there's a family of 'em. Travelled from Scotland. In pretty poor shape, I reckon." He looked at Thomas, who met his eyes directly.

"Hm, they'll be needing a bidance, then," said the Squire. He looked at Thomas again and moved on to the man standing next to him, who was healthy and strong

193

and held a riding crop in his hand. He wore riding breeches and a jacket.

Smallbone approached Thomas. "You'll be Thomas Grant," he said. "What work can you do?"

Thomas's face lit up. "I was raised on ma faether's farm in the Highlands," he said. "We kept cattle, sheep and hogs. We grew wheat and oats."

Smallbone nodded. He looked round to where John was standing. "That your horse and cart?"

"Ay," said John. "And that's ma wife, Annie." He indicated Annie, who was listening and watching. She dropped a curtsey.

Smallbone's face revealed nothing. He sucked his pipe, which had gone out. He touched his hat and waved to a passer-by.

He turned to John. "There's a cottage. Bare boards, it is. Better than a cart to bide in. Go out of town t'way ye came in. When ye reach t'inn, there's a lane opposite. Teck that lane. T'cottage is fust in a row. I'll come and talk to you termorrer." He turned and limped away, revealing a crooked back.

John beckoned to Annie. "We have a roof over our heads thenight!" He could hardly contain his relief. He hugged Annie and shook Thomas' hand. "Annie, dost want to buy food? We'll need hay for the horses, Thomas." He gave the purse to Annie. "I'll stay with the cart."

Annie and Thomas walked away, chatting excitedly.

It was late afternoon by the time they reached the cottage. The grass grew up to the door and the front garden was a tangle of brambles and nettles, with here and there a cabbage gone to seed. Hens and a cockerel scratched among the weeds, collecting what food they could find.

The family left their horses to munch the grass and went to peer through the windows. The door of the neighbouring cottage opened and a large woman emerged. She wore a dress, the laces of which had burst open at the bosom, and an apron and cap of dirty white linen. Her black hair fell in unruly tangles round her face. She swept a glance over the new arrivals and disappeared indoors.

John heard her calling, "Fred! They're 'ere!" Fred came out to greet his new neighbours.

"Eh! Ah'm reet glad to see ye!" He raised his voice. "Bring us some jars of homebrew, Mavis." Then to John, "'Ere's yer keys."

John took the keys and handed them to Thomas. He shook Fred's hand and said, "Thank you for thy advice, Fred. Mister Smallbone said he'll call themorrow."

Thomas was unlocking the cottage door. They all entered a dark, musty-smelling room. Fred stayed outside. A bird had found its way down the chimney and left a mess in its panic to get out, before dying on the window sill. Maggots were finishing off the remains. Cobwebs draped the low beams and the ashes of a fire long gone spilled out of the grate onto the floor, together with the soot brought down by the bird. John and Annie ventured up the dusty staircase, which creaked from lack of use. Two rooms upstairs were in the same state. There was not a stick of furniture or a shred of curtain or floor covering to be seen. Annie struggled to open the windows and John had to help her.

They came downstairs to find Thomas and Fred with mugs in their hands. Two more mugs stood on the windowsill. The remains of the bird had been brushed off onto the floor.

"We've been feeding t'ens," said Fred. "They belonged to t'last tenants. They're good layers, but coop fell to bits last winter. Ye'll be lucky ter find eggs that ain't addled. They're laying all ower t'place."

"There's been no-one living here for a wee while," said John as he picked up his mug of ale. He took a sip. He looked into the mug, expecting to see something dead in it which would account for the strange taste. The ale was cloudy and pale. He could not drink any more.

"Is there a well?" he asked.

"Aye. At t'end of lane." Fred waved his mug in the direction of the other end of the row of cottages. "Ye've a privy and a cow stall round back," he added.

Annie said, "Does your wife have a broom I could borrow, to clean the floor?"

"Aye. You come and talk to 'er. Ye'll want to get settled. Mavis'll give thee a loan of owt ye need." He showed Annie into his cottage.

Thomas had already gone round to the back, and John went to join him, after surreptitiously pouring his ale onto the garden. There was a cobbled yard and an area of grass surrounded by an overgrown hedge. In the middle of the grass there were the remains of a bonfire. Long ago, someone had burnt the furniture and all the contents of the cottage. There were still the charred remnants of a table leg, a scrap of cloth, a leather boot and some broken crockery. John shuddered and followed Thomas indoors. He would not tell Annie what they had seen. He and Thomas must dispose of it as soon as possible.

"We can bring the horses round here to graze," he said to Thomas. "There'll be shelter in the cow stall if they need it. The cart will have to stay in the front for now."

Thomas went to the cart and lifted Floss out and onto the ground, for her to relieve herself. She was steadier on her feet, though not bearing weight on the splinted leg. She managed to do the necessary, and Thomas called her to follow him. She gave him a sad look and sat down, holding the bad leg in the air. He went to lift her and brought her indoors, where he had made a deerskin bed for her.

That night they cooked a meal on their trivet in the back yard and ate it under the stars. They laid skins on the floor downstairs, wrapped their plaids around them and slept the sleep of the weary.

Part 3

Respite

Chapter 32   1678
Three Years Later

The barking of the dog woke John and Annie soon after they had fallen asleep. John lay listening, reluctant to get out of the warm bed.

"Is that an intruder?" asked Annie. "Floss dinna bark like that. She's warning someone off."

"'Tis Thomas' dog. He can goo and see what's amiss." John turned over and covered his ears with the quilt.

The stairs creaked as Thomas went down.

The dog stopped barking, and a while later the stairs creaked again. All was quiet.

Annie was up at dawn. She washed herself in the bowl of water which they had brought up the evening before. John waited until she had gone downstairs before he swung his feet from under the quilt onto the bare floorboards. He washed and dressed slowly and went down to the parlour to find Annie and Thomas already eating their breakfast. The fire was alight and the kettle was on the boil. John helped himself to porridge and took his place at the table.

"There were intruders out there in the night, Faether," said Thomas. "Floss sent them off. I reckon they were after the horses."

"Good thing the dog was there," said Annie. "We should have had a dog all along on the journey here."

"That dog would no' be any use if someone set upon her," John mumbled through his porridge.

"The horses should be in a stable," said Thomas. "I dinna ken why we keep them. Half ma wages goo on feeding them."

"I'll be breeding frae them soon, when I've got proper stabling," said John.

Thomas raised his voice. "We canna afford to build a stable."

"That's enough, both of you." Annie butted in. "Canna we have a meal without ye getting at each other's throats? Shall we goo into town with the cart theday, John? I've a mind to sell one or two deerskins and buy some stuff for a dress."

"They should get a good price, Mother," said Thomas. "They say that all the deer have been hunted doon in these parts. They're hunting foxes for sport now."

John looked up. "That's a good thing. We've lost two hens lately to foxes, though we shut them in at night."

"They're bold enough to come in the day," Annie commented. "I've seen them skulking in the fields."

"I'll be off now." Thomas got up and kissed his mother on the cheek. He put his jacket on over his round frock. These May mornings could be chilly. There was a frost this morning. He took the pie his mother had made for his lunch and put it in his pocket, grabbed his hat from its peg and went out into the sunshine, whistling.

"He's happy, at least," said Annie as she cleared the table and took the dirty plates to the sink in the lean-to outside the back door. Floss got up and stretched, wagging her tail in greeting.

"You were a good dog in the night." Annie poured some milk into a bowl with the left-over porridge, put it on the floor and came back into the house.

John and Annie were on their way back from town. It was market day. Annie had bought enough stuff for two dresses, and some provisions for the next week. John had enjoyed a wander round the market, chatting to the vendors and buying seeds and a few tools for the garden. It was a tranquil morning with the early summer blossom decorating the hedgerows, sending out gentle aromas as they passed.

Annie said, "I'm of a mind to take produce to market, John. I could bake a batch of bread and make jam and pickles and gingerbread sweethearts to sell."

"We could always use more siller," remarked John.

"We could do with a cow, then we'd no' have need to buy milk," Annie said "There's plenty of grass in the back. We wouldna have to feed her."

John drove on silently. He knew she was right. He knew Thomas had been right about the horses. But he clung on to his dream of breeding with them and earning some money himself. He hated having to rely on Thomas' wages.

"There's no' enough grass for a cow as well as the horses," he said.

The afternoon was fine and John took the opportunity to prepare a strip of garden for sowing the seeds he had bought. The soil was warming nicely and looked rich and brown from the dung he had spread in the autumn. He picked up a handful and crumbled it, letting it trickle through his fingers. Gardening soothed his frayed nerves. He loved the smell of the earth and to watch the seeds coming up in the spring. He thought of the beans and the peas growing up their sticks, of picking and eating a few, sweet, cool and crunchy, before giving them proudly to Annie to cook for their dinner. This distracted him from all the other thoughts pervading his mind these days.

He knew he should not be feeling like this. They had been settled here for three years. Travelling was a thing of the past. Thomas had a good job and was happy, though the money he earned did not go far. Annie had used all her home-building skills to make the cottage comfortable. When they first came here he thought it could never be home as the one they left behind in the Highlands. He and Thomas used the wood from the cart to make beds, a table and chairs. They swept the chimney and coaxed the fire into life. They built a house for the hens and enclosed them in a run to stop them scratching in the garden. They dug a hole and buried the macabre remains of the bonfire in the back.

Jemmy Smallbone came and made a deal with them. He let the cottage to them for a small rent as long as Thomas worked for him. He sometimes required the use of John and the cart for taking produce to market and grain to the mill. He was a fair man, who demanded respect.

William Todd, the owner of the farm and the big house at the top of the lane, occasionally rode by in the evening and looked down on them from his horse. He asked them if they were comfortable, and said that one day there might be a place for Annie as part of the staff in the house. But it never happened.

After the first feelings of elation, having found a place to live and work at last, John realised that he was at the bottom rung of the ladder in society. He was not his own master, as he had wanted to be when he left Scotland. He was now in the same position as Fraser and the crofters, dependant on their master for everything, and at his mercy if things should go wrong. Now he owned nothing of value except his horses.

It was time to get Shadow out and give him some exercise. John went into the house where Annie was busy cooking. The table was covered in flour and she had a lump of dough in her hands, ready to be rolled out into pastry.

"I'll be away riding, Annie." He gave her a peck on the cheek as he went past. At least they were still all together, he thought.

May blossom frothed along the hedgerows, scattering tiny white petals across the lane. Bluebells filled the woods with their scent and swallows dipped and dived over the flowery meadows. A cuckoo called, throwing his voice so it was difficult to see where he was. John rode along the lane until he came to a gate into a field. He could build up speed here, and give his horse a good gallop. Clods of earth went flying behind them and the wind in John's hair gave him a sense of freedom. They had to slow down before they came to another gate. John dismounted to open it. There were men working in this field and he kept to the edge. His neighbour, Fred, walked towards him. He pushed his hat back and looked up at John.

"That hoss can go a fair pace," he said. "You should enter him in t'York races."

"He's no' been bred for racing," John replied. "I had him for breeding."

"Have yer ever thowt of hirin' 'im to gentlefolk to sire their mares? 'E's well bred, and there's allus them as wants new stock for racin' and huntin'."

John nodded. This sounded interesting. Fred might be right. "Mm, I'll think aboot that. Thanks, Fred." He tipped his hat as he rode on, and considered this new idea all the way back. He would not need stabling if he was not going to breed horses at home. He would not have the bother and expense of raising foals.

Chapter 33
The Tavern

Thomas joined his fellow farm workers as they strode along the lane through the wood. They were chattering among themselves and he could not understand all that was said. They were friendly and would help if he needed it, but he still felt apart from them, an alien. The contrast with Highland life was leagues away. There were no hills to climb. They were not restricted by rocky outcrops or streams running down mountain sides. The only breaks in the monotony were woodlands here and there. As a result, the local people had a different attitude to life. They were not as wiry or stubborn. They were more relaxed. But they were suspicious of newcomers and 'foreigners'.

Thomas was happy. He was earning a living and learning about farming. His ambition was to take Jemmy Smallbone's place one day. Already he was given responsibilities, being put in charge of a team of pickers or mowers. He watched Smallbone and the way he kept himself aloof, but had the trust of his workers. The only drawback to all this was that Thomas' parents were dependant on him, and there was not much left of his wages for his own use.

This evening Thomas planned to take Floss with him into town. Her leg had healed, though she was still lame and would probably never have the stamina to walk far. She was his faithful companion when he was not working, and he felt easier about leaving his mother at home on her own when his father was out riding or carting. Floss was a good guard dog.

Thomas went to the tavern where his friends usually gathered. Jed and Bob were there already. He bought a pint and went to join them at their table.

"Where's Frank?" he asked. "He's generally the first one here."

"Dunnow," said Jed. "'E were 'ere last night, gettin' on everyone's wick."

"What was that aboot?" asked Thomas, taking his first frothy sip.

"Oh, 'e were rantin' on about some lasses 'e'd met. Wanted us ter meet 'em and teck 'em to t'meadow for a romp in t'grass."

"Did anyone goo?" Thomas thought that sounded interesting. He would enjoy some female company.

"Mebbe that's where t'others are now," Bob suggested.

Jed grimaced. "If I want a girl I'll find me own, and I wouldn't teck 'er out in a crowd."

They discussed their various opinions of girls and how to attract them. Floss lay at Thomas' feet. She raised her head when she heard familiar voices, and Frank and Luke came in with a couple of girls on their arms. Floss wagged her tail, but Frank, who usually made a fuss of her, had other things on his mind. The newcomers pulled up some more chairs and Frank went and bought a round of drinks.

"'E must 'ave won summat on t'osses," Jed commented. "'E never buys drinks fer us."

The girls, having come into the tavern giggling, went quiet. The one being cuddled by Luke had tired of him and pushed him away. She re-arranged her fair curls around her plump, rosy face and smiled primly when Frank brought her drink.

"Thanks, Frank," she said. "Me name's Bella." She opened her big blue eyes wide and looked directly at Bob as she took a sip of her ale.

"Hello Bella, I'm Bob," he said.

Thomas was watching Frank's girl. She was evidently not accustomed to tavern life. She sat stiff and straight in her chair, looking round her with reserve. Her dress was plain blue with a white collar and no frills. Her brown hair was tied back in a tight bun and tucked into the nape of her surprisingly long neck. Frank came to sit next to her and put his arm round her waist. She gave him a half smile. Floss got up and rested her chin on Frank's knee, gazing up at him with appealing brown eyes.

"Hello, lass." Frank put his hand down and fondled Floss behind the ear. "This is Floss, Jenny," he said to his girl.

Jenny's face softened. "Oh, you're beautiful." She bent down and cupped the dog's face with both hands. Then she looked at Thomas. "Is she yours?" He noticed what long lashes she had.

"Ay," he said, "and I'm Thomas." He could not imagine Jenny wanting to romp in the meadow, but he would quite like to get to know her. "D'you like dogs?" he asked.

She smiled shyly. "I've two of me own. Well, not exactly. They're me dad's. 'E works them on t'farm. Does your dog work?"

"Nay, she's lame. But she's a good guard dog."

Frank had one leg crossed over the other. He was shaking his foot as if irritated. The fingers of his free hand were drumming the table. "Come on. Drink up, Jen. I'll teck thee home," he said.

Jenny protested. "No! I'm not goin' without Bella." She took a few sips of her ale and looked over at her friend.

Bella was flushed, deep in animated conversation with Bob, Luke and Jed. Her eyes were sparkling and Luke's hands were straying to hidden places.

"Luke, are yer ready to teck 'em home?" called Frank.

"Aye, I'll be with yer shortly," answered Luke. He finished his ale and said, "Come, Bella, it's time to go."

"No! I'm stayin'," said Bella.

"You can't walk back by yerself, lass. It's dark. Yer don't know who's out there waitin' for yer." Luke put his hands up to his ears, pulled a face and said, "Aargh!"

"Oh, all reet. I were enjoying meself." Bella drained her mug and got up. "Nice talkin' to ye, lads." She took hold of Jenny's hand and flounced out. Frank and Luke followed.

"It'll be dark in t'meadow now," remarked Bob with a wistful faraway look.

"Aye, and cold and wet," said Jed.

Thomas stood up to go. "I'll be on ma way. Come, Floss." The others waved and carried on their conversation.

210

On his way home, Thomas could not help worrying about Jenny. He was sure Frank's intentions were not entirely honourable, and hoped she could look after herself. He thought that Bella would be too busy to look after her friend.

Chapter 34
Prospects

John was picking peas when Mr Todd came riding up to the cottages on a black stallion. His long grey wig was topped with a wide-brimmed hat. He wore a brown coat over his knee breeches and carried a riding-crop. The wives from the other cottages came out and gathered round. John stopped picking, removed his hat and waited. He was not sure what his master would think of his request.

Todd rode over to speak to him. "Good afternoon, Grant. You have a good yield of peas, I see."

"Ay, Sir. 'Tis a good year for the peas." He paused. "Could I speak to you concerning ma horses, Sir?"

"Of course, Grant. I've heard you keep a pair of fine horses."

"I've been of a mind to breed frae them, Sir. 'Twould be a way of earning us money, as I'm no fit for labour."

"That sounds a reasonable idea, but you have no proper stabling at the back there, do you?"

"No, Sir. But I might be able to hire ma stallion out for stud. I wondered, Sir, if you know of anyone who'd be interested in him."

William Todd stroked his neatly trimmed beard. "Mm, 'Tis a possibility. May I take a look at him?" He dismounted and tethered his horse to a fence post.

John thought he might be making progress. He wondered whether Todd knew anything about horse breeding. He led the way round to the back of the cottage through a gate which he had made to secure the animals. Floss got up from her resting place in the sun and came towards them, wagging her tail. John collected a leading-rein from the cow stall and walked over to the two horses, which were quietly grazing. Todd came up behind him and stood with his arms behind his back. He watched John walking Shadow round the paddock. Then he came up to the horse and looked at its teeth and eyes. He felt his legs and examined his feet. Then he stood back.

"You have a grand horse there, Grant. What are his origins?"

"I had a smallholding in Scotland, Sir. We all went in for horse breeding in a small way. He comes frae a line of sires bred by ma family for generations. A few years ago I introduced Arab stock to the Highland breed. Shadow is second generation frae them."

"That's a lovely mare too. I could offer to buy them from you..."

"No, Sir. Begging your pardon. They're all I have left of ma property. If I can earn something for hiring them out, that would be fine." John began to think he should not have approached Todd.

"I could offer you the use of some stabling and pasture, if you were willing to pay me when you have some stud money."

This man was now trying to rule his life. John felt threatened.

"No. I'd like to keep an eye on them maself, Sir. I ride them every day. They're all right in the paddock with the carthorse. Thank you kindly for the offer, Sir."

"Very well," said William Todd. He walked back to his horse and said as he mounted, "I'll make enquiries. If I find anyone who wants to take you up on it, you will have the stallion ready for inspection." He rode away.

John could not make out whether he had offended Todd, or if the man would do as he said. He was not used to dealing with English gentry, and he could not speak to him on a level. It was not in John's nature to be at another man's beck and call, and to ask for help had been hard. But he could think of no other way. He was a stranger in these parts.

He went back to the peas and decided that he had picked enough for today. He would take them in to Annie and go for a ride.

Annie was in the parlour, surrounded by the pieces left over from making her dresses, preparing them for sewing another quilt, happily absorbed. She looked up when John came in.

"That's a good pot of peas, John," she said. "They'll be fine for dinner. Who were you talking to out there?"

"Todd came by," said John. "He had a look at Shadow. Said he'd find a mare for him to sire." He sighed and felt uncomfortable. He was not sure if Annie would approve of his plans for the horse. She often scoffed at his ideas.

"They'll pay thee for siring their mares?" She looked pleasantly surprised. "That could bring in some siller for us, John. 'Tis good news!"

He smiled, relieved. "I'll be riding now, Annie." He kissed her cheek and went out into the sunshine to saddle up.

He ached for the family he had left behind. He longed for the companionship and support of the clan, the hunting expeditions and feasting and music. He wanted to be able to talk to Rob and Hamish about his present predicament and how he should resolve it. Anger burned deep down in his heart at the way they had all been split asunder and banished, bereft of all that they valued. The deed of revenge they committed as they left had done nothing to quench this anger. He had spent his life until then being fiercely loyal to the clan and his laird. His loyalty to the Covenanters had been the cause of his downfall. And now there were no Covenanters, no need for loyalty. He belonged nowhere. Even his son no longer needed him. If Jamie were still alive... John spurred Shadow into a gallop and tried to rid himself of morbid thoughts.

Chapter 35
York Races

When Thomas and Floss walked into town one evening, they found crowds of people milling around. It was the week of the Assizes. The ale houses and coaching inns were bursting at the seams. It had been a hot day and many were drinking in the streets. Thomas wondered whether he would find his friends in the usual place. He could hardly squeeze past the men at the door of The Bell. Floss was reluctant to follow him and sat down outside. Bob and Luke were there with Bella.

Thomas bought a drink and jostled his way towards them. He raised his voice above the din. "Shall we take our drinks ootside?" he suggested.

"Aye," said Bob.

The others nodded and they pushed their way through the crowds. They met Jed and Frank with Jenny and another girl at the door. Thomas indicated where they would go. Jenny and the other girl left the men to buy drinks and followed Thomas and his friends into the graveyard of a church nearby. It was cooler and quieter here. They sat on some fallen gravestones.

Bella wrinkled her nose. "'Tis creepy in 'ere. There might be phantoms."

"I'll protect thee," said Luke. He shuffled up close to Bella and put his arm round her waist.

The new girl and Jenny sat demurely on the edge of a stone slab. "This is Molly," said Jenny. "She's Jed's girl."

Molly looked around her with some concern and shivered. "'Tis gloomy. I've got goose pimples." She rubbed her bare arms and sniffed.

"Cuddle up to me," suggested Bob. "I'll keep thee warm 'till Jed gets 'ere." He went and sat next to Molly.

She looked at him suspiciously. "No thanks, I'll wait."

Thomas was watching Jenny. Floss was sitting at her feet and Jenny was fondling her ears. "Are you alright, Jenny?" he asked.

"Aye, I'm champion. 'Tis better than all them crowds."

Jed and Frank appeared out of the dusk with drinks in their hands.

"Raisin' the spirits of the dead, are ye?" called Frank. "We just passed one o' them dragging 'is ball and chains. 'Owlin' 'e were. Listen!"

"Frank, give over!" wailed Bella. She leaned in closer to Luke's body.

Frank and Jed gave the girls their drinks and sat down.

Frank leaned forward and supped his ale. "'Tis race week next week, after the Assizes. We could all teck a day off work and go to t'races."

"Aye, what day shall us go?" asked Bob.

"'Tis costly at t'races." Jed was not so keen. "It's all quality what goes there."

"We don't 'ave to bet on t'osses," said Frank. "We could just go for t'fun of it, to see all the toffs in their grand clothes, and mebbe pick a few pockets." His eyes sparkled.

"Aye, if we can all get t'same day off. 'Tis not so easy for t'lasses," Luke remarked. "Can you get time off, Bella?"

"So long as I'm back fer milkin'," she said.

"I can ask me dad. 'E'll let me come," said Jenny.

Molly said, "I'll see."

Thomas looked forward to the new experience. "What day shall we goo, then?"

"Let's say Wen'sdy," suggested Frank. "Them as can come, we'll meet at t'market cross at eight o'clock."

"Meck it nine," said Bella. "That gives us enough time to do the milkin' afore sneakin' away."

"Champion," said Frank. They all agreed that they would do their best to be there.

Thomas thought about Jenny on the way home. She and Frank were still together, but he did not know why. They were not really suited. Perhaps he would have an opportunity to be alone with her when they went to the races.

Wednesday dawned fine and bright. Mr Smallbone agreed that Thomas could take the day off with no pay. It would be harvest time soon when all hands were needed. Thomas left Floss behind with his parents. He did not tell them where he was going in case his father wanted to accompany him. He walked jauntily into town, a few coins in his pouch for a drink or two.

Frank and Jenny were waiting at the market cross with Bob, and Thomas saw Luke and Bella coming from another direction. The clocks struck nine. Jed and Molly were evidently not coming. The group of friends set off towards the racecourse at Clifton Ings. There were few people in town but many horsemen and carriages on the road, all travelling the same way. The women were wearing gaudy hats with feathers waving around as they turned from side to side, greeting friends and gossiping with their travelling companions. The coachmen sat on their high seats wearing livery and hats perched on top of curled wigs, their crops hovering over the backs of their horses. Men waved their hats to the women, bowing as they passed. Messenger boys dodged and dived among the wheels and horses' legs, backwards and forwards as if their lives depended on it. The nearer they all got to the racecourse, the more congested the crowd became.

Frank took Jenny's hand and beckoned to the others to follow. He pushed through a gap in the hedge. He had been here before. The others crept through after him and found themselves on the turf surrounding the horse course. There were stalls selling pies, ale, sweetmeats and all kinds of delicacies. There were betting booths and men with waggons selling hay for the horses. All were shouting their wares to the milling crowds. The gentry had left their carriages and horses with their grooms and coachmen, and were now on foot. Thomas caught a glimpse of some riders on their horses at the far side of the field.

"Shall we goo and take a look at the racehorses?" he called to the others. He made his way through the crowds to the enclosure. It was quieter here. Thomas looked in admiration at these beasts. There was some good stock there, he thought.

"Ma faether's horses would match them any day," he said to Bob, who admitted he knew nothing about horses.

The girls were enthralled. They gazed at the handsome heads and rippling muscles.

"I never knew thy Dad 'ad 'osses, Thomas," said Jenny.

Bella said, "I ain't been this close to grand 'osses like that. I've only seen 'em running across the fields after t'fox."

A race was about to start. The friends walked along the course until they found a good viewing place and sat on the grass.

"Stay there while I gets us a drink," Frank said to Jenny. He went to a booth selling ale.

Chapter 36
Jenny

Thomas took the opportunity to talk to Jenny. "You like horses do you, Jenny?"

"Aye, they're fine, strong beasts, yet so gentle. 'Ow many 'osses does thy dad keep?"

"Two. A stallion and a mare. He's a mind to breed frae them, but we've no proper stabling or pasture." Thomas' thoughts wandered for a moment to what might be if he had his way.

"Did he buy 'em?" Jenny was awestruck. She looked wide-eyed at Thomas.

"Nay. We travelled on them frae Scotland. Ma faether bred them when we lived in the Highlands."

"Oh, ye must have been rich people. Why did ye leave?"

Thomas would have liked to pour it all out to her but Frank arrived back with the drinks. He squeezed into a gap between Jenny and Thomas.

The horses were under starter's orders and the race began. The spectators cheered and shouted as the riders and their steeds thundered past. The atmosphere was exhilarating. Thomas was breathless with excitement. After two more races had passed them, the friends helped each other up from the grass. They stretched their legs and brushed the debris off their clothes.

"I'll buy you a drink," Bob said to Thomas. They walked over to the booth.

Frank called after them, "We're going to t'other end of t'course, by t'finish." Luke and Bella followed Frank and Jenny.

"Let's teck a look around," said Bob.

Thomas wandered after him with his ale. They talked about how different their lives were compared to the gentry, their rich clothes and strange behaviour. They watched the way the men posed and flirted and the women preened and fluttered their fans. Thomas wondered how they had all become so affluent and marvelled at how tedious their lives must be with no work to do. Bob said they owned land and businesses, and spent their time speculating and trading.

A shout behind them caught their attention. They turned round and Thomas saw Mr Todd striding towards him with a well-dressed couple.

"Thomas Grant?" Todd slowed and caught his breath. "I'm glad to see you here. I wonder if you could take a message to your father?"

"Certainly, Sir."

"He was asking me the other day if I knew anyone who was looking for a stallion to sire his mare."

"Ay, Sir"

"This is Mr Bromet. He has a mare he wants to breed from." He turned to his companion who held out his hand.

Thomas shook it. "Pleased to meet you, Sir." He bowed his head.

"Good afternoon, Grant. Can I come and see your father's stallion tomorrow, first thing?" he asked.

"Ay, Sir. I'll tell him."

"Thank you. Good day to you, young man."

The two gentlemen and Mrs Bromet walked away, deep in conversation.

Thomas and Bob stood looking after them then walked on.

Thomas said, "Mm, that's ma boss. Faether will be pleased. It's what he's been waiting for."

They came across a great, cheering crowd, facing what looked like a gibbet over a scaffold. As they watched, a man with his hands tied behind his back was pushed up the steps. The noose was placed round the neck of the miscreant. The cheering became roars, rotten fruit and eggs went flying through the air, hitting him in the face and dripping down his clothes. Thomas turned away as the floor fell down. When he looked again the man was hanging, his body writhing in the death throes. Thomas retched and went to be sick on the grass.

Bob was by his side. "Sorry, I should 'ave warned you," he said. "The criminals who were tried and given t'death sentence at t'Assizes last week, they bring 'em here to give people entertainment between t'races. 'Tis traditional."

Thomas was recovering. "If that's what they call entertainment, they must be sick in the heed," he said. They walked away.

Bob suggested that they should go over to the pie stall. Thomas was ready to eat now and they headed that way. He caught sight of Jenny wandering around looking lost. The two men went up to her.

Jenny was relieved to see them. "Frank's 'ad over much to drink," she said. "'E's gone off to put some money on a hoss." Her brow wrinkled and her eyes were watery.

"Dinna fret, Jenny," Thomas said. "Come with us and I'll buy you a pie." He tucked her arm under his, and Bob walked the other side of her.

"I wish I 'adn't come," said Jenny.

They bought pies and drinks and took them to the edge of the course. Jenny sat between Bob and Thomas, and seemed to cheer up after she had eaten. They watched a few races and bet with each other on which horse would win. Thomas caught sight of Frank on the other side, waving a paper and shouting as the horses came to the finish. He raised his fists in the air then covered his face with his hands. Evidently he had lost his bet.

"Shall I take you home, Jenny?" Thomas asked. "Frank will no' be in a fit state by the look of him."

Jenny looked into his eyes and smiled. "That would be champion, Thomas."

Thomas stood up and helped Jenny to her feet. He said to Bob, "If you see Frank, will you tell him we've gone home?"

Bob nodded and got to his feet. "Aye. I'll see ye in T'Bell next week." He gave them a wave and wandered off among the crowds.

Thomas bought some sugar mice on their way off the horse course. He linked arms with Jenny and they sauntered away. Jenny lived on the other side of town, and Thomas had his wish. They talked about their homes and their parents. Thomas told her a little about life in the Highlands and the journey south. Jenny told him about her brothers and sisters.

As they drew near the farm where Jenny lived, Thomas stopped and turned to face her. He put his arms round her slim waist and looked into her soft brown eyes.

"Will you be ma girl, Jenny? I dinna think Frank is truly interested in you."

Jenny nodded. "Aye, Thomas. Frank don't treat us like a lady as you do. But 'e'll be mad at yer for bringin' us home."

"We'll keep away frae him for a while. He'll soon find someone else." Thomas kissed her on the forehead, then on each hand. Jenny reached up and kissed his cheek. They parted. Thomas kept turning round as he made his way along the road, and she stood and watched him until he turned the corner. The place on his cheek where she kissed him was tingling all the way home.

Annie was serving the dinner when Thomas walked into the parlour.

John looked up, "Where hast been? Fred said you've no' been at work theday."

Thomas smiled a satisfied smile and sat down at the table. "Smallbone let me have the day off. I went to York Races with ma friends."

Annie looked up at him, the spoon in mid-air, dripping stew back into the pot. She looked at John and put another spoonful and a dumpling into his bowl.

John felt unreasonably annoyed. "I could have come with thee. Why did you no' tell me?"

Annie filled a bowl for Thomas. "He's got a life of his own now, John. You could take me to the races if you've a mind," she said. "Tell us all aboot it, Son."

227

Thomas tucked into his meal before speaking. He looked infuriatingly pleased with himself. John waited to hear the news.

"There were crowds of grand people there. Real Quality, some of them. The race horses were fine, strong beasts with good breeding." He took another mouthful. "I wouldna mind racing with them one day."

"You'd have to find a good horse. Ma stallion was no' bred for racing," John said.

"I dinna ken why we couldna train him, or Clover for that matter. They had mares there racing." Thomas carried on eating, glancing at his father between mouthfuls.

John felt undermined. Why did Thomas have to challenge him?

"Tell us what else you saw," said Annie, her eyes glistening.

Thomas described the clothes people were wearing, and the way they posed and flirted. Then he said, "They had a scaffold there. Criminals who'd been sentenced to death at the Assizes last week, they were hanging them to keep people amused between races."

Annie looked horrified. "Och! No! I wouldna want to see that!" she said.

Thomas emptied his bowl. He looked at John. "Mr Todd introduced me to Mr Bromet. He's got a mare he's planning to breed from. He's coming to look at Shadow first thing themorn." He pushed his empty plate away. "That meal was champion, Mother!"

Chapter 37
Winter

Thomas saw Jenny regularly. They went walking when it was fine. Sometimes, Thomas rode on Clover to her house. Jenny met him and he allowed her to ride while he walked alongside. The evenings were drawing in, and soon the fires would be lit. They went to The Bell in town to meet their friends. Frank was not there when they walked in.

"Look 'oo it is!" called Luke to the others. "Cum an' join us you two." He pulled up two chairs from another table.

"Ee, it's right good to see ye," said Jed.

"We've been keeping oot of Frank's way," Thomas explained. "I didna reckon he'd like me stealing his girl!" He and Jenny looked at each other, their eyes sparkling.

"'E ain't been 'ere ower much," said Jed. "Allus were moody, that one."

They caught up with all the latest news and made friends with two strangers, George and Lucy. Jenny and Bella had not seen each other for some time. They sat together and gossiped. Everyone was deep in animated conversation, enjoying the cosiness indoors. Thomas looked around. Faces became more flushed and the voices and laughter grew louder.

Floss was lying by Jenny's feet. Her ears pricked. She sat up and looked towards the door.

The door opened. Frank staggered in and made his way towards Thomas.

"I heard you was 'ere. I want a word with you, outside."

"Nay, Frank, lay off!" cried Jenny. "'E ain't done no 'arm."

Floss laid her ears back.

Frank's face was close to Thomas' now. His breath reeked of ale.

"You can say what you want to say in here," said Thomas quietly. He knew Frank would come off worst if Thomas accepted the challenge.

Frank rocked around and reached out to the back of a chair to steady himself.

He shouted, "You stole my girl!"

Floss growled, and the other customers stopped talking. All eyes were on Frank.

"You left us when we was at the races," complained Jenny. Thomas had never heard her raise her voice like that.

Frank grimaced at her. "You baggage!" he snarled. He looked at Thomas. "You can 'ave 'er. She ain't worth fightin' ower." He bowled over to the door and slammed out.

Thomas, relieved that he had avoided a fight, raised his arm and called to the barman, "Another round if you please." He found his money pouch and emptied it into the barman's hand. Bob, Luke, Jed and George cheered and the camaraderie resumed.

Floss settled down again.

Winter took them by surprise. They were still not accustomed to the weather patterns in this part of the country. In the Highlands they were able to predict when the cold weather would curtail all outdoor activity. In Yorkshire the autumn days were often balmy and they were not ready for the sharp frosts and strong winds of November.

There was not much John could do in the garden, so he foraged for wood for the fire and stored it under the lean-to by the back door. They had to remember to bring pails of water indoors at night in case the frost covered it in a thick layer of ice. The wind rattled the shutters, keeping them awake, and John went round making them more secure. Annie made woollen socks and waistcoats from the wool she had spun in the summer.

Stores of oats and flour were running low. John and Annie made an extra journey into town to buy more, in case they were snowed in, as happened last winter. They bought salted beef and bacon to keep for emergencies.

The snow arrived on Christmas morning. Thomas looked out of his window to see a covering of white over everything. The wind had dropped and the sky was eggshell blue. He had two days off work and planned to see Jenny tomorrow. Hopefully it would not snow again until later. He dressed and went downstairs.

Floss was indoors in this cold weather. She got up from her deerskin bed and stretched before coming to greet him. They went out into the back pasture. Floss sniffed the snow and went to relieve herself, leaving footprints and a damp, yellow hole. Thomas stooped to collect enough to make a snowball and threw it into the air. Floss caught it and wished she hadn't. She shook her head and leapt about, crouched on her forepaws and barked. Thomas threw another snowball.

A window opened above them and John's head in a nightcap poked out.

"Happy Christmas, Faether!" called Thomas.

John looked grumpy and retreated, slamming the window shut.

Annie roasted a capon with some bacon for their dinner which they ate with potatoes, carrots and winter greens. There was plum pudding for desert. They celebrated the day with a bottle of wine and spent the afternoon and evening by the fire, telling stories and talking about the old days. John found his pipe and managed a few tunes to accompany Annie's and Thomas' singing.

It froze overnight. Thomas saddled up Clover and he and Floss crunched their way over to see Jenny. He had been invited to have dinner with her family. Her parents were honest, hardworking farming folk and welcomed him into their home, pleased to meet the man Jenny had spoken of. It was a big, friendly farmhouse with log fires and comfortable furniture. Thomas dreamed of the time when he would have a place like this.

After dinner they wrapped themselves in their coats and hats and went outside. Thomas lifted Jenny up to ride in front of him. He relished the feel of her warm body between his arms. She held onto Clover's mane and they spent the afternoon riding along the snowy lanes. Floss ran alongside until she tired and Thomas slowed Clover down. They dismounted and had a snowball fight. Floss played pig in the middle.

The next few weeks were colder and work on the farm became laborious. They moved the cattle under cover and dug up the last of the turnips for fodder. The ground became solid and there was little else they could do. Smallbone allowed the men to go home early.

More snow fell and bound them indoors. Their time was spent digging pathways to the well and the men took a whole day to clear the lane up to the farm. They hitched the horses up to a snowplough and drove it to the road into York. Other farmers were doing the same and eventually they could all link up and exchange provisions and supply the elderly and poor with water, food and fuel.

Chapter 38
Carting

Shadow visited three mares that spring. Word had spread and two or three landed gentry were waiting to see the results before they approached John for the use of his stallion. The family had extra money to pay for new clothes and a few pots and pans for Annie. John painted the walls indoors and was now thinking of the possibility of building stables.

The summer was coming to an end. John was clearing away the spent pea and bean haulms. He stood up and stretched his back. The sun was low in the early evening sky and he had to shade his eyes to see who it was coming down the lane towards him. Smallbone swung his walking stick as he ambled along, his other hand in his pocket and a piece of straw protruding from the corner of his mouth. He stopped when he came to John's garden.

John jabbed his fork in the ground and walked over the clods of earth to meet his manager. "Good evening, Sir," he said.

Smallbone never wasted words. "Grant," he said, "we could use an extra cart to teck wheat to t'mill termorrer."

John had planned to take Annie to market with some produce. This had become a regular source of income. She would miss it. "Ay, Sir. That'll be fine," he said obediently. It was not worth objecting and he would be paid for it.

Smallbone grunted. "Fust thing, mind," he said as he set off up the lane.

John returned to his garden. He took the fork and lifted the haulms into the barrow, left the fork on top and wheeled it to the compost heap. Two more journeys to and fro finished the job and he took the barrow and fork to the shed he had erected in the back garden. He would be glad to have a wash at the well before the men came home, and take off his leather glove. The stump was sweaty and sore.

Annie looked up from the stove as he came in. "I saw Smallbone talking to thee," she said. "What news?"

"He wants me to take a cartload of wheat to the mill themorrow," he said, watching Annie's face.

She grimaced. "That means you'll no' be taking me to market," she said crossly. "The quilt I was going to sell can wait, but there's the eggs and the gingerbread I made. They willna keep."

"Can you no' sell them to the neighbours?" suggested John.

"I doubt if they'd be willing to pay for them. I'll have to give them away." Annie sighed and went back to the pot on the stove.

"D'you want me to buy some flour? You could bake a batch of bread for the next market." He regretted having to disappoint her.

"Mm," said Annie with a mouthful, having tested the stew for seasoning. "So long as you dinna have to goo carting again."

Thomas came in, hot and tired. "'Tis a good harvest this year. We've been threshing theday, and there's more to do themorrow." He slung his knapsack over a

236

chair and ran his fingers through his thatch of hair. "I'll goo and swill doon at the well, Mother." He went over and kissed the top of Annie's head before taking off his round frock and tossing it into the corner. He walked out, stretching and rubbing his chest.

Next morning John harnessed the carthorse and hitched him up to the cart. He enjoyed these days carting. He felt better when he was contributing to the family income. The sun was rising as he made his way along the lane to the farm. There were two other carters loading the sacks of grain when he arrived. Although he was quite capable of picking up a sack and putting it on the cart, they saw the hook on his left arm and loaded up for him. He was embarrassed but felt obliged to thank them. He would try to arrive at the mill after they had delivered their loads.

The roads were almost straight and flat. There was no view except of buildings and windmills. John drove the cart past farms and meadows, wheat fields and vegetable crops. His heart still ached for his home country. He could not get used to the vast skies coming down to the ground. He felt exposed and vulnerable in the open spaces.

The white sails of the windmill came into sight. They creaked as they rotated with the wind. The other carters waved as John drove into the yard. They were carrying the last of their sacks into the mill. John did not want them to help him. He jumped down off the cart and went round the back, hauled the first sack of grain onto his shoulder and strode into the mill. He heard a shout behind him. He ignored it and carried on, dumped the sack on the floor next to the others and turned to collect the rest of his load.

Only then did he notice a trail of wheat from his cart to the door of the mill. His heart jumped into his throat. In his haste, he had forgotten to remove the hook from his left arm. It had pierced the bag. He turned back and saw a mounting pile of wheat trickling out of the hole.

The other carters shook their heads as they lifted the other bags off John's cart, muttering to each other. They came towards him.

"Yer should've let us help yer," said one of them.

"That's one wasted sack, unless yer can stop it leaking," the other commented.

John looked again at the result of his haste and stubbornness. He grabbed a shovel and pushed it under the mounting heap of grain.

"That won't stop it." The miller was coming down the stairs. "Here, Davy, gi' us a hand." He grabbed an empty sack and between them they lifted the leaking one into it.

"It'll cost yer," said the miller crossly to John.

John had nothing to say. The evidence was clear enough. He wondered if he would ever be given the job again. He hung around waiting for the receipt for the wheat, which he would pass on to Smallbone. He and the miller would settle up later. John would have to confess to Smallbone what happened and pay for the lost wheat. He hoped the miller had not charged for the whole sack. He took the piece of paper and walked back to his cart. The other carters followed him. One patted him on the shoulder as they parted.

John looked at him and smiled ruefully, shrugging his shoulders. "Forgot to take the hook off," he said.

"Ee, ah don't know," said the friendly one, shaking his head as he climbed onto his cart.

John cursed his stupidity all the way home.

Smallbone was angry and charged him for the whole sack.

John unhitched the horse and let him into the pasture, went into the house and straight to the whisky bottle.

"Not a good day, then, John?" Annie knew the answer. "I dinna suppose you remembered ma flour." She turned back to her spinning.

John took a glass and the bottle to the chair outside the front door and sat down. His hand shook as he poured the golden liquid into the glass which he had placed on the uneven ground. He replaced the cork carefully into the bottle. He did not want any more accidents today.

Chapter 39
An Old Acquaintance

Musty black earth crumbled off the potatoes, leaving them clean and smooth in his hand. John dug another forkful. He was pleased with his produce this year. There was enough to share with his neighbours. Fred showed no enthusiasm for gardening and his results were poor. The evening sun slanted through the changing leaves. A cold wind chivvied some of them to flutter to the ground and chase along the lane. John stood up to ease his back.

The men rumbled down the lane scuffing their boots and talking roughly, their coats over their shoulders. Their working day was over. Thomas emerged from the group and came up to his father.

"There's a hunt meeting themorrow, Faether. Mister Todd has some visitors biding frae Scotland. He wants to hire thy horses. You're to goo up to the house with them first thing."

John considered. He was not sure he wanted other people riding his horses.

Thomas raised his voice. "Faether, it's another way of earning siller. Besides, I dinna reckon you have a choice. Mister Todd is your maester."

Of course, Thomas was right. "Ay. That'll be fine. We'll ride them there themorn." He was curious to meet these visitors from Scotland.

Thomas picked up the sack of potatoes and took it in to Annie. John upturned his spade and fork, rested them each on the hook on his left arm, wiped off the remnants of earth with some tufts of long grass in his right hand and took them round to store them in the cow stalls.

A mist floated over the low ground the next morning. The locals called it *white ladies*. It was a portent of a fine day, they said. John and Thomas gave the horses a polish with bristly brushes before saddling them. They rode up the lane towards the big house.

No-one was about except the groom. He handled the horses respectfully and said, "Don't worry. We'll teck good care of 'em...Mister Grant. I'll have 'em ready for you to collect around five. Good day." He lifted his cap an inch off his head with his crop, and led Clover and Shadow away over the cobbles.

John stood looking after them, feeling bereft.

Thomas said, "I'll be off to ma work, Faether. Why dinna you follow the hunt when they get going? 'Tis a grand sight with all the Quality folks in their fine riding habits galloping over the fields." He strode away whistling.

John turned and walked back down the lane. The sun was burning the mist away now, leaving wisps like wraiths among the hedgerows. It seemed a long day. John could not even go riding without his horses. He gathered all the potatoes in and dug over the earth to catch the winter frosts. Annie was busy making jam and pickles and did not want him hanging round the house. He went foraging in the woods for blackberries and nuts until it was time to go to collect Shadow and Clover.

The stable yard was milling with horses and people. Hooves clattered on the cobbles and loud voices and laughter filled the air. John felt out of place. He looked for Shadow and Clover, searching deeper into the crowds. A tap on his shoulder made him turn. Shadow was there. A familiar figure held the reins.

"John Grant?" the man asked. Recognition opened his face into a delighted smile. He removed his hat. "By God it is!" said Alex MacPherson.

John gaped at this apparition from the past. He had aged considerably, but then John suspected the same might be said of himself. He took off his hat, tucked it under his left arm and held out his hand.

"'Tis a pleasure to meet you again, Sir."

MacPherson held John's hand in both of his. A warm glow spread through John and emotion caught his breath.

"This must be your horse. I thought I recognised the Scots breeding. We've had a grand ride together today." MacPherson slapped Shadow on the hind quarters.

The groom came and took the reins. "I'll just give yer horses a rub down afore you teck 'em, Sir."

John nodded.

A lady appeared at MacPherson's side.

"This is an old acquaintance of mine, my dear, from Covenanter days. Tell me Grant, how you came to be here."

John recounted some of the adventures the family had experienced on the long journey from Scotland. "And you escaped the gallows also, Sir," he said.

"Ay. When it became evident that our lives were in danger we fled to France. My eldest son, who had Royalist leanings, took over the estates and was not challenged about my allegiance. I rarely go back to

Speyside now. Ludovick Grant cleared all that part of Scotland of Covenanters and has since been named the Highland King. He still struts around in his tartan trews. His father was my greatest friend, but I never took to Ludo, even when he was a lad."

"D'you miss the auld country, Sir?" John asked.

"Ay, we do. There's nowhere like the Highlands. I live in Sussex now, which is also beautiful. There are rolling hills and forests, deer parks and plenty of sport. This land is abominably flat. But we had good sport today."

John nodded. "I still have a hunger for the wild mountains and moors," he said softly. He looked up and saw Thomas coming towards them. "This is ma son, Thomas," he said.

Thomas shook hands with MacPherson and his lady.

"This is the Laird MacPherson, Son. I knew him when I was a Covenanter."

Thomas nodded and stood back. "'Tis a surprise to meet a Highlander in these parts, Sir. Did ye have a good ride theday?"

"Ay, your father has two fine horses. 'Twas a pleasure to ride them." He replaced his hat and said, "We must go and dress for dinner. We'll be staying here a week or two. We might see you again before we go home." He took his lady's arm and lifted his crop in salute before walking off to the house.

John and Thomas went and collected Shadow and Clover from the groom, mounted and made their way home. John mulled over the pleasure it had been to meet an old friend. But the yearning for his roots intensified.

244

Chapter 40
Disaster Strikes

Annie had been cleaning the outside privy. She came into the parlour scratching her legs, and lifted her skirt to see what was biting. John watched her from his chair by the hearth.

"Struth!, Annie! You're covered in fleas!"

She screamed and ran outside. "Bring a pail of water, John," she shouted.

John leapt from his chair and grabbed the pail they had brought in for cooking. He took it out to where Annie had kicked off her patens and lifted her skirt around her waist. She plunged both feet into the water and stood there scooping it up her legs and swilling it down. No-one was outside next door. She took off her skirt and shook it violently. When she was satisfied that no fleas remained, she stepped out of the pail and replaced her skirt.

By this time John was laughing. "I've never seen thee move so quick!"

Annie caught the humour and giggled. "They were biding in that privy for me to goo in there and disturb them!"

"There's been rats lurking around there," John said as he picked up the empty pail and started up the lane to refill it at the well.

Annie was preparing the dinner when he returned. "Thomas'll no' be back for a meal thenight. He's taken Clover to meet his girl again," John announced.

"All the more for us," Annie retorted, as she chopped up carrots and turnips for the stew.

Thomas did not return until after John and Annie had gone to bed. John heard the back door close and the stair creak before he dropped off to sleep.

The next morning Thomas appeared for breakfast with a long face.

"Has thy girl given thee the push?" teased John.

"No, it's worse than that." Thomas sat down. His hands were shaking, his face was pale.

"What's amiss, Son?" Annie stopped stirring the porridge and was staring at Thomas.

John was thinking of all the possible disasters to worry Thomas like this; someone had died; he lost his job; Floss...

Thomas drew a deep breath. "Someone stole Clover."

Annie sat down.

Thomas stared at the table.

John felt his anger rising... "How didst let that happen?" he burst out.

There was silence.

Thomas looked up at his father. "She was tethered with the other horses outside the coaching inn. I was in The Bell with ma friends. When I came out with Jenny to take her home, Clover was gone." He shrugged his shoulders and shook his head sorrowfully.

John shouted, "I knew I shouldna have let thee take her into town!" He banged his fist on the table, then put his head in his hand.

Annie slowly and quietly served out the porridge. "Get that down thee," she said to Thomas. "You need to eat before going to work."

Thomas took a few mouthfuls and pushed his plate away. He got up and lifted his coat from its hook on the wall, opened the door and walked out into the autumn morning.

John sat around brooding all day. He could not settle to anything.

Annie said, "'Tis no use sulking, John. We canna do aught to bring the horse back. Thomas is as upset as thee. 'Twasna his fault. 'Twere just bad luck, I reckon."

Thomas did not return that evening.

"'E must've gone into town looking for Clover. Floss is gone. Likely he came to fetch her after work and said naught," said Annie as they prepared to go to bed.

"I didna hear him come home after work," John said.

"No, but thy hearing's not so good these days." Annie chuckled.

There was no sign of Thomas the next morning, and no Floss.

Annie was shivering. "I'm worried, John," she said.

By midday Annie was feeling ill. Her limbs ached and she was hot. John tried to persuade her to go to bed. He would ask Fred's wife Mavis to come. Annie refused.

When the men returned from work that evening, John went and knocked on Fred's door.

"Was ma son at work theday, Fred?" he asked.

"Nay. Smallbone were mad. We ain't seen 'im for two days. I were coming to ask you where 'e is."

"We havena seen him either," said John. "And now Annie's ailing and I canna leave her to fetch the doctor."

Fred looked alarmed. "Does she have a fever? Is 'er neck swelled?" he asked.

"Ay. She's hot, but shivering," John said. "What's wrong, Fred?"

Fred had backed away and started to close the door. "Them as was in your cottage afore you, they 'ad the plague. Sounds like the same. They all died. Go inside and shut your door. Keep away!" He closed the door. John heard him shoot the bolts home.

He stood staring. He had heard that the plague reared its ugly head from time to time in York, wiping out large numbers of the population. He knew that it was highly contagious, but that not everyone caught it. He remembered the remains of the bonfire in the back when they arrived. Everything in the house had been burnt.

But how did Annie catch it? She only went into town once a week, and had not made any friends. As far as he knew there was no epidemic in York. Maybe it was not the plague, and Fred had been hasty in his judgement. Whatever it was, he had to go and look after Annie. It appeared that Thomas had deserted them. No matter if John caught the plague. If Annie died, there would be nothing left to live for.

Chapter 41
False Accusations

Thomas worried about Clover all day. He was angry, too. He suspected that Frank had something to do with the disappearance of the horse, but could not believe he would steal her. As far as he knew, Frank could not ride. It could be a vicious prank. He would take Floss into town and try to track Clover down. Maybe someone would know where Frank lived.

He finished work early and sneaked round the back of the cottage without his parents seeing him. He did not want an argument with his father. He collected Floss and they walked into town. The taverns were open and a few men hung around the market square. Most people had gone home from work before coming out for the evening. A street vendor was setting up his stall. Thomas waited until he was ready then bought two pies. He went and sat down on a bench at the side of the square and shared his pies with Floss. They watched as more vendors came along, couples in love, and groups of young folk on an evening out. One or two horsemen rode up and hitched their horses onto the rail where Thomas had left Clover the previous evening. A coach clattered in. It stopped to deposit its passengers, before going round to the stable yard for a change of horses.

Thomas got up and walked over to The Bell. There might be someone there who knew where Frank lived. The barman was polishing the tables, ready for his first customers. He looked up in recognition as Thomas and Floss walked in.

"D'you happen to ken where Frank lives, Josh?"

"Nay, not for sure. Somewhere Fulford way I reckon." Josh continued wiping down the tables, then went behind the bar. "Care for a mug of ale? You look all-in."

"Ay. I'll wait for the others." Thomas paid for his drink and took it to sit on the bench outside. He settled there to watch people coming and going. The sun retired and lights were lit in the surrounding buildings. Thomas thought of Jenny. They had planned to meet again tomorrow. He wished she was with him now, cuddling up to him on the bench. She would give him encouragement in his search for Clover. She might even know where Frank lived. He watched a couple of lads scrapping in the dust by the cross. One of them landed on top of the other and pinned his adversary down. More boys came and cheered him on. The day he stood by the market cross waiting for Smallbone to come along and hire him seemed a long time ago now.

His legs were getting stiff sitting down. He stood up and took his empty mug into the bar. He and Floss took a turn round the square. They came to the coaching inn and stopped to look at the horses tethered there.

He looked again. Floss wagged her tail and sniffed at the grey legs. Clover snickered and stamped her foot. Thomas went to greet her, fondling her muzzle and whispering in her ear. Waves of relief flowed through him.

"I've found thee, lass. Where've ye been?" He did not wait to see who had brought her here. Whoever it was, was a thief. He loosed the reins and mounted. But he did not even have time to turn Clover round.

"Hey! Stop, thief! That's my horse! Stop him, Harry!"

A man came in front of Clover, preventing any forward progress. There was a shout nearby and a constable ran up. They took the reins and dragged Thomas off the saddle. Floss barked. A crowd gathered.

"That's ma horse!" Thomas protested. "She was stolen yest'reen."

"Nay. 'Tis my horse. I bought her yesterday, didn't I, Harry? You were with us."

Harry confirmed this fact by a vigorous nodding of his head.

The constable had a firm hold of Thomas. He said, "What is your name?"

The supposed owner said, "Grundy. Tom Grundy."

"D'you know the name of the man who sold you the horse, Sir?"

Grundy shook his head. "Nay, I can't say as I do. I know where to find 'im though." He looked at the constable and nodded.

Thomas said, "'Tis ma faether's horse. He'll vouch for me."

The constable looked down his nose. "You're one o' them foreigners, ain't yer? How do I know yer ain't in partnership with yer father, stealing horses?" he sneered, kicking out at Floss who was snarling at him. "You're coming down to t'gaol, 'til you can think of a better story." He looked at Grundy. "Bring that man who sold you t'horse to me, when you find 'im." He led Thomas away.

Thomas had been in this stinking, dimly lit, cold hole for a few days. He did not know how many. There was a bucket in which to relieve himself. This was taken and emptied now and again. A silent old man shuffled in periodically with a meagre meal of gruel and stale bread. No-one else had come in to ask him to explain himself. They all believed that he was a horse thief. His father would never forgive him for losing Clover. Thomas lay on the wooden bench and stared at the ceiling through the gloom, wondering if Floss had given up waiting for him and gone home by now, and whether anyone had come into town looking for him. Jenny must be wondering why he had not met her as agreed.

He was confused and angry. He kept going over the occasion of his arrest in his mind. Why hadn't someone come and confirmed his story by now? He had not been given a chance to explain. They had just flung him into gaol.

A rattling of keys and the sound of the lock turning brought him out of his reverie. This was his next ration of gruel, no doubt. The door opened and someone entered carrying a lantern. The door was shut behind him.

"Thomas Grant?" a gruff voice asked.

The light dazzled him and he could not see his visitor clearly. "Ay," he said.

"I have to tell you that the man Grundy has not returned with the person who sold him the horse. But the constable who arrested you clearly saw you attempting to steal it. If we have no proof that you are telling the truth, you will be kept here until the Assizes next August, to await trial."

Thomas gasped. "That's nine months!" His heart pounded. He felt sick. He stood up and shouted, "I canna stay here! Ma faether and mother need ma wages. They'll have to leave the cottage if I'm no' earning." He sat down again and leaned forward, his head in his hands.

"Is there anyone who can vouch for you, that you be telling the truth?" The stranger sounded sympathetic.

"No, only ma faether. 'Twas his horse. But the constable said you'll no' trust him."

"Who is your employer? Surely, he knows about your father's horse."

Thomas thought for a while. Then he remembered the loan of the horses for the hunt. Why had he not thought of it before? "Ay! Mr Todd! He has a visitor frae Scotland, the Laird MacPherson. He hired ma faether's mare and stallion for the hunt. They'll vouch for me!" He began to feel hopeful. "But if you canna find Grundy, then you canna find the horse."

"You're not likely to get your horse back, if it is yours. But you might get your freedom, lad. I happen to know Mr Todd. I'll send a messenger to fetch him."

By now Thomas could see the man's face in the light of the lantern. His eyes shone blue and kindly from under bushy eyebrows. His mouth spread into a re-assuring smile. He turned to go, leaving Thomas in semi-darkness once again with his thoughts. The key turned in the lock, and he returned to his bench, praying that he had not been dreaming for the last half hour.

Chapter 42
The Plague

Annie lay on the bed, feverish and restless, drifting in and out of consciousness, crying with pain. Her neck was swollen and there were great black lumps in her groins and new ones in her armpits. John had spent the last two days bathing her in cold water and trying to persuade her to sip the gruel he had made from the few ingredients he could find in the food store. He had eaten all the bread, and cooked himself porridge when he felt he could leave her. He had to keep up his strength until the end.

Floss came to the back door, looking sorry for herself, her head hung low and her tail between her legs. She was ravenously hungry and thirsty. Thomas must be dead, John thought. Floss would never leave him otherwise. Even if she could lead him there, John could not leave Annie. He fed Floss on porridge. She stayed by the back door in her usual place. When John had the chance, he checked on Shadow, alone in the cowstalls, and the carthorse, and topped up their haybags. The grass in the back had stopped growing and there was little for them to graze. He collected the eggs and fed the hens, then went back to Annie.

He kept checking his own body for signs of the disease. He felt well, if a little weary through lack of sleep, and had no pain in the places where Annie's swellings were.

It was night. John had drifted off into a welcome sleep and Annie was quiet. He was woken by her hands reaching for him. The moon, shining through the window, revealed her white face, hollow-eyed, searching for his own.

He sat up. "Annie, love, what is it?"

"Thomas. Is Thomas home?"

"No, lass. I reckon he's no' coming home." John could not lie to her.

She sank down onto the pillow. "God bless him, wherever he is." She grabbed hold of John's hand and turned her head to look at him. "I'm no' long for this world, John. You goo and seek Thomas. He'll look after thee." She shut her eyes and groaned.

"Rest in peace, Annie. God bless thee." John held onto her hand until it relaxed. She would soon be out of pain and in the loving arms of her Maker. His duties were over. He lay back feeling alone and wishing his own days were at an end.

He woke with the dawn. He could not lie there waiting to die. He would have to leave the cottage. Thomas was no longer around to pay the rent.

He rolled over and kissed Annie's cold face, got out of bed, washed himself in the pail of water and dressed himself in clean clothes. He took the pistol out of its drawer, with some bullets in a box, collected together the old plaids they had brought with them, and anything else he thought he might need, and took them downstairs. He went out and brought the cart round to the back, and rooted out the old trivet and some cooking pots, bowls and spoons from Annie's cupboards.

The fire had not quite gone out and John chivvied it into life. He went out and fed the animals, collected the eggs and started loading the cart. He cooked himself a hearty breakfast of crowdies and spent all day packing anything he might need on a long journey. He killed a chicken, plucked and gutted it, and put it in a stew pot with water, potatoes and vegetables and herbs from Annie's store. This he left bubbling over the fire until he reckoned it was cooked. He ate some for his dinner and was impressed with his efforts. He gave some to Floss and stowed the pot containing the leftovers in the cart.

When night came, John went into the back garden. He fetched his spade and fork from the cow stalls and dug a deep hole. He went up to where Annie's body still lay on the bed. He wrapped it lovingly in the quilt she had made and carried it to the hole, laid the body carefully down, and covered it with soil.

"Sorry, Annie. 'Tis the best I can do," he whispered. He stood a few minutes by the makeshift grave before going back into the house.

John had not had the need to write for a long time, but there was just a chance that Thomas, if he was not dead, would come home to an empty house. There were some old papers in the corner of the room. John took a piece of charcoal from the now spent fire and wrote:

MOTHER DEAD GONE SOUTH FLOSS WITH ME

He hoped that Thomas would be able to read this, and wished he had made the time to teach him to read when he was a boy. Maybe he could find someone else to read it to him.

When he was sure that all was done, John blew out the candle in the parlour and left the house by the back door. He put a harness and leading rein on Shadow and hitched him up to the cart. The carthorse backed into the shafts willingly and Floss jumped in when John called. They set off down the lane, away from the nightmare of the last few days, and started on another journey south.

Chapter 43
Reprieve

The Justice of the Peace sat behind his great desk in his spacious office. There was a carpet on the floor and chandeliers hung from the ceiling. The long windows were adorned with heavy drapes and the walls were painted with luscious fruit, fantastical flowers and exotic birds. His Lordship stood up as his visitors entered.

"Good morning, Alex, William. Thank ye for coming so promptly in this inclement weather. Pray, take your seats."

Thomas, who was standing to one side of the desk, the gaoler and the constable on either side of him, gave a thankful sigh as the two familiar figures sat down on chairs facing the desk. The bewigged butler closed the door quietly behind them.

Lord Fairfax, Justice of the Peace, wearing a long white wig and a suit of dark blue velvet, returned to his seat and turned his powdered face towards Thomas. "Thomas Grant, you are accused of stealing a horse outside The Black Swan in York market place. I believe you have denied this charge on the grounds that the horse was stolen from you on the previous evening."

"That's correct, your honour," Thomas asserted.

"Constable Baker, you were present and witnessed the occurrence. Please tell us what happened."

Constable Baker wheezed and coughed before accurately reporting that, although Grundy said he bought the horse, he failed to re-appear with the man who sold it to him.

"Grant, be kind enough to describe to us the horse, which you referred to as your father's, and which you attempted to reclaim."

"Ay, your honour." Thomas bowed his head. "She's a dappled grey mare standing fifteen hands. She has Highland blood in her veins and a dark spot, the shape of a Clover leaf, on her right shoulder. She snickered in recognition when I approached her."

The Laird MacPherson spoke up. "That's a very accurate description of the mare my wife rode to the hunt last week."

"D'you know this man?" asked Lord Fairfax.

"I do. His father hired me the mare for my wife, with a black stallion for myself. We are known to each other from our previous lives in the Highlands."

"William Todd, d'you know this man?"

"Yes, Sir. I have employed him as a farm worker for four years. I can vouch for his honesty and reliability as a conscientious worker with a promising future in farming. He would be sorely missed on my estate."

"Well, young man, that is a very glowing report from two reliable witnesses. I believe you are telling the truth and have been duped. As it happens, my mare was sired by your father's stallion. It looks as if you've lost your father's mare, unfortunately. But I can now allow you to go free and resume your work on Mr Todd's farm."

"Thank you. Thank you kindly, your honour." Thomas bowed again, and turned to his liberators. "I canna thank ye enough, gentlemen." He went over and shook their hands.

"Thomas, I am pleased that we could be of help," MacPherson said warmly. "William, could we give the lad a lift home in the trap? 'Tis unpleasant weather to be walking, and I'm sure he will be eager to get back to his parents, who will be worried."

"Of course," said Mr Todd.

They walked out of the building together.

The trap made its way out of town in the pouring rain. Thomas felt light-headed and could not believe he was free and travelling with gentry. He was anxious to get home and explain his disappearance. He hoped Floss had found her own way back.

Mr Todd cleared his throat. "Grant, I'm afraid I have bad news for you."

Thomas looked at his master questioningly.

"I have reason to believe that there is plague in your cottage."

Thomas's heart stopped for a moment. "Who...? How...?" The words stuck in his throat.

Todd continued. "A few days ago your neighbour, Fred Clark, reported to Mr Smallbone that your mother was ill with what sounded like the plague. The family who lived in that cottage before you, all died of the plague. It is possible that your mother caught the disease from something that was left in the house, though it is some years ago."

Thomas was speechless. He had to go and find out for himself.

He gaped at Todd, who said, "I would strongly advise that you stay away from your parents until the crisis is over, one way or another. We can get a message to them to say that you are safe. If you go to the cottage, I cannot guarantee to keep your position open for you. The disease is highly contagious and you will understand that I do not want the whole of my workforce infected."

There was a pause, in which Todd allowed Thomas to take in the situation.

"I can allow you to bide in one of the rooms in my stable block in the meantime, and you'll be able to get back to work." Todd finished by saying, "I am truly sorry to have to bring you this news."

Thomas' mind was in a whirl. It would be sensible to take Todd's advice. But the thought of leaving his parents to die without help was too much. He had to go to the cottage to find out the situation for himself, even if it meant losing his job.

He shuddered as he drew in a deep breath. He said quietly and firmly, "Please drop me off at the cottage, Mr Todd. I'm grateful for your advice, and will be mighty sorry to lose ma job with you. But I need to see ma mother and ma faether before they goo."

Todd raised his eyebrows. "Just as you wish. You're a brave young man."

Alex MacPherson had been listening to the conversation with grave concern written across his brow. Now he spoke. "I have not taken the trouble to free the man to condemn him to a life of vagrancy. I will alight from the trap when we reach the cottage. I will not enter or go near it. But I will wait to see if I can be of any assistance, then walk up to the house if I am free from contamination. If I do not return to you within the hour, I will send a message to you, William, from The Black Swan, with instructions for my wife to join me there."

Todd nodded. "You also have great courage, my friend. I will await news." They shook hands.

The trap started on the last leg of its journey up the lane. It stopped at the cottage. Thomas and MacPherson alighted and it continued towards the big house. Thomas ran round to the back, leaving MacPherson standing in the rain.

Chapter 44
Bad News

Floss was not sitting at the back door. Shadow and the carthorse were missing. The cart was gone. Thomas' heart sank to the soles of his boots. But then he snatched at the possibility that the whole story was a mistake, and maybe they had gone into town. He opened the back door cautiously, afraid of what he might find. The parlour was empty. He ran upstairs to his parents' chamber. The bed was unkempt and coverless. His own chamber was as he had left it.

Back in the parlour he was unsure what to do next. Were they both dead? If so, who had gone off with the cart and the horses? He wandered round, looking for a sign. He sat down at the table. There was a piece of paper with writing on it. He picked it up, feeling that it was important, but he could not read it. He ran outside to where MacPherson was waiting.

"There's a note, Sir. I canna read it." He held it up for his friend to read.

"*Mother dead. Gone south. Floss with me.*" Mac Pherson looked at Thomas. "I'm sorry for your loss, Thomas. I expect you'll want to go and look for your father."

"He canna have gone far," said Thomas. "The fire's still warm. But I dinna ken how I can find him with no horse."

"May I suggest that you stay in the cottage for tonight. Get some rest. My wife and I will be returning south in the morning on the stage coach. You can walk into town and I'll meet you at The Black Swan at nine

265

o'clock. I will pay for your fare to wherever you need to go. We might see your father on the road. The coach will travel faster than him. What d'you say?"

Thomas once again felt overwhelmed with gratitude. "Och, Sir. Thank you. You've been unco kind."

"We have to look after our fellow countrymen, Thomas. I admire your father and his courage in such adversity as he has endured. He needs you now, and I hope I can alleviate some of his suffering, and yours. Now, we are soaking wet, and I must make haste to find my wife, who will be anxious. I'll see you in the morning." He turned and walked up the lane.

Thomas stared after his friend, and took his father's note back indoors. He realised he had not eaten properly for several days, which might account for his light-headedness.

He searched the cupboards and shelves for food. There was a small amount of oats in the crock, and some potatoes and root vegetables. Then he remembered the hens. He went outside and collected the eggs. He noticed that there were fewer hens in the coop. He killed one, plucked and gutted it, throwing the entrails onto the grass for the birds and foxes. There was a freshly dug mound of earth and he went to look at it. This was his mother's grave. He crouched down and touched the wet earth. Tears welled up and spilled over, falling to join the raindrops.

"Goodbye, dear Mother," he whispered. "God bless and keep thee."

With a deep sigh, Thomas went indoors and prepared himself a meal, as his father had done the day before. While the stew was cooking, Thomas draped his wet jacket over a chair in front of the blazing fire and went upstairs to change his clothes. There was nothing in the house that he needed now.

After a good night's sleep, Thomas rose from his bed, went downstairs and cooked a meal of crowdies with the oats and eggs, wishing he could have made it with milk instead of water. He put on his dry jacket and his hat and went out into a fresh, bright morning, hoping that he would find his father on the cart, trundling up the road, with Shadow tied behind and Floss up in front, looking out for him.

Part 4.

The Search

Chapter 45
The Long Journey Resumed

John drove through the outskirts of York heading in what he hoped was a southerly direction. He would know when the sun rose. It was raining hard. Floss was huddled up in the cart among the plaids, covered with a cow hide from the floor of the cottage. John's mind travelled back to the events which brought him to this situation. He had been angry with Thomas and felt sorry that they parted on bad terms. He hoped that his son was still alive somewhere and that one day they might find each other. His dear Annie, though, he had lost for ever. This thought brought tears to his eyes. He allowed them to run down his face, mingling with the rain. He remembered her bright face, her common sense and her faithful attention to his needs. How would he manage without her? He was a vagrant again. He thought of Sam, near Alnwick. That man spent years wandering the countryside, poaching and foraging. John considered that was giving up on life, which he was not prepared to do. He must cling onto the hope of ending his days in some comfort and security. MacPherson had spoken of hills and woodlands in Sussex and John would travel until he found them.

He could see the dawn breaking on his left hand side. That was a good sign. The road stretched ahead of him through the gloom. He had a little money on him, but it would not last long. The time had come to sell Shadow. He should get a good price. It would be a big wrench but the cart and horse were more use to him now.

Cottages and farm buildings on each side of the road heralded their approach to a small market town. The houses became closer together and grander in style. John could see a busy market place ahead of him. He left the horse and cart in a back street, told Floss to stay on guard and led Shadow, with his saddle on, to a coaching inn in the middle of town. He went into the yard where an ostler emerged from one of the stables.

"Can you tell me if there's a horse fair hereabouts, where I can sell ma horse for a good price?" John asked.

The ostler looked John and Shadow up and down. "There's nowt round 'ere. Hoss fairs go to York or Wetherby." He shook his head and stroked his chin. "But there's a man has a racing stables t'other side of town. 'E's allus lookin' for new stock."

John nodded eagerly. "Where would I find him? Can you tell me the way?"

"Jim Fellowes, 'is name is," said the ostler. He waved his hand in a southerly direction. "Carry on through town on this road, about a mile, there's a lane oop on t'right, wi' a notice and a picture of a race hoss, wi' *FELLOWES* written under it in big letters. Go oop there. You'll find 'im."

John searched in his pocket for small change and gave it to the ostler, who thanked him and touched his cap as he closed his hand over the tip.

The rain poured down. John began to feel cold. He led Shadow back to the cart and tied him on. They continued along the road out of town. It was not long before he found the entrance to Fellowes' place. The road up to the stables was long and rutted, with big

272

stones which made the cart lurch and shudder. They came into a large courtyard with boys running round with loads of hay, barrows full of dung and leading horses in and out of stables. The clatter on the cobbles was incessant and the shouts of the boys echoed round the enclosed yard. John felt apprehensive as he approached.

A foreman wearing a green jacket and long leather boots over his breeches saw him arrive and stopped him in his tracks.

"No carts in 'ere, Sir. What's yer business?"

John jumped down from the cart and brought Shadow round. He explained Shadow's origins and gave the man the names of the two gentlemen whose mares had been sired by him recently. The foreman examined Shadow carefully, looking in his mouth, eyes and ears. He ran his hands down his withers and hind quarters, picked up each foot and commented on the poor condition of his shoes. He quoted a figure.

"Excuse me, but I was of a mind to sell him for a better price than that." John was disgusted. He started to lead Shadow away.

"Wait!" the man called. "What d'you reckon he's worth, then?"

John quoted the highest figure he could possibly hope for, which was twice that which had been offered.

The foreman looked at Shadow again. "I'll meet yer half way," he said.

John met the man's eyes and thought he could push him a little further. After more bartering he decided he had pushed far enough. They agreed a final price and the deal was done.

"You'll no' regret it," John said as he counted the gold coins. He handed the reins over and gave Shadow a final pat before turning back to the cart. He did not want the man to see the anguish on his face.

Tears rolled down John's cheeks again as he drove the cart down the lane, leaving Shadow behind. The rain persisted. He began to feel giddy and his hands started to shake. They had gone only a few miles when he came across some ruined farm buildings at the side of the road. He drove the cart into the entrance and round the corner to hide it from view. Floss jumped down to relieve herself and sniffed around the area. There was a pile of rotting straw in one corner of what was once a barn. Although the roof had gone it was relatively dry and sheltered there. John was shivering and hot at the same time. He felt his neck. It was not swollen. He lit a fire with what dry material he could find and broke up some rotten rafters to add later. He set the trivet over the fire and put the pot of stew on it to heat up. The whisky he had brought with him was there somewhere, and a spoon to eat with. After rummaging around he found all that he needed, including a bowl for Floss and a bag of hay for the carthorse.

Now he could look after himself. He took off his coat, heavy with water, and hung it on a hook on the wall. It dripped steadily onto the earth beneath it. He found the plaids which he had managed to keep out of the rain and wrapped them around himself. Whisky was the next priority. He knocked back a whole mugful in one. Feeling light-headed, he doled out the stew into a bowl, and some for Floss. He set the empty pot out in the rain to catch water overnight, and settled down to eat his meal.

That felt better. But he was drowsy now, and perspiring. Another mug of whisky should do it. He lay back on the straw and sipped the soothing liquid. He felt Floss creep in beside him as he was dropping off to sleep.

Suddenly he was awake. It was dark. Panic had roused him. He could not remember what he had done with the money he had for Shadow. He felt for his money purse around his waist. There it was. He opened it and felt the coins. His fingers were shaking as he closed the purse, and he was shivering again, but burning hot and perspiring. He groped around for the whisky bottle and took a long draught. If he was going to die of the plague he may as well go with the taste of the golden liquor on his lips.

Chapter 46
The Stage Coach

A crowd was gathered in front of The Black Swan when Thomas walked into York market place. The air hummed with the voices of the spectators as they pointed and nodded at the spectacle. Stagecoaches had only been running for a few months. Each departure attracted a great deal of attention.

He was a little early, and he took the opportunity to call in at The Bell.

"Josh!" he shouted to the barman from the door.

Josh looked up from what he was doing.

"Tell the others I'm going south. I'll no' be back for a while." He did not wait for an answer, and ran over towards The Black Swan.

He pushed his way through the crowds to find Alex MacPherson and his wife in the forecourt with the other passengers, waiting to board. They watched the baggage being packed into the boxes before and behind the coach. These boxes also provided seating for the driver, the guard, and the passengers who travelled outside. The remainder of the luggage was piled onto the roof. The coach was a magnificent sight, with the name of the coach company on the doors in black and gold and coats of arms painted below. The seats inside were covered in red velvet. Ostlers harnessed the four horses into their traces and held them steady while the passengers climbed aboard.

MacPherson said, "If you're quick you can get a seat on the front bench next to the coachman, Thomas. That will give you a good view of the road and an early sighting of your father on his cart. We'll be inside. 'Tis more comfortable."

Thomas waved his thanks and went to climb up onto the front bench. The coachman was already there, holding the reins in one hand and a long whip in the other.

The church clocks chimed and struck the hour of ten.

The guard checked the desired destinations of the passengers then climbed onto his bench at the rear. He blew his horn.

The ostlers jumped away as they pulled the covers from the horses' backs.

The coachman flicked his whip and his team sprang into action, striding across the square towards the bridge over the River Ouse and Micklegate, the southern gate of the city.

The spectators made way, shop boys stopped in their tracks, their barrows rested on the cobbles. Housemaids stood and stared with brooms in their hands and figures appeared at upstairs windows as the coach dashed past. Animals and pedestrians fled in terror as the horses, pulling the loaded coach, negotiated the narrow streets. Passengers perching outside held on tightly to their seats and each other. Thomas was crammed between the coachman and a stout passenger who was in danger of falling off the end of the bench. The baggage was piled so high on top that they only just made it through the archway of the city gate without losing any.

The going became less hazardous as they joined the highway out of town and encountered fewer pedestrians. The recent rain had left ruts and puddles.

Muddy water splashed up on all sides. The horses soon settled into a steady stride. They passed horsemen, farm carts and small herds of animals being driven to and from the market. There was the racecourse where Thomas had spent the day with his friends. He felt sad that he would not be seeing Jenny again. Perhaps one day he would return... The coach drove through countryside, green pasture and stubble fields where the farmers were gathering in the harvest. Thomas marvelled at how swift the horses were.

Tadcaster was the next town and the coach stopped at the inn to change horses. Thomas alighted and went to find an ostler, who was busy leading one of the fresh horses from its stable. He had no time to stand and chat, and he pushed Thomas out of the way.

Thomas followed him and shouted, "Have you seen a man with a cart, leading a black stallion, in the last two days?"

The man continued walking. He turned round and shouted back, "There were a man leading a black stallion askin' where 'e could sell it. That were yusterdy mornin'"

Thomas ran back to the coach and climbed into his seat. The fresh horses were backed into the traces and the same procedure started them off. The coach lurched forward and they built up speed until they were hurtling down the road again. There was no traffic in front of them. If John had the cart and he had sold Shadow by now, he would be half a day ahead of them.

Thomas said to the driver, "I'm looking for ma faether. He left York yesterday with a horse and cart and a collie dog, going south. He was hoping to sell a black stallion."

"We'll surely see 'im if 'e's on this road," said the driver.

They passed the entrance to a long drive. There was a notice with the picture of a racehorse. "That's Jim Fellowes' place. It's possible yer father sold 'is stallion there."

Thomas watched the man's skill with admiration as he controlled the four horses, avoiding large potholes and other travellers.

"How long did it take you to learn to drive?" he asked.

"Nobbut a few days."

"Who pays you?"

"The coach company. I gets me pay when I hands ower the fares." He paused and slowed the horses. "I have ter stop. There's a woman waving us down."

They came to a standstill and a woman at the side of the road came and offered the driver a bundle wrapped in a cloth and a letter.

"Can yer teck this to the landlord of The Angel Inn at Ferrybridge? He'll know where to send it."

The driver took the letter, handed the bundle to Thomas and motioned him to unwrap it. A warm pie appeared in the folds of cloth, releasing an appetising aroma. The driver flicked the horses into action, took the pie in his free hand, and munched his way through it. "This is by way of payment for tecking the letter," he said through a mouthful.

The horses galloped on. The condition of the road improved and there was more traffic: gentlemen riding fine horses, carts laden with flour, grain or vegetables and a variety of traps and private carriages. There were walkers carrying sacks or baskets of produce from the local market. Everything slowed down when a herd of cattle was driven across the road, and they had to wait several minutes before the way was clear. They stopped at coaching inns along the route, where the horses were changed, some passengers left and more joined the coach. At the Angel Inn at Ferrybridge the coachman announced that they would stop for refreshments. They had twenty minutes in which to eat a meal provided by the inn. Thomas joined the MacPhersons for the snack which they barely had time to eat before the coachman put his head round the door.

"All aboard, ladies and gentlemen, if ye please."

Towards the end of the day Thomas started to look out for his father again. The sky lost its light and the stars began to appear.

The driver said, "We'll be stopping at the next inn. I've done my stint. The coach will drive on through the night. I reckon your father's long gone. You might catch up with 'im termorrer."

Thomas climbed down and went to find the ostler to ask if he had seen his father with the cart. No-one with a cart had been near the inn that day.

MacPherson met him as he came back to the coach. "We'll not be driving on with this coach, Thomas. We'll have a good meal and a comfortable bed for the night, and catch the first coach coming past in the morning. Most passengers travel overnight, but 'tis very tedious this time of the year." He found his baggage in the box under the driver's seat and the driver lifted it out.

"I'm leaving you now, Sir," said the driver. This was a signal for all the passengers to give him a tip, and he went round collecting the money before bidding them good night.

He disappeared into the bar of the inn.

The guard's horn blew, and the coach rumbled off into the dark.

Chapter 47
Friends

It was good to stop travelling. Thomas felt as if all the bones in his body had become disjointed and his head hummed with the galloping of the horses and the jingling of their harnesses. They walked into the inn and were given their room keys. The porter took the MacPherson's baggage upstairs.

Alex said, "We'll see you at dinner, I hope, Thomas."

Feeling self-conscious in his rough clothes and his tousled hair, he said, "I've no clean things to wear. D'you really want me eating with you?"

"I have a clean shirt you can have if you're so concerned," said MacPherson with an amused smile. "But I'm sure it doesn't bother us, does it, Peggy?"

"No, but the puir lad would feel more comfortable, I believe." Lady MacPherson's eyes twinkled. "Let Alex give you one o' his shirts. I shall enjoy your company, Thomas."

So Thomas was given a clean shirt to wear. He took it to his chamber and thought how fortunate he was. How could he ever repay this generous couple? He gave himself a thorough wash in the water provided, rinsed his hair and ran his fingers through it to make it lie down. He looked at himself in the glass and nodded, wondering whether his father would be able to find a comfortable bed for the night.

An idea had begun to form in his head. He was not ready to talk to his friends about it yet, but he was conscious that he must become independent as soon as possible. He could not expect them to support him all the way to London, and as the time passed the search for his father was going to take longer than he had thought.

The MacPhersons were pleasant companions. They wanted to hear more of the journey from the Highlands, and they told Thomas how they went to France and of their time living there. He found it difficult to talk about his parents. He realised that he would never see his mother again, and had grave doubts that he would ever find his father. He spent a restless night seeing them in his dreams.

Waking early, he looked out of the window to see that the world was shrouded in fog. It swirled around the inn, muffling all sound. He wondered how the coach would make any progress at all in this weather.

The previous evening, Thomas had the forethought to pay the chambermaid to launder his shirt. He carefully folded up the one MacPherson lent him and put it in his jacket pocket for the next evening. The passengers had a good breakfast and gathered outside ready to board the coach.

"How long does it take to get to London?" Thomas asked his companions.

"Just over a week if there are no hold-ups," said MacPherson. "I would sooner travel on horseback, but I cannot leave my wife to travel alone. If you travel overnight you can do it in less time."

"I'll be sitting up in front again, Sir," said Thomas. "I want to know how much I owe you for my bed and board."

MacPherson frowned. His bushy eyebrows met in the middle. "First of all, Thomas, it's time you used our first names. I cannot have my travelling companion calling me *Sir*. Secondly, I will not hear another word from you about paying for your bed and board. I said I would pay your fare, and that includes everything. And I will pay the chambermaid next time you have your shirt laundered." He smiled at Thomas and clapped him on the back. "Go and sit with the driver before you miss your seat." He climbed up into the coach and shut the door, leaving Thomas gasping.

Thomas jumped onto the bench and sat beside the new coachman, who was crouched over in his seat. He looked at Thomas with a sullen expression and nodded. An unpleasant unwashed aroma surrounded him. The horn blew, and the eager horses were given rein. The coach came out onto the highway and lurched forward. Vapour poured from the horses' nostrils into the misty air. The sun peeped through and lit up the frozen puddles. The coachman beside Thomas sniffed at intervals.

Thomas' thoughts turned to Jenny. He was missing her shy smiles and her gentle ways. He wondered whether she was worried about him. Perhaps she had gone back to Frank. Thomas did not expect to return to York. Maybe when he found his father and settled down somewhere, he would find a way of getting a message to her. She had been a good friend.

Chapter 48
A New Skill

This seemed to Thomas like the longest day of his life. Even the days the family travelled from Scotland in the pouring rain had not lasted as long as this. Fog swirled around them, catching at their breath and seeping through their clothes. Other travellers loomed out of the gloom almost before the coachman could take avoiding action. The horses stumbled on the rough road. Progress was slow. There was no scenery to look at and the chances of finding his father were small. The coachman continued to sniff.

The only light relief came when the horses were changed at their stages. Thomas took the opportunity every time to alight and make enquiries about his father. He was glad to stretch his legs and stamp the cold out of his feet. There was no news and he was losing hope. This was the third day John had been on the road and the coaches might have overtaken him by now. He would have to make more stops in towns to buy food. Perhaps he had wandered off the highway in order to find shelter.

When they stopped at Markham Moor for refreshments, Thomas joined the MacPhersons again. The passengers were bemoaning the fact that they hardly had time to warm up enough to eat anything before starting off again. Alex and Peggy were relatively warm and dry. Thomas wanted to share his thoughts with them while they ate.

"I've a mind to learn to drive these coaches," he said.

Alex looked up from his plate and raised his eyebrows.

Thomas continued. "If I were on the coaches travelling up and down this road, I'd have a much better chance of tracking ma faether doon." He picked up a mouthful of food to give Alex the chance to absorb this information.

Alex said, "You mean you want employment as a coachman?"

Thomas nodded, "I think 'twill no' take me long to learn. I've driven two horses on ma faether's cart."

"'Tis a hard life, and I imagine it takes great skill to drive these horses. They're not carthorses, Thomas."

"I'd be earning ma keep. And I've no other ties. I mean to find Faether if I can, and this seems the best way."

Alex nodded. "How long d'you reckon 'twill take you to learn?"

"I'd like to think that I can start now and be capable by the time we reach London. I mean to ask the coachman to teach me along the way. 'Twill depend on him."

The coachman looked in and called, "Time's up, ladies and gentlemen."

Alex laid down his knife and fork and wiped his mouth on the napkin. He looked concerned. "You must do what you think is best, Thomas. We'll talk again this evening."

They all rose and left the inn. The coach was ready and the new horses restless to be off. The guard blew his horn and they were away. The fog was clearing and it was easier to see the road ahead.

Thomas said to the driver, "Ma name's Thomas. I've a mind to learn how to drive these horses. Can you teach me?"

The driver looked at him and away again. He had not been the best of travelling companions so far today, keeping to his own thoughts. But he did not seem averse to the idea. He sniffed.

"'Ave yer driven 'osses afore?"

"Ay, I've driven a pair of carthorses frae Scotland to York.

The driver took another look at him. "Yer needs all yer wits about you to drive this lot." He nodded at the four in hand. "But I'll gi' yer a go. See how you gets on, like. Me name's Bill. Watch my hand…" He demonstrated to Thomas how each of the four reins was arranged in his hand and which controlled which horse. "These are the wheelers, the ones at the back. You have ter meck sure they keep well back from the leaders, who set the pace…"

Thomas watched carefully. Bill's hand was making adjustments all the time.

"Yer have ter be able ter do this and be watching the road at the same time. Potholes or a swerve to avoid another carriage could topple the whole coach. We're going slow today because of t'fog. In clear weather we'll pick up speed, so yer reactions must be quicker. After t'next stage, I'll let yer handle 'em."

Thomas watched the coachman carefully until the next stop. He again took the opportunity to enquire after his father. There had been no sign of him.

The coach started with new horses in improved conditions. A wind picked up and sunshine helped to disperse the remaining patches of fog. Thomas climbed up with a lighter heart to sit next to Bill, who also looked more cheerful. He had stopped sniffing.

"I'll start 'em off, then you can have the reins. I'll keep t'whip for now," he said.

Thomas nodded and waited with a mixture of excitement and fear. His time came and he took the reins cautiously.

"You have ter 'ave a firm hold. Each pull on the reins must be strong, to send a clear message to t'hosses. You're in charge," said Bill.

Thomas looked ahead. There was no other traffic in sight. He played with the reins and felt the horses' reactions. He began to enjoy himself. He avoided some potholes and felt he had the hang of it.

"Ye needs practise 'til 'tis second nature," Bill said. "Don't get carried away."

They drove on, Bill calling instructions when he thought it was necessary. Now the fog had lifted more coaches and horsemen were on the road. People walked along the verges, wheeling barrows and carrying children. The driving became more difficult. Thomas slowed the horses down so that he would have better control. He forgot to look for his father and his cart.

Chapter 49
On the way to Grantham...

After a few miles Bill said, "We'll be at Grantham soon. I'll be leaving you there. You'll have to ask the next driver if he'll let yer drive. You're doin' well, but you won't be ready ter drive by thisen for a day or two. An' driving at night's more difficult."

"Thank you kindly for your help, Bill," said Thomas. "I can see 'twill be a while before I can manage on ma own, but you've given me a good start."

"It's been a diversion, that's for sure. Life gets tedious as a coachman on these stages. You won't put up wi' it fer long. I'd like ter go to private coaches, but the toffs won't 'ave us because of me looks." He looked at Thomas ruefully.

Thomas looked in his companion's face for the first time, then quickly back to the road. His face was red and pitted with smallpox scars. His nose was bulbous and covered in warts and his grey beard and hair were matted. The aura of unwashed body and clothes hung around him.

"If you care to take ma advice, Bill, you could clean yourself up. No-one would notice your face if you didna smell so bad." Thomas hoped he had not offended the man.

As they were talking, Thomas became aware of a change in their surroundings. Swampy land with small copses and bushes here and there had taken the place of the farming country they had been travelling through. The road was narrower in places. He kept away from the edges to avoid sinking in the mud. Another coach appeared in the distance, rapidly approaching.

Bill stood up, waved his arms and shouted, "Move over! Slow down!"

The guard blew his horn.

Thomas pulled on the reins, realising that the two coaches were on a collision course.

Bill sat down and took the reins from Thomas. The horses swerved towards the edge of the road.

The oncoming coach came closer.

Thomas braced himself for the inevitable.

The inside wheels of the two coaches collided with a splintering crash.

Women screamed, horses reared up, and the coachmen cursed each other.

The other coach slewed round on the road and stopped, its wheel shattered but still holding the coach upright.

Silence roared in their ears.

Thomas felt his seat tilting towards the left.

A tremendous creaking broke the silence. More screams came from within the coach as its wheel slowly sank into the mire.

Bill and the outside passengers jumped down whichever way they could scramble. Bill ran to the horses to release them from the traces. Thomas went to help. Other people assisted the inside passengers as they struggled out of the uppermost door. Passengers poured off the other coach before it, too, leaned over and settled on its broken wheel.

The road was blocked by the two coaches.

Everyone stood around, dazed, the women crying, the men comforting them.

The guards were deep in conversation, shaking and scratching their heads and pointing at the damage.

The two coachmen shouted and waved their fists at each other. A horseman rode up to them. They stopped and looked at him.

"Can I be of assistance, gentlemen? Your passengers will require transport to the nearest inn. Are any of them injured? You will need re-enforcements to collect the baggage and clear the road..."

Bill said, "Aye, Sir. Thank you. 'Tis not far to The George at Grantham, which is where we was heading, and I believe the other coach came from there. Though Ed 'ere is that drunk 'e don't know whether 'e's comin' or goin'." Bill glowered at his fellow coachman. "I'd be obliged if you could ride to The George, Sir, and tell 'em what's occurred. We're in need of two new coaches and their 'osses, and, as you say, men to clear the road."

The horseman saluted with his crop, wove his way through the jumble of coaches and stranded passengers, and rode on towards Grantham.

Bill examined the state of the two coaches and looked at the passengers. He took off his hat and wiped his brow. He said to Thomas, "These people must be shepherded to a safe place. I suggest between the wheels of our coach. 'Tis the worst place to be held up by highwaymen. They hide in gangs in t'woods, waiting for an occurrence such as this. In fact it wouldn't surprise me if that gentleman on a horse were one of 'em. 'E's probably gone off to get a band of robbers together afore coming back. Ask the gentlemen if they carry guns of any sort, or swords, to be prepared ter use 'em." He went over to the passengers of the other coach and brought them over the road.

Thomas herded his group into the shelter of the carriage. Alex came to him and asked if he could do anything to help. Thomas told him of the possible proximity of highwaymen. He asked if anyone was injured.

"They're shaken but not hurt," Alex said. "I have a gun and am prepared to use it. It seems to me that we should unload the baggage and use it as a barricade around these people."

"We can get some of the men to help," agreed Thomas.

Bill came over to talk to everyone. "I've a mind to lift that coach out of t'road so other travellers can get through," he said. "Any gentleman willing to 'elp, follow me."

The men, glad of something to do to keep them warm, set to work to rescue the baggage and move the coach. Ed, the other coachman, sat on the side like a sulky boy. Thomas kept his eye on the patches of woodland nearby, his hand on his dirk. He was constantly aware that they could be attacked at any moment. He hoped that the horseman was honest and had indeed gone for help. The two coach guards paced up and down, their guns at the ready.

The light was going from the sky. Their work done, there was nothing left but to settle down and wait for assistance. Maybe the robbers were waiting for darkness before attacking.

Chapter 50
John Wakes Up

A thin mist lifted from the barn as the sun broke through. John opened his eyes and gradually became aware of his surroundings. He tried to remember how he came to be here. There were rough stone walls around his straw bed. He saw his coat hanging up, just as it had in the cottage. Perhaps this was the cottage, and the roof had blown off in the night. Birds chirruped in the trees outside. He looked up and saw pale blue sky with wisps of white cloud sweeping across. Mare's tails, they called them...

Clover was missing. So was Thomas. John turned his head carefully, aware of tenderness in his neck. Why was he here?

He had been there for some time, in and out of consciousness, dreaming of bodies rising from a plague pit. They tried to drag him into the mass of putrifying human remains. Then he was on fire. He must have gone to hell. Jamie and Annie appeared to him in shining white light, their arms held out in welcome.

He raised himself into a sitting position. His throat was parched; his head hurt and his clothes were damp and sticking to his body. It was raining when he came here. Slowly he remembered, and wondered how long he had lain there, tossing and turning. He needed to drink, and to eat something.

Floss appeared in the entrance of the barn, her eyes bright and her ears cocked. She carried a dead rabbit and came to drop it by John's side with a wag of her tail. She licked his face.

John pushed her away and said, "Good girl."

He moved all his limbs and, though stiff and feeble, he concluded that he was well. He rolled onto all fours and pushed himself into a kneeling position. He had forgotten to remove the leather glove from the stump of his left arm before going to sleep. It was lucky he had not injured himself on the hook. Annie always insisted that he took it off before coming to bed…

He sat back on his heels. Annie was dead. His eyes smarted with the approach of tears. He took a deep breath. It was no good feeling sorry for himself.

Where was that water? He remembered leaving the stew pot outside to catch the rain. He found the mug he used for whisky, stood up shakily and lurched out into a bright autumn morning. There was water in the pot. He dipped the mug and swallowed several great mouthfuls.

It took the whole morning for John to light a fire, find hay for the horse, prepare the rabbit leaving the entrails for Floss, and start to cook a meal. After washing his hands and face as best he could, he shared the remains of the water between the horse and Floss and found ale for himself. The clothes he was wearing dried in the light breeze, aided by his proximity to the fire. He sat on an upturned bucket and ate his dinner.

He spent the afternoon taking stock of the supplies he brought with him and making a mental note of the things he needed to buy in the next town. He remembered the money he had from the sale of Shadow and checked in his money purse again. There it was, intact. It would be a good idea to put the bulk of it in a safe place and only have his immediate needs in the purse. After much thought, he tore off the hem of his shirt, counted out the coins and wrapped them in the cloth. He took his gun out of its holster and placed the package inside, then replaced the gun. A highway robber would have to search for it.

There was a crock of oat biscuits on the cart. Annie had cooked them the day before she became ill. John took a handful and went to sit by the fire with a mug of ale. The light was fading and he was weary. Floss came to lie by his feet and he shared the biscuits with her.

"I've no been verra friendly with thee, Floss, have I?" he said. "I was angry with Thomas for rescuing thee. Didna want the responsibility."

John munched a biscuit and took a sip of ale. "Come to think of it, I've been angry most of ma life. 'Twas Annie kept me cheerful." He sat staring into the fire. He had to manage, somehow, without Annie or Thomas.

"If I find Thomas I swear I'll never be angry again," he said aloud. "Did you hear that, lassie?" He looked down at Floss, but he was really saying it to Annie.

He broke off a piece of the last biscuit and put the rest in his mouth. "You're a good, faithful friend, Floss. I'll never forget thee." Floss looked up at him, ears alert and he threw the piece of biscuit into the air. She caught it without needing to get up. John finished his ale and stood up to go and lie on his bed of straw. Floss followed and lay down beside him. He put out a hand and patted her side.

"We'll move on themorn, lass," he said.

297

Chapter 51
Parkin

The sun's rays peeped round the entrance to the barn and fell on John's face. He felt better, though still weak. Apart from the biscuits there were only dry oats to eat. It was urgent that he find a town where he could buy supplies. He staved off the hunger with a few oat biscuits and a mug of ale. He gave dry oats to the horse and Floss. Then he packed the plaids and hide, the pots and crocks and the trivet and prepared the horse and cart to continue their journey. Floss jumped on to the seat next to him and they turned out onto the highway.

John was surprised to see how busy the road had become. Gentlemen on horseback saluted him as they rode past in the direction of York. Carts laden with corn were on their way to the mill and geese driven by women and children seemed to be all over the road. Smart private carriages passed him and a heavily-laden stage coach flew by. He wondered why everyone was in so much hurry.

In the distance ahead he could just make out the figure of a small boy going in the same direction. He carried a heavy sack almost as big as himself. When he reached him, John stopped the cart horse a little way ahead and as the boy drew level he called down to him.

"Are you going far, young man? D'you want a ride?"

The boy stopped and looked up at John with a troubled frown. He dropped his sack. "I've only a few more mile ter go, Sir… But I'd like a ride, if you please." His face broke into a wide grin.

John jumped down and lifted the sack onto the cart. "That's a heavy load for a young lad."

The boy clambered up. "I'm teckin' them potatoes to me Gran. They'll last 'er all winter, Mam ses."

John clicked the horse on and they plodded over the lumps and bumps in the road. The boy settled himself on the pile of plaids. Floss went and sat down beside him.

"I like your dog," the boy said. "What's 'er name?"

"Floss," said John. "D'you have a dog?"

"Nay. But me Gran has a big dog. Scrapper, she calls 'im. 'E fights other dogs, an' he don't like strangers."

"What's your name?" John asked. "Mine's John."

"Me name's Moses, but they calls us Mo," said the boy.

"You'll tell me when we get close to your Gran's house, Mo, where I can drop you off?"

"Aye, 'Tis not far now." He got up from his seat and scrambled over to stand behind John, legs apart, and swaying unsteadily with the motion of the cart. "See them trees?" He pointed to the left of the road.

About a mile away a group of poplars swayed in the wind, their autumn brightness sparkling in the sunshine. John nodded.

"Me Gran's 'ouse is just around t'corner from there." Mo sat down suddenly as the cart lurched.

In a little while they drew near to the trees. The wind whispered in the branches, sending leaves fluttering to the ground to make a carpet of gold. John could see the cottage now, hidden by more trees, well back from the road. He could hear a large dog barking. He halted the horse and looke horse and looked at Mo.

A voice shrieked from the open cottage door. "Scrapper! Come away 'ere!"

Mo said, "That's me Gran. She'll tie the dog oop, then you can drive in." He jumped down from the cart and ran round the corner through the entrance of what John now saw was a farmyard. Hissing geese flew towards him, squawking chickens scattered to all sides.

All was suddenly quiet. Mo reappeared and beckoned to John.

John clicked to the cart horse, who cautiously approached the entrance and pulled the cart into the yard. John climbed down.

An old woman emerged from one of the barns. "That's tecken care of them," she said, and came to meet John, beaming all over her crinkled brown face. "They keep the intruders away," she said. "But they frighten the visitors! Not that I 'ave many!" she cackled. Her white hair was tied up under her bonnet and her smile revealed lost and decayed teeth. "I believe you've brought Mo wi' me tatties. Come in and rest awhile. I don't see many people these days." She hobbled into the house. "Put t'kettle on, Mo."

John followed her into a stone flagged entrance leading to a flight of wooden stairs ahead. To the right and left there were two doors. The right hand door opened into a homely parlour. Lace curtains hung at the windows, and a big iron range faced him. A fire blazed in the hearth. A rug, woven with rags of all colours, lay in front of the fire and a large black cat sat in the centre, his eyes shut and his front paws tucked neatly under him. By the window there was a table covered with a cloth. In the middle a round pot with a spout stood on a ceramic tile.

Gran went over to the table, holding onto the furniture for support as she passed. She picked up the pot and took it out to a further room which must be the kitchen. Mo waited in the doorway for her to pass, then came in carrying a large kettle, blackened by wood smoke, and hung it over the fire.

"Sit down, Mister John. Me Gran won't 'ave no-one standin' around in 'er parlour." Mo pulled a chair out from under the table. Its back was made of a single length of wood, curved, to make each end fit into the back corners of the seat. Wooden spindles came from the top to slot between the corners into the back of the seat. The wooden seat was shaped to fit a person's thighs comfortably. Arms came from the back of the chair, supported on more spindles which slotted into the sides of the seat. John studied the chair carefully before sitting down. He would like to be able to make a chair like that.

Gran came in with the washed pot and replaced it on its stand. "I gets me tea from me son." She grinned her toothy grin. "'E's a mariner and works from Knottingly. 'E brings us all manner of fine things that only the gentry can buy." She reached up and found a wooden box among many crocks and a number of ornaments on the dresser by the fire. The box contained tea, which she carefully spooned into the pot. Then she took the boiling kettle from its hook over the fire, poured water into the teapot and replaced the lid. "I thought we'd treat usselves, seein' as we've a visitor," she said. She took three pottery mugs from the dresser, put them on the table and sat down on a chair opposite John. "Mo, can you get t'crock wi' t'parkin from t'cupboard out there, and bring it in? There's a love." She reached out, picked a large plate off the dresser and put it on the table.

John watched in speechless anticipation. He had very little for breakfast that morning and it must be well past noon. He worried that the gurgles coming from his stomach could be heard. It would be interesting to taste tea for the first time, not to mention the parkin.

Mo came in with a large crock, grinning his Gran's grin, though his teeth were intact. "You'll surely like me Gran's parkin," he said as he removed the lid and dipped in.

Gran's gnarled hand came up from her lap and slapped Mo's wrist. "Not so fast, child. We'll put it on a plate for the visitor to help hisself, fust."

Mo withdrew his fingers from the crock and licked them.

With a trembling hand, Gran picked out six blocks of dark brown cake and arranged them on the plate. She handed the plate to John.

"Sit yer down, boy. Thy turn will come," she said.

Mo sat down and rested his elbows on the table, his chin on his hands. Gran ignored him. She watched John's face as he picked up a piece of parkin and took a bite.

He chewed the sticky soft cake, savouring the taste of black treacle. The cake melted and a soft, burning sensation followed. He swallowed, enjoying the warmth in his mouth. "Mm, that's a wondrous fine cake, Ma'am." He had another bite.

Gran was happy. She let Mo have a piece, and took one herself. Then she poured the tea into the three mugs.

"Now then, Mister John. I've let you into me parlour and given you me best parkin, an' I don't know nothin' about yer, except that you were kind enough to help me grandson wi' t' tatties. Have yer travelled far? You look to be in a bad way, if you don't mind us sayin'." She filled her mouth with parkin and sat back to wait for John to speak.

"I'm greatly obliged for your hospitality, Ma'am. Your parkin is a godsend. 'Tis true, I'm in a bad condition just now…" For some reason, though habitually reticent, he found himself pouring out all his troubles to this kind old woman. It was difficult to speak when he came to Annie's death, but he avoided breaking down. Gran and Mo listened in astonishment. Gran nodded and *mmmed* and *ahhed* at intervals in sympathy. Mo forgot the half-eaten piece of parkin he held in his hand.

"…so you see, I really need to find a town where I can buy food for maself and the animals. I dinna ken how far I'll have to travel to Sussex. But that is where I want to be…" John's voice trailed off, and he took another sip of his tea which had gone cold. He preferred it hot, but would rather have ale.

Gran picked up the teapot and poured more into John's mug. "Well! For once in me life I don't know what to say! I cannot imagine the pain you must be sufferin'. But you're a brave man, and you're not beaten yet!" She bit into her second piece of parkin, shaking her head and murmuring in her throat.

Mo stood up, still munching his last mouthful. "I'm goin' out ter give Floss a drink an' play with 'er for a bit." He left the room.

Chapter 52
The George, Grantham

At last Thomas sat down to a late dinner with Alex and Peggy. It had been a long day, but certainly more entertaining than Thomas had anticipated. After a tedious wait with the disabled coaches, help had come in the shape of one replacement coach with a number of ostlers and labourers aboard. This was all that the landlord of The George could spare. The passengers were taken to the inn in two loads. It was decided that Ed was in no fit state to drive a coach, and his passengers were given accommodation until another driver could be found to take them to York. Bill's coach, after it was pulled out of the mire, was discovered to be intact. Bill drove it to Grantham to be checked over in daylight. The other coach was left on the road until morning. The ostlers walked the four horses to The George.

"There were moments when I was sure I saw robbers creeping up on us," said Alex. "I was ready to take aim and fire at shadows!" He laughed at the memory.

"I've never been so afraid in my life," said Peggy. "Thank the Lord we had such gallant men to protect us!"

Thomas smiled. "The highwaymen missed a great opportunity, surely. We were sitting ducks! They must have been busy with another coach, elsewhere."

"D'you still want to be a coachman, Thomas? 'Tis not uncommon for them to be attacked on the road." Alex poured himself another glass of wine and offered it to Peggy. She shook her head.

"Ay. I'm no' bothered aboot that. I had a turn with the reins and found the driving enjoyable." Thomas took another sip of his ale, nodding his head.

When they had finished the meal they bid each other goodnight and retired to their chambers. Thomas had been told that, due to an extra load of customers, he would have to share his chamber with another young man. When he opened the door he found his bedfellow already there. He went in and offered his hand.

"Thomas Grant. Pleased to meet you."

The young man was of slender build and well-dressed in brown knickerbockers over white hose and shoes with large buckles. He had removed his hat and coat. His black hair fell in curls around his shoulders. He was not wearing a wig, as was usual with older men. He took Thomas' hand and shook it with a firm grip. "Charles Turner. I hope I don't intrude." His voice was a pitch higher than Thomas'. "We didn't expect to be staying the night here, though I must say I shall be glad of a comfortable resting place."

"How far have you come?" asked Thomas as he sat down on the edge of the bed.

Charles joined him. He had travelled from London and was on the way to York. He was to be indentured to his father's cousin, an apothecary, to learn the profession.

Thomas told him about York and how he had a girl there who would be wondering where he was. He should have met her the day before yesterday. He explained to Charles the reason why he was not able to do so.

"Perhaps I could find this lady and give her a message for you?" offered Charles.

"I'd be obliged if you would. I wish I could send her a letter, but I never learned to write." Thomas looked down, embarrassed.

"I'll write it for you if you can tell me what to say. Can Jenny read?"

"I believe she can," said Thomas. "That would be very civil of you." He sat and thought about what he would say.

Charles went to his baggage and found paper and a quill and ink. He went over to the washing table and removed the bowl and jug of water, putting them to one side, and sat on the stool. He dipped his pen in the ink. His long slender fingers hung poised to begin to write.

"*Dear Jenny, I am sorry I left York with no word to you. I found Clover and was going to ride her away, when the constable caught me and imprisoned me for attempting to steal her. 'Twas the kindness of my master that saved me two days later. When I reached home the house was empty. Father left a note. Mother is dead of the plague and he had to leave the cottage with no siller for rent. He didna ken where I was. He's on the road somewhere travelling south in the cart with Floss. I have to find him, Jenny. I know you will understand. I am learning to drive a stage coach so I can look for them on the road. If you care to write to me, I can collect a letter from The George at Grantham. Charles Turner wrote this letter for me and said he would find you when he reaches York. He is a kind upstanding young man. I miss you, Jenny. God bless thee.   Thomas.*"

Charles finished writing. Thomas went over and put his cross where his name was. He shook Charles' hand again but could not speak. There were tears in his eyes. He blinked them away as he went back to the bed. He took his shirt and breeches off and slipped under the covers. He was very tired.

There was no sign of Charles in the room when Thomas awoke. His baggage had gone. Thomas had no idea whether he had shared the bed. He rose and washed and dressed in haste, hoping to see the young man before he left.

Downstairs, the passengers for the journey north were already gathered. Thomas sought out Charles and shook his hand again.

"I canna thank you enough. I wish you well in your new life in York. If you leave the letter for Jenny at The Bell in the square, the barman, Josh, will know how to get it to her."

Charles smiled warmly. "I hope you find your father, Thomas. God speed!" He climbed into the coach.

Thomas went to talk to the landlord. He was the official owner of the coach route between Stamford and Doncaster. He employed the coachmen and the guards. He provided the horses and hired the coaches from a coach company. Thomas talked to him about the possibility of his being employed as a coachman.

He told the MacPhersons at breakfast, "The landlord is willing to employ me if I learn to drive by the time we get back to Grantham on the return trip from London. He's spoken to Bill, who recommended me to him, and to the driver of the next coach."

"But you'll have a break between stints. How long will you be driving?" asked Alex.

"Eight hours," said Thomas. Then we get an eight hour break before driving again. I'll be starting the next stint in the night."

"Then we'll be parting company this evening," said Alex. "If ever you tire of coaching, or if you find your father, you'll be more than welcome at my estate at Warminghurst, near Ashington in Sussex. I hope to see you there one day. There will be work for you." He smiled at Thomas and raised his glass. "A toast to a successful future, young man."

"You've been verra generous, Alex, and I've enjoyed your company, both of you. Pray God I will see ye again." Thomas raised his tankard and took a long draught of his ale.

That day the coach made good progress. Thomas drove most of the way. The coachman, Toby, was a jolly, rounded fellow, with a ruddy complexion and curly grey hair. He made Thomas feel comfortable and showed him different ways of handling the reins. He pointed out features in the landscape as they passed, telling stories and repeating local gossip and myth.

"That there is Gunnerby Hill." He indicated a tall hill, raised like a pimple from the plain around them. "I've heard tell that there's witches living in the woods up there. 'Tis a curious feature. People come from far away to see it."

Further on, he pointed out a large manor house. "Now that's Lord Shotley's place. 'E 'as three sons. The eldest is a rogue. They say 'e goes out on his hoss at night and holds up the coaches with a gun. Can't say as I've ever seen 'im meself, like."

"What about the other two sons?" asked Thomas, intrigued.

"The middle un. 'E's run off with a local girl. 'Is father's disowned 'im! The younger un, I believe e's doin' as 'e's told and meckin' sure 'e receives 'is inheritance!" Toby chuckled.

"Have you been driving coaches for long?" asked Thomas.

"Aye, since I were your age. Private coaches then. But the stage coaches is better. I like the fresh air and the people I meet."

"D'you have a house and a wife?" Thomas was curious about the lifestyle of a coachman.

"Nay. A wife would never put up with us bein' away driving, though it brings good money in tips an' all. I 'ave me frolicks wi' the barmaids sometimes, but I couldn't settle to one woman. Youngsters like you don't put up wi' drivin' for long. The masters are allus looking for new drivers."

Thomas was not surprised. He was just starting, and could see already that this was not to be the life he would want for long. He fell to wondering where his father was. There was a possibility he might be dead of the plague...

"And what about you, young man? What brought yer so far from home? I can tell you're from Scotland. I know that speech from other people I've met."

Thomas paused while he avoided a coach coming the other way. He still had visions of the collision yesterday. Then he started telling the story of the long journey to

312

York. There were intervals in his narrative when a tricky manoeuvre distracted him, and when they passed a horse and cart he wanted to see who was driving.

They changed the horses for the last time. Toby told Thomas that the next stop would be Huntingdon where their stint would end.

"I hope you find yer father, lad," he said. "You're a good driver, but I reckon you'll not want to do this for long."

"No," affirmed Thomas. "It'll do for now. At least I'll be earning ma keep." He had eight hours now in which to have dinner, say goodbye to the MacPhersons and to snatch a few hours' sleep before the next stint started at two in the morning.

Chapter 53
The Angel, Ferrybridge

On the road again, John was thinking of Gran and Mo. The taste of parkin was fading, but he would not forget the little cottage and its occupants for some time. He travelled through farmland, mainly flat with a few low hills to break the monotony. The wind was cold. John buttoned up his jacket and pulled his hat down firmly onto his head. Floss snuggled up close to him on the bench. Farm carts passed him and a stage coach seemed to fly by on its way to York. The handsome horses with their long striding gait rattled their harness as they went. "What a way to travel!" he thought.

Gran had told him that the next town was Knottingly and there was a coaching inn at Ferrybridge called The Angel, where she told him that he would be very comfortable and well looked-after. Her cousin was the landlord and if John cared to mention her name, Nellie Clarkson, he would be given special attention. John looked forward to a good meal and a comfortable bed, and relished the thought of a proper wash.

The day was fading when the inn came in sight ahead. The ostler was lighting the lanterns in the stable yard as John drove in.

"Can I leave ma cart and horse with you for thenight?" he called down to the man who was approaching him.

"Aye, leave 'em wi' me. What about t'dog? I can feed and water 'er too."

John patted Floss who sat up when the cart stopped. "She'll sleep in the cart, but I'd be obliged if you'd see to her needs." He climbed down. "I'll pay you."

The ostler nodded and led the horse with the cart to a corner of the yard. "There's nowt of any value on t'cart, is there? I can't be watchin' all night."

John looked in his purse for a tip. "No," he said. "Naebody'll want what's there." He handed a coin to the ostler.

"D'you have a son who might be seeking you?" the man asked, dropping the coin into a small pocket in his waistcoat.

John's heart missed a couple of beats. "Ay," he said, and waited for more information.

The ostler looked at him. "A young man were 'ere two or three days ago. 'E were travelling on a stage coach to London. They stopped for a bite to eat and 'e came to me an' asked if a man such as you with a cart an' a dog 'ad been through. 'E talked like you. Shame 'e missed yer." He shrugged his shoulders and turned away to unhitch the cart horse.

John walked in a daze into the inn. He bought a dram of whisky and went to sit down in a dark corner, sipping as he went.

Thomas was alive.

John took time to absorb this information. Thomas must have gone home and found the note John had left. So he knew his father was travelling south and he was trying to find him. But what was he doing on a stage coach? He must have money to be able to pay for that kind of travel. He might have found Clover and sold her. But it would have been better to be riding her. John

316

shook his head, gave up his speculation and had another sip of whisky, which was going to his head. It was time he had something to eat.

He called the landlord over, enquired about a room for the night and ordered a meal. He mentioned Nellie Clarkson.

The landlord's face lit up. "You're just in time. There'll be a crowd of passengers on the next stage coach in. They'll be in a hurry to eat and continue on their journey."

"How long does it take to get to London on a coach frae here?" asked John.

"Fower or five days," said the landlord. "Depends on t'state of t'roads and t'weather, and if they have an accident 'twill teck longer.

John nodded and sat back in his dark corner, savouring his whisky and watching customers come to the bar for drinks.

His dinner was brought to him before the coachload poured into the inn, stamping their feet and rubbing their hands together. John ate his meal, savouring the beef pudding and carrots with lots of gravy. He watched the travellers finding places to sit and ordering meals. They were a hotch-potch of all ages and conditions. Women and children were accompanied by their men, all well-dressed. There were tradesmen and professional people, elderly men and young scholars. They ate their meals quickly, talking little, and soon the coach driver called them to join their transport again. John tried to imagine Thomas as part of this crowd. The space they left behind them was littered with dirty plates and cutlery and half tankards of ale, unfinished. The barman cleared the tables and all was quiet.

John continued eating. He began to feel better, more relaxed and hopeful. He would enjoy sleeping in a bed for the night, but knew it might be the last time for a while. He could not afford to stay in an inn every night.

Chapter 54
A Kindness

Knottingly was a large, bustling town. John left Floss with the horse and cart in the outskirts and walked into the centre. He was astonished to find that this was a sea port. The river was wide enough for ships to come inland. There was a quay with ocean-going vessels moored. Carts were waiting to be loaded with cargo from the ships' holds; huge chests and sacks full of all manner of cloth, spices, pottery and things that John had never seen before. There were strange animals in cages, and birds with coloured feathers. The noise was deafening; the shouts of seamen and tradespeople were raised above the braying of the horses and donkeys and the barking of dogs. Seagulls swirled around the masts, squawking and calling. Creaking noises came from the ships as they rolled around in the swell. Clatter of hooves on cobbles provided accompaniment. The strange aromas of faraway countries were set free, having been stored in airless holds for months. Underneath there was the stench of dead fish, horse manure and kitchen slops, mixed with the smell of ship's tar.

John stood mesmerised for some time, watching the furling of sails and the comings and goings of ships up and down the river. Merchants in their rich clothes stood in groups, bartering, or shouting orders at the mariners. So this was where Mo's Gran got her tea. He pulled himself away and went in search of food and ale, and water and hay for the horse. He would try eating fish for a change. It would be fresh here. The market was as busy as the quay. The stallholders were selling exotic food as well as the recognisable meat and vegetables. He bought oats, some vegetables and a pie for his bait. Milk and eggs and some cured ham would keep a day or two. He still had potatoes on the cart. He would need a supply of ale and a bottle of whisky. Laden with produce, he walked back to the cart and brought it into town to load the items he could not carry.

It was another cold day, and as he drove across the bridge over the River Ayre the wind snatched at his hat. He caught it before it escaped into the water and he jammed it back on his head. The bridge was only wide enough for one vehicle at a time, and John wondered how the coaches managed to get through without scraping the sides. He came off the bridge and encouraged the horse into a trot, determined to make better progress today.

He passed several people on foot, their heads bent against the wind. Men pushed carts, women drove geese, and children played tag as they went. He did not want to be delayed by passengers, and drove on when the temptation came to give someone a lift. Around midday he pulled over onto the grassy verge and went to sit on the back of the cart to eat his pie and have a mug of ale. Floss ran off to relieve herself in a ploughed field and wandered around finding attractive scents to investigate. More travellers passed them by.

A woman approached along the road. She looked different. She wore a long dark cloak with the hood up and she walked slowly, as if in difficulty, stumbling on the rough ground. She carried a bundle in her arms. Her head was bowed as she went to pass, and she nearly collided with the cart. She stopped and hung onto the corner, unsteady on her feet. She looked up at John with anguish and fear on her young pale face.

He jumped down from his perch and caught her arm to stop her fall. "Steady now, lady," he said gently. "Come and sit here. You're no' fit to be walking oot." He led her to the grass and lowered her down.

The girl let her bundle roll to the ground, revealing that she was in the late stages of pregnancy. She buried her face in her hands and wept.

John did not want to be intrusive but he could not leave her on the roadside. He went to fill his mug with ale and offered it to her.

The girl looked up. Her face was streaked with tears. "Thank 'e, Sir," she whispered as she took the mug with a shaking hand and drank the contents, her other hand over her swollen belly. When she had finished she handed John the mug and struggled to stand up.

John helped her. "I'm John," he said. "Can I take you somewhere you can rest? You're all-in."

"I have ter get to Doncaster," she said. "Me name's Fanny. Father's thrown us out. It were t'squire's son what 'ad me, and 'e denies it. Me sister might teck me in." She looked ready for more tears.

John said, "Can you climb up with ma help?" He indicated the cart.

Fanny nodded and came over. She held on with both hands while John offered her his left arm for her to sit on. He levered her onto the edge and she swung her

321

legs over. John picked up her bundle and handed it to her.

"Goo and sit on that pile in the corner there." He called to Floss, who leapt up to see who the passenger was. They set off at a trot.

John was annoyed that he had been compromised into giving this girl a lift. She had got herself into the family way and now expected her sister to help her out.

"Where does your sister live?" he asked.

"Oh, don't teck me there. She might send us away like Father did. I'll walk from town," said Fanny. "I must find work, for I 'avent no money, an' if I can't support meself I'll have to go to t'poor 'ouse." She sniffed.

John did not want to know any of this. There was nothing more he could do. If he gave her money it would not solve her problems. He just wanted to deliver her somewhere safe and get on with his own journey.

Fanny's wheedling voice reached his ears. "I could come and work for you, Sir. I'm a good worker, an' you're a kind man…"

"You wouldna want to come where I'm going, lassie. I'll drop you off in Doncaster."

They drove past rolling parkland with tree-lined avenues leading to imposing mansions. Herds of deer stood in the shelter of trees, and woodland stretched for miles into the distance. On the outskirts of the town there was a huge stable surrounded with paddocks where handsome horses grazed. John thought of Shadow and was relieved he would be well looked after now.

Doncaster was a small market town. The houses were substantial and the people were well-dressed. Perhaps they kept the less fortunate people locked up in the poor house. John hoped that Fanny would find work as a maid until her time came. The market place was crowded with stallholders dismantling their stands and packing their goods away. John pulled up at the side and turned to look at Fanny.

"Will this do?" he asked.

The girl nodded and crawled to the back end of the cart, where she swung her legs over and dropped to the ground. "Thank you kindly, Sir," she said. She picked up her bundle and stared after him as he drove away.

Chapter 55
The Cock and Bull, Huntingdon

Driving at night was a different experience for Thomas. He kept the horses at a steady but slower pace. There was not so much on the road, but he had to watch out for the lights of oncoming coaches. It was difficult to see the edge of the road. His coachman tutor was a young fellow not much older than himself. He was companionable and enjoyed a laugh. But he took his driving seriously and was a good teacher. When there was no grass verge to guide Thomas, Matt leaned out and shouted if the horses were veering off the road. As they drove on, Thomas' eyes became more accustomed to the dark. He was relieved when they stopped for refreshments.

They drove through two large towns before the stint was over. By now the dawn was breaking and the going became easier.

"We'll be stopping at Huntingdon, Thomas," said Matt. "You look ready for a break. D'yer want me to take over now?"

Thomas was relieved to hand over the reins. He would be staying with Matt until they returned to Grantham, and looked forward to getting to know him.

Soon the guard blew his horn to warn the ostlers at The Cock and Bull Inn of their approach. Matt slowed the horses and he and Thomas climbed off their box, shaking out the stiffness in their legs. They helped the passengers down, saying, "I'll be leaving you here, Sir,

Madam," and held their hands out for the obligatory tip, saying, "Thank you, and have a pleasant journey."

They unloaded the baggage of the passengers whose journey was over, while the ostlers led the horses away. The travellers went into the inn where a fire and a good breakfast awaited them. Matt and Thomas went up to the bar and claimed the tankards of ale which had been set there for them. They both took a long draught before finding a table to sit at.

"You did well for yer first night's driving," said Matt. 'Tis hard to keep awake when 'tis so cold."

"Ay, but I'm accustomed to the cold. In the Highlands it's far colder than this in winter with the snow and ice," said Thomas.

"We'll get some o' that too. After Christmas, I rackon. Then yer fingers and toes'll freeze 'till they're senseless." Matt chuckled at the thought. "It seems like they'll never get warm again." He looked towards the door where a group of customers had entered. He put his tankard down and said, "I'll be back, I've a score to settle."

One of the new arrivals saw Matt and turned round to make his escape.

Matt leapt across the room. "Oi! not so fast!" he shouted. "I've got yer this toime." He caught up with the fugitive and held him by his hair, pushing him out of the door. The other men followed them.

Thomas remained in his seat. He did not want to get involved in another man's fight. He was too tired to be of any use. Matt seemed to have limitless energy. Thomas supped his ale and his breakfast was brought to him by the barman. What a welcome sight! As he ate the ham and eggs and potato cakes he began to warm up and was feeling sleepy when Matt came through the door with the men who now appeared to be his friends. He and the fellow he had collared both had bloody noses and cut lips, but they came in with their arms around each other, joking and laughing. Matt disentangled himself and they all came over to where Thomas was sitting.

"These're moi friends," he said. "Jim here, 'e went orf wiv moi girl while I were on the road. She's gorn orf wiv anuvver coachman now!" He and Jim creased up with laughter. Then Matt waved his hand to the barman, "I'll have me breakfast now, Lennie." He sat down and the others gathered round on stools. Some of them went to buy ale at the bar.

Thomas introduced himself. "Matt's teaching me to drive the coach," he said.

They were a friendly bunch. They chatted among themselves and to Thomas, recounting stories about Matt which Thomas thought were wildly exaggerated. They asked him about his own story and were intrigued by his Scottish way of speech. At last he could keep his eyes open no longer, and got up to go to his bed, agreeing to meet Matt later in the day. The next stint would start at six o'clock that evening.

Matt told Thomas a little about himself over dinner. He was born in London. When he was ten, his parents and brother and sisters died of the plague and his aunt took him in.

"She weren't bovvered about me," he said. "I were an independent nipper and took to roaming the streets, foinding ways to fill me belly, 'cos me aunty never fed us proper. The best places ter foind food was the back yards of inns. They threw out their leftovers an' I had a good few tasty meals for nuffin'. I watched the ostlers handlin' the horses and earned meself a few pennies givin' 'em a hand, feedin' the horses an' rubbin' 'em down."

When he was old enough Matt got himself a job as an ostler, which eventually led to him driving coaches.

"D'you see your aunty?" asked Thomas.

"Na. She fell ter setting up a boarding house fer gentlemen. There's all sorts goes on in that place now. I bet she's forgotten about me."

"I've never been to London," said Thomas. "It sounds like a rough place."

"Na. 'Tain't all rough. There's plenty of smart houses being built after the Great Fire. That were ten years ago. I'll show yer a bit of it when we gets there."

The luggage was stowed and strapped down; the passengers boarded; Matt and Thomas climbed onto their seats; Matt shouted, "To London!" The guard blew his horn and the cloths were dragged off the horses as Thomas whipped them into action. They plunged forward into the dusk.

Thomas always enjoyed this moment. The drama excited him as he prepared himself for another adventure. He had given up looking for his father. They were sure to have left him far behind. On their return journey they might see him. Thomas was looking forward to seeing London, the busy streets and the people. It would be quite different to anything he had experienced before.

"We'll finish this stint at The Saracen's Head in London," said Matt. "We'll have a kip then I'll show yer the sights before we head back to Grantham."

Chapter 56
London

It was dark when they arrived and Thomas could see nothing of his surroundings. This was the end of the journey for the passengers, and Matt and the guard raked in a good few tips which they shared with Thomas. The coach would be starting the return journey with new horses and drivers in the morning. Matt and Thomas retired to their beds until dawn woke them. They ate a hearty breakfast and set off on a quick tour of the city.

Matt led Thomas up narrow passages, through markets and past terraces, crescents and squares of grand houses. Thomas could not believe how anyone would want to live in such crowded conditions. There was no landscape, only stone and brick buildings as far as the eye could see. In the markets and poor areas the stench of daily living was overpowering. There were taverns and churches at regular intervals wherever they went. Carriages and carts, horses and pedestrians fought their way along the streets, all in a hurry, except for the urchins and beggars who hung around in dark corners with vagrant dogs, eating scraps of rubbish. Matt and Thomas dodged and dived their way through the crowds until a space opened up before them, and a sight which Thomas would never forget. They stopped and stared.

"That's St Paul's Cathedral," said Matt. "'Twas destroyed in the Great Fire. They're rebuilding it."

A giant skeleton of scaffolding towered into the sky, with men the size of ants climbing about carrying what appeared to be buckets and hods of bricks. The ants were hauling up stones by ropes and pulleys. Mountains of building materials lay on the ground everywhere, with more men sawing wood, chipping away at hunks of stone and mixing mortar.

Matt tugged at Thomas' sleeve. "There's more, come on." He turned and walked swiftly down another street and soon Thomas saw water in front of them.

"That's the River Thames, wot runs all froo the city," said Matt.

The river seemed like the sea to Thomas, though he could see the other side. There were wherries full of people being rowed up and down to steps in the banks which led up to the streets.

"'Tis quicker to travel this way." Matt led him to a flight of steps and hailed a wherryman who brought his craft alongside and they scrambled aboard. "Westminter, if yer please." Matt handed over some coins and they pushed out onto the river.

Thomas sat down suddenly. He had never ridden on water, and felt unsafe and bewildered. There were warehouses along the banks with merchant ships unloading their cargo. One was setting sail on its next journey, the sails billowing as they caught the wind. The wherry rocked over its wake.

A vast building came into view with a church in the background. A bridge spanned the river just here. Thomas and Matt alighted at another flight of steps and stared at The Palace of Westminster.

"Parlyment meets in this building," Matt informed Thomas. "They make the laws and decide who's the next one to have 'is head chopped orf and how much we should pay in taxes." He set off again, shouting above the din of the city, "We've got to hurry back. We're starting the next stint at ten o'clock!" Thomas had difficulty keeping up with him as he dodged the traffic and dived up narrow alleyways.

Negotiating the London streets was the greatest challenge to Thomas' newly acquired driving skills. Matt directed him along cobbled lanes, some of which were only wide enough for one vehicle. It was a race with other drivers to be the first to squeeze between the houses. Once they had to stop while Matt leapt down from his seat and argued with the driver of a smart private carriage coming the other way. When Matt rolled up his sleeves in preparation for a fight the occupant of the other carriage called to his driver to back away, much to Thomas' relief. He could not imagine how he would reverse four horses and a laden carriage out of this tight corner. The guard blew his horn to warn other vehicles to make way, and they trotted through.

They were soon free of the confines of the town and could pick up speed. The countryside emerged from streets of houses and farmland opened up. They travelled through villages and the road became rougher. Fog came down and visibility was poor at times. Swathes of mist swirled around the carriage when they drove across streams and boggy areas.

"We'll be coming to Finchley Common soon," said Matt. "There's bands of robbers lurking out there, ready to pounce if we 'ave ter stop. This wevver's wot they loikes best. They can creep up on us before we knows it. Keep yer eyes skinned."

Thomas kept the horses going at a steady pace. He avoided driving too close to the verge, as he could see it was soft in places. There were mostly farm carts on the road today, loaded up with vegetables and timber. Pedestrians and horsemen were evidently staying indoors. It would not be long before Thomas would be looking for his father again. He wondered how he would manage in the London streets and hoped that he would have the sense to skirt around the city. Thomas had heard that Sussex was the other side. He was sure that that was where his father was heading…

A stone hit Thomas on the face. He ducked and put his arm up to shield his head from another blow. The horses swerved as he almost lost control. Dark figures ran and capered in the mist around them.

"Speed up!" shouted Matt. "They're trying ter drive us orf the road!"

They pulled their hats down to protect their faces. Matt took the whip from Thomas and cracked it over the horses' ears. They plunged forward. The carriage rocked on the stony ground. Passengers hanging on the sides of the carriage shouted in fear of being flung off. The guard blew his horn to warn other traffic to steer clear. More stones were hurled at them and Matt gave a shout of pain.

The horses galloped on.

Thomas's heart was in his mouth, thumping enough to choke him. He kept the carriage on the road by some miracle. Stones flew past his face, some hitting the horses and the carriage. The attack seemed to go on for ever.

As they thundered on, he became aware that they were alone on the road again. All was quiet, except for the jangling of the harness and the clatter of the horses' hooves. The figures in the mist had been left behind.

Matt said, "Yer can slow down now, Thomas. Let the horses 'ave a break."

Thomas looked at his companion. He was holding his head. Blood was pouring down his cheek and his hands were covered in it.

"Shall I stop?" Thomas asked.

"Na, 'tis nuffin'. We'll be at the next stage soon." He continued holding the wound as he gave the whip back to Thomas.

Chapter 57
The George, Grantham

It had been a cold damp night, sleeping under the cart. John stirred as the first light reached him. He rolled over and felt an urgent need to vomit. He staggered out into the pouring rain and emptied his stomach onto the grass. That fish had not agreed with him. He was glad to be rid of it. He found a costrel of water on the cart and poured some into his mouth to swill it out, then stood in the rain wondering whether he would ever make it to Sussex. The weather was not going to get any better for months. He would likely catch a fever and die out here, with no-one to bury him. Thomas would never find him…

Thomas would be in London by now.

There was no point in trying to light a fire. He did not feel like eating anyway. He gave some oats to the horse and Floss, wrapped the plaids in the hide to keep them as dry as possible and prepared to leave.

It was a long day, plodding through the driving rain. They were drenched, but they kept going. John was in a daze. He remembered times like this when Annie and Thomas were with him, fleeing from the Royalist militia. There was more urgency then. Somehow that made it easier. They did not have a choice. Today, John did have a choice. There was no-one chasing him. Knowing that Thomas was alive was enough. John had given up hope of them finding each other. The lad had his own life to lead, and he wished him well. John was seeking comfort and security. It did not matter where he lived. He could earn enough as a carter to keep himself anywhere…

He came into a town and approached a coaching inn. He could see the lights beckoning to him through the twilight, and drove the cart into a well-lit yard where ostlers were scurrying here and there, attending to the horses. He arranged for them to look after Floss and the horse and wearily made his way into the inn. He had had enough of travelling in the rain and dreaded the thought of another night in the open. He asked if he could have a room for the night and gave the chambermaid his wet coat to dry in the back parlour. He went as close as he could to the fire and felt the warmth seeping through his clothes, aware that he was steaming. The barman saw him and brought his whisky.

"What inn is this?" John asked.

"This is The George at Grantham. One of the best coaching inns, Sir," said the barman.

John nodded. This would be an expensive night. But what else did he have to spend his money on? He ordered a meal.

≈ ≈ ≈

Matt and Thomas had come to the end of their stint. Matt was in no fit state to carry on. The flow of blood from the injury on his temple could not be staunched. The doctor was called. Thomas would pick up his next coach in the middle of the night. Matt told him he would have to go unsupervised to Grantham.

"Good thing you was with us," he said. "They would have had to foind another driver."

338

Thomas woke at two o'clock, lit his candle and went to look at Matt sleeping in the other cot. His head was bandaged. There was a red stain where the blood had soaked through. His face was white as the sheets.

Thomas dressed and went down to meet the coach as it came trundling in. It was dripping with water in the heavy drizzle. He did not relish the thought of driving through this for the next eight hours on his own. He hoped he would meet Matt again one day. He had enjoyed his companionship.

He drove through the rain all night. The journey was uneventful, and the passengers beside him on the bench were wrapped in their own thoughts. Daylight pierced the heavy grey clouds which were laden with more rain. They stopped to change horses. Thomas was cold and soaked through. He went into the inn for a tankard of ale. He could not wait until the next stop at Grantham.

≈ ≈ ≈

John set out from Grantham with dry clothes. Floss had spent the night on straw with the horse and they both looked happier. But it was not long before the persistent rain had penetrated to their skins. The carthorse plodded along the deserted road. They came to another inn where a coach was changing horses. Floss sat up, ears pricked, sniffing the air as they drove past. She whined and looked at John, mouth open, tongue hanging out, panting.

"'Tis no time to be stopping again, Floss. We'll have to put up with this rain for theday," John said, and hunched his shoulders, driving relentlessly on. He felt alone and friendless. He longed to have a conversation about other things not connected with his family and the situation he was in. He was getting depressed and had no way of bringing himself out of it. Peering through the rain, he thought he could make out a figure ahead of him. He slowed down. Walking in this weather must be even worse than riding on a cart.

≈ ≈ ≈

Thomas reached the George at Grantham. He said goodbye to his customers and collected a good few coins to slip into his pouch. He reported to the landlord and received his first wages and a coat and trousers in the coach company's livery colours; light and dark blue. A letter was waiting for him and he put it inside his shirt. He would have to ask someone to read it to him. Before having his breakfast he went to ask the ostlers if there had been a man with a dog on a cart going through.

"Aye. A man of that description left here early this morning, heading in a southerly direction. He had a look of thee about him."

"That was ma faether," Thomas said. He walked slowly and despondently indoors, wondering how they could have missed each other this morning. At least he knew now that John was still on the road.

Chapter 58
Mary Stevens

She was an upright, handsome woman dressed in a hooded cloak. She strode along the road carrying an empty basket. As John drew alongside, she looked up and revealed an honest and open face.

"Can I give you a lift home, Lady?" asked John.

"Thank thee, Friend, but my home will be well out of thy way."

"'Tis no matter," said John, climbing down from the cart. "Your company would be welcome." He offered her his hand and helped her up onto the bench. "'Tis no weather for a lady to be out walking. I'm John Grant, Ma'am."

As he started driving, the lady looked at him again, in a way that warmed his heart, and said, "My name is Mary Stevens. I have been on an urgent errand to my ailing brother and sisters. I believe the Lord has brought us together."

They settled into a companionable silence as John drove on. He was surprised at what she had said, but made no comment. The rain lashed their faces and soaked through their clothes. Soon they came to a crossroads.

"Turn right here, John, and keep going until thou reach a turn to the left. 'Tis a mile or so along there to our village," said Mary.

John turned into a narrow road with tall hedges on either side. The regular passage of carts along here had worn deep ruts into the ground. Water had collected

341

and formed rivers which flowed down the hill towards them. The wheels of the cart sprayed water out onto the hedgerows.

"We'll have to get off and swim soon, Ma'am," said John, trying to make light of the trouble he was having to keep the cart from leaning over.

"'Tis not far now to the turning. The lane to the village is not so rutted," said Mary, seemingly unperturbed by the roughness of the ride.

They negotiated a corner and the left turn came into sight. John skirted a pond which had formed, and drove onto a smaller track going downhill. The muddy water flowed along with them. By the time they reached the village it was pouring off the surrounding fields and they continued through a torrent into the flooded village street. John kept the horse going. The water came up to the axles of the cart. He glanced at his companion who appeared to be praying. The road started to go uphill again and the horse pulled them clear of the water.

"That is my house, ahead of thee," said Mary, indicating a cottage close to the road. "There's an entrance to the back yard just beyond it. Thou must come in and rest awhile, and I will dry thy clothes."

John had not intended to delay his journey, but the temptation to rest was strong. He drove into the yard where there were stables. He halted the horse and jumped to the ground, then handed the lady down. A man emerged from the back door.

"This is my husband, Joshua," said Mary. "John has brought me most of the way home, Husband."

"Thou should never have gone out in this weather, Wife. Thou could have become stranded on the road. Come along indoors, both of thee."

John hesitated. Floss had leapt down from the cart and was shaking herself vigorously. "Would it be possible to allow ma dog and ma horse some shelter in the stable, Sir?" he asked.

Joshua looked at the two animals. They both had their heads down and were standing dejectedly in puddles of water. "Aye, of course. The second stable is empty."

John went to take the horse out of the shafts, and found some dry hay under the hide on the cart. He took him over to the stable and called Floss. When he had settled them both he came to the back door which had been left ajar for him, and walked in, hat in hand.

This couple lived simply. The floor was of stone flags and the furniture plain wood. The chairs reminded him of the ones at Grammer's house, which he had so admired. A fire burned in the iron range. There were no soft furnishings. A single candlestick stood in the middle of the table. Framed extracts from the Bible hung on the walls. John started to read one of them:

John 1:9. The true light, that lighteth every man that cometh into the world...

"Let me take thy coat, Friend," Mary spoke from behind him.

John turned round and allowed her to help him with his coat, which she hung on the back of a chair in front of the fire. "I'll no' be staying long, Ma'am, but thank you for your kindness," he said.

343

"Where dost thou live? Hast thou a family waiting for thee?" Joshua asked. "The rain will not ease today, and the water is already too high to drive through."

"No, there's no family. I'm travelling south to find a home for maself," replied John.

"So there's no hurry to be gone," said Mary, smiling. "Thou art welcome to stay here for a while, Friend. We have a spare chamber aloft."

John stood next to the fire and warmed himself.

Joshua said, "Can I lend thee some dry clothes? Thou wilt be more comfortable."

"I will show thee thy chamber," said Mary. "Change thy clothes up there." She opened a door in the wall of the parlour, revealing a narrow flight of stairs, and beckoned to John to follow her.

It seemed he had no choice in the matter. It was easy to do the bidding of his hosts, relieved of having to make any more decisions for himself.

When he came down to the parlour, dressed in a clean dry shirt and breeches, and carrying his wet clothes, Mary was busy putting food on the table. She sat down and took Joshua's hand and said, "Let us join hands and wait upon the Lord." They both held their hands out for John to hold.

John was embarrassed by this unexpected command. For one thing, they must have noticed that, instead of a left hand, he wore a leather stump with a hook attached. And why should they hold hands before a meal? He held out his right hand to be taken by Joshua, and watched Mary's face as he presented her with his stump.

Mary, without flinching, took hold of his arm above the stump and held it gently. Joshua took his right hand. There followed a long silence which disturbed John at first, but then a strange feeling of calm came over him. The longer they remained in this position, the more comfortable he became. Mary and Joshua sat with their eyes closed, smiling peacefully.

At last Mary said, "Amen." Joshua followed suit, and John added his "Amen."

They started eating. It was a simple meal of broth and a loaf of bread, with milk to drink.

John felt better, though the absence of ale worried him. He looked round the room, then at his hosts. "I have some provisions on the cart that I can give ye in return for your hospitality," he said. "'Twould be a shame to let them goo to waste."

Mary nodded. "Bring them in later, John."

Joshua went to the window and looked out. "The water's still rising, Mary. 'Tis almost to the doorstep. We should move upstairs."

Mary joined him at the window, then went to the back door and opened it. "'Twould be wise to move thy cart into the barn, John. 'Tis dry in there. Joshua will help thee."

John was pleased to note that the stables and barn were on higher ground than the yard. The water almost surrounded the house. Joshua helped him pull the cart into the barn and they collected straw for the horse and Floss. John found the oats on the cart and took some into the stable with some water. Then he and his host unloaded and took the provisions into the house.

Joshua saw the ale and whisky. "Don't let Mary see those, Friend. Best hide them away under thy cowhide. Our religion doesn't allow strong drink."

John looked at him in astonishment. How could he live without his whisky? He would not be staying here long. He would come out here when they were not looking and have a draught.

They splashed back to the house through the flood, which was already seeping over the doorstep. Mary was in the kitchen collecting provisions to take upstairs. When they had taken what they needed, they took chairs, and emptied the shelves and cupboards of books and papers, and Mary's sewing materials and patchwork. By the time they had finished there was a thin film of water covering the floor. The table stood in its place with chairs on top and the wet clothes hung on a line over the range. Mary lit the candle and they left the parlour. John hoped it would not be for long.

It was getting dark. They all went into Mary and Joshua's chamber and Mary sat down. Joshua and John followed her example. They again joined hands and bowed their heads. There was another period of silence, then Mary spoke.

"Let us think of all who go abroad this night, and send the guiding spirit of the Lord, that they may keep their faith in Him and come safely home."

"Amen," said Joshua.

"Amen," John echoed.

Silence again. John had never felt so peaceful. He felt at this moment that his future was blessed; that whatever happened, he would be safe.

His head started spinning. He could hold his hands up no longer. It was as if he had consumed a whole bottle of whisky. His body swayed and collapsed into someone's arms.

Chapter 59
The Search Continues

Thomas sat at the bar after eating a hearty breakfast. The barman was cleaning up after the last batch of travellers had passed through. Thomas took the letter from under his shirt. It was damp and smudged.

"D'you know anyone who could read this for me?" he asked.

"Aye, the cook can read," said Daniel. "You've a girl somewhere, then?"

"Left behind in York," said Thomas sadly. "I'm no' likely to see her again..." He gazed into his tankard before putting it to his mouth and drinking the remaining contents. "Thank you Daniel." He slid off his stool and went to find the kitchen.

The cook, Jacques, was pleased to read Thomas' letter. He wiped his hands on his apron, broke the seal and began:

"Dear Thomas,

I hope your fortunes are improving since we met, and that you have found your father.

I delivered your letter to The Bell in York, and went there for a sup of ale several times before I met your Jenny. She was surprised and delighted to hear from you, as she had been worrying, thinking you had had some misfortune. I am writing this to you on behalf of us both.

Jenny is a delightful girl as you know, and as we have made our acquaintance since we met, I can now say that we have become close in our feelings for each other. I hope, some day to make her my wife, when I become established as an apothecary and have a small income.

This might come as unwanted news, as I know you were fond of her. But as there seems to be no prospect of your meeting her in the future, we felt that you would understand. She remembers you with affection, and we both thank you for bringing us together.

If you could send a letter to The Bell in York, we would be pleased to hear news from you.

Sending best wishes from us both,
Yours respectfully, Charles Turner."

Jacques peered at Thomas, falcon-like, his beady eyes over the hooked nose searching for a reaction.

Thomas drew a breath. "Well, that's that."

He shrugged his shoulders. He was pleased that Jenny had found a respectable replacement for himself. But he still missed her. He went to his chamber and sat on the cot, remembering his life in York and his friends there. It all seemed far away now. And his mission to find his father was not yet fulfilled. He must go on searching. The next stint would take him to Doncaster, then he would be returning to drive to Stamford. He was now committed to coach driving for the next few months. If he had not found his father by the spring, he would go to Alex MacPherson and ask for the job he had offered.

He undressed and lay down on his cot. Sleep came easily, with dreams of a woman's arms enfolding him against her soft breasts, whispering comforting words...

For weeks Thomas drove up and down the route between Doncaster and Stamford through wind and snow, ice and rain until he knew the road intimately. Every stage inn, every barman, every team of horses and every ostler became familiar to him. He made friends with the local barmaids, but was never tempted to take them to his bed. He got to know the other coachmen in passing and met Matt briefly several times, but had no time to spend with him. He had interesting conversations with the passengers who sat next to him and told him their stories. He experienced agonising pain in his cold feet and hands and realised that his body was becoming weak with lack of exercise.

At first he kept his eyes open for a sight of his father on the cart, but as time went on his hopes faded. John had either wandered off the main road or had settled down somewhere, having given up his wish to reach Sussex.

Around Christmas the roads became busier and there were more passengers, all carrying more luggage and braces of game. There were new passengers at every stop, coming and going to stay with friends and relatives for the festive season. Thomas and the guards were tipped generously. All were in high spirits

Thomas accumulated a large amount of money which he deposited in several different places, in nooks and crannies of inns and stables, in case one of them was discovered by a dishonourable colleague or traveller, or should he be set upon by a highwayman. There was little opportunity to spend it, but he would need some of it for his journey to Sussex when he was ready. He felt increasingly lonely and by the end of February was yearning for freedom from the incessant driving.

The next time he reached Grantham he said to the landlord, "I'm thinking of giving this up. I can drive to Stamford and back one last time, then I'll be handing in ma livery."

The landlord gave him a long hard stare. "Didn't think you'd stick it this long. But you're one o' the best. If I give you a break of a week or two would you be willing...?"

Thomas interrupted. "No, thank you, Landlord. I'm hankering after ma farming life and I know someone who will give me work."

"I'll be sorry to lose you, Thomas. You're a reliable worker, not like some of the other young drivers. They can be real trouble, running off to see their girls in the middle of a stint, and picking fights with the passengers. Do the route to Stamford and back, lad, and we'll call it a day."

He held out his hand and Thomas took it with relief. He shook it hard, with the energy which surged up through his weary body at the prospect of freedom. He began to feel alive again.

Snow floated in fat flakes from a leaden sky. It covered everything in a white blanket. It crunched under the carriage wheels as they rolled down the familiar road, now transformed into a silent wonderland. Only the movement of the horses and their harness shook off the clinging soft down.

Thomas was wearing as many clothes as he could fit under his heavy coat. He had wrapped a scarf round his mouth and nose to keep out the cold air and put a rug over his knees, covering his legs and feet. An inch or so had settled on the top of his hat, shoulders and lap and those of the passengers who sat outside. Only those inside the coach were protected, and even they were experiencing flurries of feathery flakes blowing in through the windows, melting on their clothes and leaving puddles on the floor.

It was hard to see the road now. There was no other traffic to guide him, and no recent tracks. Thomas began to realise that they would not get further than the next stage. He slowed the horses down and stopped, removed the blanket and shook off the snow. He jumped from his perch and was nearly ankle-deep in the stuff. Walking round to the guard at the back of the coach confirmed his concerns.

"Will you goo along in front, Sam?" he called. "I canna see the road, and we must get to the next stage before we give up."

Sam took his hat off and banged it against the coach and replaced it. He brushed the white covering off his shoulders and climbed down. "Struth!" he said. "I'll not be able to run in this!" He looked at Thomas and grinned. "Here we go!" He plodded off ahead of the horses.

Thomas climbed back up to his seat and clicked his tongue. They set off slowly behind Sam who was bending forward to find the way, kicking the snow away in places. It was taking forever. The deeper the covering, the heavier the horses' load. They would not be able to pick up speed. Not being accustomed to pulling, they tossed their heads and snorted, puffing clouds of steam into the damp air.

Sam stumbled but righted himself. He was getting tired.

Thomas stopped the horses and alighted. He waded to Sam who was trudging on, oblivious of anything around him. Thomas patted him on the shoulder.

"Can you drive the horses? 'Twould give you a break. I'll walk in front. We must get to that staging inn."

Sam nodded and went back to the coach. Thomas watched as he took the reins and the horses walked on. He set forth, searching for signs that they were still on the right track. Whiteness surrounded him. He became disorientated. There was only the jangling of the harness to re-assure him that he was not alone in this vast wilderness.

He stood up straight to ease his back and looked ahead. The dove grey sky on the horizon was diffused with hues of pink and yellow. He could see into the distance. The snow had stopped falling. The shapes of the trees became visible and he recognised some landmarks; a hump by the side of the road which he knew was a milestone, the lacework of wrought iron gates at the entrance to a long drive, with lodges either side, their windows peering out through a layer of snow clinging to the walls. They had kept to the road and, if he was not mistaken, there were the lights of the stage inn ahead of them. He shouted for joy and bounded over the snowdrifts to get back to the coach.

"We're there!" he shouted to Sam. "Come down and we'll lead the horses."

The passengers had seen the lights and some dropped off their perches like great black bats, eager to stretch their cold, stiff limbs. They pushed their way through the mounds of soft snow towards their destination, shouting with relief.

Sam and Thomas held the harnesses of the leaders and encouraged them the last few hundred yards to the welcoming lights and the warmth of dry stables. It would be a day or two before anyone could continue their journeys.

Chapter 60
The Quakers

John became aware of voices some distance away. He was not sure where he was and, before opening his eyes, he felt his body with his right hand. It was clothed, but not in shirt and breeches. He was lying in a strange bed covered with a soft quilt. He opened his eyes and saw a beam of sunlight shining through a window onto a picture on the wall in front of him. There were dust motes dancing in the sunshine. It had stopped raining. He could not remember how he came to be lying here in a strange room. The voices outside the window were friendly, laughing, happy.

He sat up to look more closely at the picture on the wall. It wasn't a picture. The words shone out at him, lit by the sunbeam:

"Be still, allow that of God to rise within thee and to guide thy thoughts."

John lay back on the pillow. He recalled the evening he came to this place; the strange feelings of warmth and comfort he had experienced. It was as if he had been bewitched. These people were very religious, and John was uncomfortable now. He felt he had no control over what became of him. All this talk of God and the Lord unnerved him. He had never paid much attention to God. What was He anyway? An ominous figure in the heavens, threatening hell and damnation to all sinners. He had always done his best to be honest and fulfil his duties as a husband and father. He had sometimes failed, but things had happened that were of

357

other peoples' making. He did not consider that he was a sinner. He would meet his Maker one day and take the consequences.

So what was all this about God rising within him? He did not understand, and was not sure he wanted to. He shut his eyes again. He was weary, weary of travelling, fending for himself. What was the point of it all? He drifted off to sleep.

Suddenly he was awake. Someone was in the room, moving about. He opened his eyes, and recognised Mary, the woman he had given a lift. She was carrying a tray.

She smiled and said, "Thou art awake, John. Welcome. I've brought thee some food."

John sat up and realised that the leather glove had been removed from his left arm. The stump had been bothering him lately. It had become sore and weeping. Now it was bandaged.

Mary said, "I put some salve on the arm. Canst thou manage without the cover until it heals?"

John nodded, "Thank you, Ma'am. You're unco kind."

"Call me Mary, John. We're all Friends here." She placed the tray on his knees. "Thou needs to build up thy strength. How long hast thou been travelling?"

John could not remember when he left York. "A while now. I stayed a night or two at inns." He remembered Floss and the carthorse. "Ma dog, and…?"

"Do not worry, John. They have been cared for. Joshua is quite taken with Floss, but she's missing thee. Eat up, then perhaps thou wilt feel able to dress and come downstairs. The water has subsided."

She turned and left the room.

John uncovered the dishes on the tray.

Porridge! Mary had made him some porridge! How could she have known? It was not crowdies. That would have been asking too much. Again, he was overcome by the thoughtful kindness of these people. He ate slowly, savouring every morsel. There was a hard-boiled egg wrapped in a cloth, and bread and butter, spread with honey. No ale, but a drink of milk went down well. He pushed the tray away, and swung his legs round. The bare floorboards were icy cold after the warmth of the bed. His head started spinning. He took a few breaths and sat there awhile, looking around him. Clothes lay on a chair by the bed, just within reach. There were some stockings. He put them on. He pulled the nightshirt off over his head and leaned forward to take a woollen undergarment from the chair. He dressed slowly, sitting down until it was time to stand and pull the breeches up over his hips. He was missing the hook on his left arm. As he stood, he felt wobbly and had to lean against the bed for support. At last he wriggled into the breeches and tucked in his shirt. He sat down to fasten them at the waist, and shuffled his feet into his waiting boots. A waistcoat and his jacket remained on the chair. He put the waistcoat on and picked up the jacket, draping it over his left arm. He could not believe how weak he was, and wondered how long he had been in bed. He stumbled down the dark stairs and opened the door into the parlour.

The room was full of sunshine and a homely aroma of baking. The warmth from the range met him as he entered. Mary and another woman were standing by the table, their sleeves rolled up and their hands covered in flour, kneading dough. Mary looked up, her face flushed. A curl of brown hair had escaped from her bonnet. She brushed it away with her wrist, leaving a streak of flour across her cheek.

"John, this is my neighbour, Sarah."

"Pleased to meet you, Ma'a… Sarah," said John as he closed the door behind him. I left the tray up there, Mary. I couldna…"

"Don't worry about that. I'll fetch it later," said Mary. "Sit thee down and rest. Thou art still weak. 'Twill take a while for thee to build up thy strength." She nodded to an armchair by the window.

John walked slowly across the parlour and was glad when he reached the chair. He draped the jacket over the back and sat down. He could see the village green from here, and the road where they had driven through the floods. There were children playing with a ball. He could hear them shouting and laughing in the sunshine. He sat back and watched, enjoying the warmth and peace. His eyes closed. The smell of baking bread went to his head, which dropped forward as his mind drifted.

He would not be going anywhere for some time. How fortunate that he had met Mary on the road. He settled into the Quaker routine of meeting twice a day with whoever was in the house, joining hands and contemplating. He still had no idea why God should rise up within him, but he no longer thought of his Maker as ominous, but rather as a benign Presence who would provide what was needed to those who had faith.

When she was not visiting the poor, or baking bread for them, Mary spent hours sitting by the window in the daylight, sewing hexagonal pieces of fabric together to make patchwork quilts. While he was recovering his strength, John sat with her, watching her nimble fingers flying through the air as she stitched. He asked about her charitable activities and she told him about the sick, and those in prison for their beliefs, and how she became a Quaker.

Most of the village had become Children of the Light, as they called themselves, after a visit from George Fox, their founder, a few years before. He travelled the country, disrupting church services with his ministry. He was accused of blasphemy by the Anglican priests and had spent long periods in gaol. He had inspired many followers with his revolutionary teaching, and with them he had formed the Society of Friends.

"There is God in all beings," she said. "We are all equal in the eyes of God, and each one of us is His minister. The power of the Lord works through us. That is why we do not enter steeple houses or need priests to baptise and marry us. Thou wilt find God in everyone if thou looks for Him, John."

John thought it was a risky business being a Quaker. But the old Scottish rebel in

him admired their courage and fortitude in living up to their beliefs.

Chapter 61
Village Life

As soon as he had the strength to walk outside, he put his jacket on and went to see Floss. She nearly turned herself inside out in greeting him, running round in circles, whining and uttering little barks of pleasure. She led him to Joshua's workshop next to the barn, and sat outside the open door, panting, tongue hanging out.

Joshua looked up from his work and laughed. "Thou hast found each other, then! Floss has missed thee, John. She's a good companion."

"Thank you for looking after her, Joshua. I'm glad you've enjoyed each other's company. May I come and see what you're doing?"

"Please, come in," Joshua nodded.

The smell of wood greeted John as he entered. The floor was deep in shavings and a thin layer of sawdust covered everything. Joshua was planing down a piece of wood, the curls dropping to bury his feet. The parts of a chair lay to one side. John recognised the same pieces that made up the chairs in the house, and those he had admired in Grammer's cottage. He went over and examined them, caressing the smooth wood and putting it to his nose to breath in the aroma.

"They're ready to polish, John, before I assemble the chair. Wouldst thou like to do that? There's a stool over there by the bench." Joshua went over to a shelf where he found polish and rags. "Thou knows how to do this?"

John's heart gave a leap. "Oh, ay!" He took his jacket off and went to sit at the bench where Joshua had put the polish. His stump had healed and he had the leather cover on again, with the hook. There was a clamp nearby and he put one of the chair parts into it to hold it between his knees while he polished. This was going to be a pleasure, working with wood again. Memories of making furniture for Annie when they first set up house together flooded back, and of doing the same when they came to York. Sadness came over him and he had to put all his mind and energy into polishing to dispel the emotion.

The harsh winter crept up on them and, before they knew it, Christmas had come and gone. The weather kept John safely tucked up in the cottage. He had no desire to start travelling again.

He spent most of his time in the workshop with Joshua, and learnt how to make a chair. He offered to pay for his keep, but Mary refused to take any money. So he took them into the nearest town, a few miles away, on the cart, loaded with furniture and quilts to sell in the market there. They bought more wood and fabric and Mary offered to make John some shirts and knee-length breeches. She bought some wool, and she knitted stockings and vests for them all.

John began to get involved in village life, something he had never experienced. He soon found that it was like being in a large family as it was in the Highlands among Clan Ciaran. He took his carthorse to the blacksmith for new shoes. He stood and watched as the bellows puffed the fire into life, reaching red hot in no time. Harold beat the shoe into shape as the flames flew. John recalled his childhood stories of the god Odin.

When all the shoes were replaced, John said, "How much do I owe you?"

Harold's red, greasy face broke into a smile. He removed his dirty cap and scratched the back of his head. "Well, John, last week the wind did some damage to a fence by my hog pound. I've heard tell you're handy with carpentry tools. Could you mend it for us?"

John smiled back. "Show me," he said.

They walked to the back of the smithy and John examined the damaged fence. "I'd be pleased to do that, Harold." They shook hands. "I'll be back later."

That afternoon, John went to mend Harold's fence. Halfway through the job, the blacksmith appeared, carrying two mugs of ale. "I reckon you've earned this, John." He stood and took a mouthful while John put his tools down. His mouth filled with saliva at the prospect of ale. He had finished his own supply weeks ago. He took the mug gratefully and relished the first taste as if it was heavenly mead. "Thank you kindly, Harold," he said, and took another gulp.

"You don't abstain, like Mary and Joshua, then?" Harold looked at John directly with a twinkle in his eye.

John shook his head. "I'm no Quaker. But they're verra kind, and took me in when I was needy."

"I've no objection to their strange ways," said Harold. "They do a lot of good work. No-one else would go near the filthy gaols. But there are some in the village who have a different opinion, and won't have nothing to do with them."

"You've no' considered joining the Quakers yourself, then?" John asked.

"Nay. I'd rather stick to the rules, and do as I'm bid. I don't want no trouble." He

grinned and took John's empty mug. "I'll let you get on, then," he said, and went indoors.

That evening when John came home, he told Mary what he had been doing. She

looked at him accusingly, but did not mention that she had smelt the ale on his breath.

The Quakers held Monthly Meeting in each other's houses. John felt reluctant to go, but obliged, as he was staying with Mary and Joshua. So he went along with them to Sarah's house. Others were there, sitting in the parlour with the table pushed to one side. John recognised some that he had come to know who were there with their husbands. Mary and Joshua sat down with John next to them.

After a few moments, when all were settled, Mary spoke. "Be still in the presence of the Lord and hear His voice within thee."

They sat in silence for a long time. There were no hymns or prayers. Occasionally someone stood up and read a passage from the Bible.

Martha's husband rose from his chair, and said, "Remember that there is God even in our enemies. We must look for Him in them and show them."

John pondered on this, and did not feel inspired. This religion was not for him. He could never forgive the Laird Ludovick for his treatment of clan Ciaran. He longed for his whisky and ale. They were his life blood and he could not understand why they were forbidden.

The village priest saw him in the street one day. He removed his hat. "Good day to you, Sir. I believe we have not met. Are you living in the village?"

John knew that the vicar would be well informed. He did not want him to think he was a Quaker. He raised his hat. "Good day to you, Sir. I am John Grant. I was travelling south from Scotland and became ill on the road. I was taken in and have been cared for most kindly by my hosts."

"I hope you have recovered now, and that I shall see you in church on Sunday. How long will you be staying, may I ask?" The priest held his hat to his chest, and leaned forward with his head on one side, smiling benignly.

"I dinna ken, Sir. I'm no' yet fit enough to travel, and living in the open is harsh in this weather," said John, avoiding the subject of church.

The priest's face darkened. "You have been lured into a web, John. Beware of false prophets." He gave a curt bow, replaced his hat and walked on.

Chapter 62

Spring in the Air

It became generally known that John had a horse and cart. There were not many in the village. Those who owned them had them in use constantly. John found himself carting logs for people and was paid with a bag of corn or a chicken. He was walking up the street one day with Floss on an errand for Joshua, when a woman he had not met before ran out of her house towards him.

"Oh, Sir," she called, "can you help us?"

John stopped as she approached. "What's the trouble Ma'am? I'll help you if I can."

"My child's sick with the fever. I cannot carry her all the way to the doctor in town, and my husband is laid up with a broken leg. Can you take us in your cart?"

John said, "Go and fetch your child. I'll be here with the cart presently. Come Floss."

He retraced his steps to Joshua's yard and called through the door of the workshop, "I have to take a sick child into town, Josh. I'll fetch the beeswax you wanted later."

Joshua came to the door and called "That's all right, John." He disappeared inside.

John was already taking the horse from the paddock to the cart, which was standing ready in the yard. He went to get the harness from the stable, put it on the waiting horse, and backed him between the shafts. Floss had jumped on, eager to be driving again.

As John helped the woman up to sit beside him on the driver's bench, he asked her name.

"Prudence, Sir," she said.

It did not take long for John to drive Prudence and the child into town. The woman was too concerned to talk much, and spent the time caressing and crooning to the small bundle in her arms. They found the doctor at home and John waited outside on the cart.

Prudence soon came out of the house and climbed back up to her seat. She was calmer and the child seemed to be sleeping.

"He's given me a potion and said 'e would come and see us tomorrow," she said. "I dunnow what Wilf'll say when he knows I arsked you for help." She shook her head and frowned.

John twitched the reins and the horse moved off. "Why's that?" he asked.

"He don't like the people you're staying with," she said. "He says they're witches. They've got the backs up of the vicar and the Squire. There's trouble brewin', I reckon." She looked at John. "You ain't one of 'em, are yer?"

John sighed and said, "No, I'm only passing through. But the Quakers are no' witches. You have nothing to fear from them."

Prudence sniffed. "You'd be well advised to move on, Sir, if I may say so."

They were entering the village. "Thank you for yer kindness, Sir. I ain't got nothing to pay yer with. We've no money on account of Wilf's leg. If you stop here I'll walk the rest of the way."

John pulled the reins in. The horse stopped and Prudence handed him the child to hold while she clambered down. She took the child from him and walked away.

At the beginning of March, John was with Joshua in the workshop. They were polishing a table which they had been making.

John stopped rubbing and said, "I'm thinking of moving on, Josh. You and Mary have been verra kind and I canna thank ye enough. But I canna stay here for ever. The weather's improving and I'm fit enough, thanks to ye both."

Joshua continued polishing until John had finished speaking. Then he looked up.

"I guessed thou wouldst be getting itchy feet." He smiled. "It's been a pleasure, John. I shall miss thee. Thou hast put up with our Quaker ways patiently. I know thou art not entirely comfortable here." He shook John's hand warmly.

"I shall need to do some repairs to the cart before I start ma journey. Can you spare me for a day or two?" asked John.

"I'll be pleased to help thee with whatever is necessary, Friend."

A few days later, nature took over and the snow started falling. Their lives were disrupted for over a week. The road to town was head-high in drifts. All those who were able stopped their work and took shovels out to clear paths between the houses, the animals in their barns and the log stores. The children took makeshift sleds to the hills behind the village. Their cries of excitement rang out into the icy air, mingled with the barking of dogs. They piled loads of provisions onto the sleds to take to the elderly and infirm. Sometimes they hitched up the farm dogs to do the pulling.

John was walking up a back lane with his shovel to check that it was clear. The roars of a distressed cow reached his ears. He stopped and looked around but could not tell where the cow was. Nicholas Weaver panted up the lane behind him.

"Is that your cow, Nicholas?" John asked.

Nicholas was a thin weasel of a man. His red-rimmed eyes were small and close together. His wispy ginger hair and beard surrounded his shoulders.

"Aye, it is that. Dunno what's wrong now. She's forever hollerin' like that," he grumbled.

"Maybe she's sick. Shall we goo'n take a look?" John knew a bit about cows.

Nicholas nodded. His nose was running and he wiped it on his sleeve. He went ahead of John and they came to a barn where the cow stood bellowing over the half–door. Going inside, John caught his breath at the stench that met him.

"You'd do well to clean this place out," he said. "And when did you last milk her?"

"Just coming to do it now," Nicholas replied. "I ain't got no straw or hay left. The neighbour gets it for me, but he's laid up with his leg."

"Bring her out into the fresh air. I'll clear a space in the snow, and you can milk her while I fetch some fodder. She needs water, her bucket's empty." John was shocked at the poor condition of the cow. He took the bucket and filled it with snow. "That'll melt soon," he said, and left Nicholas to do the milking.

An hour later the cow was back in her barn on clean straw with a bag of hay to munch, and with water in the bucket.

Nicholas was still sniffing and grumpy. "What did you want to help us for, anyway?" he asked as John walked down the lane with him. "I ain't got nuffin' to pay yer wiv. You're the body who's livin' wiv those Queer folks, ain't ye? Satan's followers, they are, the vicar says. Puffed up above their station. Think they can get away wiv not paying their tithes like the rest of us have to do. No respect for the gentry..." He grumbled on, complaining about the Quakers and their misdeeds.

John did not say anything. Nicholas had fixed ideas which he had gleaned from the local gossip, and there was no point in discussing them. When they parted company, Nicholas carried a full bucket of milk up the path to Prudence and Wilf's house and knocked on the door.

Chapter 63
Crisis

Thomas was at last on his way back to Grantham. It took a week to struggle through the snow to Stamford, though it had stopped snowing and had thawed. Then it froze over, making the going even more hazardous. He brought the passengers safely to their destination, and the return journey was easier as the thaw set in.

The sun shone warmly on his back, the birds sang lustily and the grass was green again. The road was a slushy mess however, and the horses and carriage wheels had to be cleaned off at each stage.

He started thinking about his journey south. He would get to Grantham first thing tomorrow morning and hand in his uniform, collect his final wages and book a room for a day and a night. He would have a large breakfast and go to sleep until dinner time. Then he would have a good meal, enjoy a social evening at the bar and go to bed at a normal time for a whole night's sleep. The next morning, he would leave The George and go and buy a horse, before setting off towards a future of farming with friends.

≈ ≈ ≈

In the village, the ditches ran with water. The grass appeared on the green and at the roadsides. Snowdrops nodded their heads under the trees.

Joshua said to John, "Wilt thou take the cart into town with me to collect the tools I ordered for the workshop?

Then we'll get the cart ready and thou canst start thy journey whenever it pleases thee."

John agreed and they set off with Floss in the bright spring sunshine. Along the road they saw Nicholas Weaver walking into town. John slowed the horse down, wondering whether the man would accept a lift after the last conversation they had.

Nicholas looked up and scowled at Joshua when he saw him. None-the-less, he climbed up and sat in a moody silence in the cart.

Joshua said to John, "Mary said before we left that she's arranged Monthly Meeting for today, as we missed it last week. We'll finish our business in town as soon as we can, to be back in time."

John nodded and drove on. As they entered the little town, Nicholas jumped down, tipped his hat to John and walked away.

The town was busy with a market and it took a long time for John to find a place to leave the cart. He left Floss on guard while he and Joshua went to collect the tools. A large crowd was gathered in the market place, and they had difficulty pushing their way through.

There were shouts of "Hunt them down!", "Flush them out!", "They're a blight amongst us!"

John's flesh began to creep. He looked at Joshua who appeared not to have heard or to be aware of what was going on.

What should have taken a few minutes took over an hour. The ironmonger's shop was in a state of chaos. A large queue waited for attention.

The man in front of Joshua turned to them as they arrived. "Someone broke into the shop last night and took a lot of stock, small stuff mainly. Some was orders waiting to be collected."

Joshua said to John, "We'll have to wait. I need those tools."

When they reached the shop counter, the flustered ironmonger shook his head. "Sorry, Josh. All thy tools have gone. I'll have to make some more. It could be a few weeks, there's been so much taken..." He shrugged his shoulders and shook his head again.

Joshua left the shop despondently. "I know one other ironmonger in town. There's just a chance he'll have what I want."

They walked through the backstreets to avoid the crowds. The second ironmonger had a few of the tools Joshua wanted. He bought them for twice the price he would have paid, and they hurried back to the cart.

"We're late for Meeting," Joshua said.

The mob in the market place had dispersed. Joshua stowed the tools and John clicked the horse into a trot. The road was still muddy from the melted snow, which slowed their progress. As they approached the village, they heard angry shouts from a large number of people. John turned the corner and reined in the horse.

"Josh, get out of the cart and goo home out of sight. They're raiding the Meeting and if you show yoursell they'll take you too."

Joshua hesitated. "I must go and be with Mary."

"You'll be more use to her out here if she's taken to gaol."

Joshua leapt from the cart and ran to a gap in the hedge where he disappeared. John drove the horse and cart slowly up the main street.

Chapter 63
A Purpose in Everything

A crowd surrounded one of the cottages. There were shouts of "Blasphemy!" "Illegal assembly!" Someone saw him and came running over. Floss growled. John was dragged from his seat. Floss followed and caught the leg of the captor in her teeth. He yelled and let go of John. "This is one of 'em!" he cried. John stood still and Floss came close, baring her teeth. The crowd backed away.

A figure in black approached. The vicar said, "This man is not a Quaker. He has done no wrong."

John touched his hat to the vicar and climbed back up to his seat. From here he could see the Quakers. Mary was there with the men and women who were at the last Meeting. They looked calm and were allowing themselves to be led away by four constables. John caught sight of Nicholas Weaver at the edge of the crowd, picking stones from the road and hurling them at the prisoners. Mary's face was bleeding.

Anger boiled up in his breast and burnt his throat. "Stop that!" he roared, and leapt down from the cart. He strode over, feeling for his dirk. He clamped the hook on his left arm over Nicholas' shoulder, and pointed the dirk at his throat. He led his captive to where others were throwing stones.

"Leave off, ye fiends! I could use this on all of ye. 'Twould be over in a trice." The culprits looked shocked and dropped their stones.

"Look out!" a woman's voice cried.

John felt a thud on the side of his head. He staggered, braced himself on Nicholas' shoulder, and let go. He swung round to meet his adversary, his arms up and prepared to fight. The muttering mob surrounded the two men.

John faced a burly hulk, a stout stick in one hand and supporting himself on a roughly made crutch. He looked menacingly at John.

John straightened up and lowered his dirk. He thought of what he had heard in Meeting; "*There is God even in our enemies.*"

"You must be Wilf," he said. He could not see the slightest glimmer of God in this man, but he would not fight with anyone with only one good leg. The crowd went silent.

"How is your daughter?" John asked.

Prudence pushed her way through and joined her husband. She took the stick from his hand and said, "She's well, thank you, John. You're a kind man." She led Wilf away and the crowd turned their attention back to the Quakers.

John made his way to Floss and the cart. Two constables had their heads together. Floss wrinkled her nose and bared her teeth.

"Sir, is this your cart?" one of the constables enquired.

John nodded.

"You're obliged to take these prisoners to Grantham House of Correction, to await trial. The law demands it."

John was shocked. The constable had started handing the Quakers into the cart. He had no choice. Then he realised that they would have a more comfortable journey than walking miles along the muddy roads. He looked for Mary and went to help her up.

"I'm sorry this has happened, Mary," he said softly.

"It is the Lord's will. There is purpose in it," she said.

"Goo and sit at the front, behind me," John suggested.

She scrambled over the legs of her companions and sat on the pile of hides which were still on the cart. John climbed into the driver's seat. Floss sat beside him.

A constable called, "Proceed!"

John turned the horse round and set off up the road out of the village, aware that his passengers might not see their homes again for a long time, if at all. The loaded cart swayed and rocked over the ruts, splashing the legs of the constables who walked alongside. Some of the rabble who had come from town followed the cart, shouting insults, until they came to the junction with the road into town. John turned right, while they all went to the left.

John heard Mary behind him. "John, the children. They're hiding in Felicity's cottage, where we had the Meeting. Canst thou seek them out and take them to Joshua? He'll care for them. The eldest is Ruth; she can help him."

"I surely will do that, Mary. Joshua has gone home and is waiting for me to join him. I'll soon be starting ma journey south. I want to thank you for all your kindness. You saved ma life."

"God saved thy life, John. There is a purpose in everything. Remember, God is with thee always."

In Grantham John delivered his passengers and sadly watched them being led away. Never in his life could he remember a need for whisky as strong as now. It was nearly dark, and he had to get back to Joshua and the children. But he could not resist the call of the bar at The George.

He turned the cart and headed in that direction. It would not take long to knock back a dram to prepare himself for the journey. He could feel Mary's disapproval as if she was still behind him.

He walked into the bar and thought of the last time he was here. It seemed like years ago. He felt a different person now. There were a few early customers sitting at the tables. He ordered a whisky and felt in his money pouch to pay…

"Faether?"

John froze. He turned round.

It was Thomas! Thomas was there, facing him. His son, looking as if he had seen a ghost.

"Thomas!" John fell into his arms. Tears flooded down his face. His head swam and his knees gave way. He was led to a seat and his whisky was brought to him. He took several deep breaths and looked at his son, still trying to believe what he saw. He shook from head to foot. Mary's voice echoed in his ears: *There is a purpose in everything, John.* He took his whisky in one mouthful.

Thomas sat down to face his father. He had bought himself a dram and raised his glass to John before emptying it down his throat. The two looked at each other, savouring the moment before saying anything. John stopped shaking.

Thomas was the first to speak. "I'd given up looking for you. I searched for months, up and down the road."

"Where were you when thy mother was dying, Son?" John asked.

"In prison. I found Clover and they accused me of stealing her."

John did not understand. He did not need to now. They sat quietly for a while. He remembered Joshua and the children.

"I have to go back to the village, Thomas. They need me there."

"I'm no letting you out of ma sight, Faether. If necessary, I'll come with you. Then you can tell me all aboot it on the way."

"Come and see Floss," said John, getting up from his chair. He sat down again quickly. He felt giddy again.

"When did you last eat, Faether?" asked Thomas.

John shrugged. It had been a long day. "Breakfast," he said.

Thomas called the barman. "Bring two dinners, Daniel. I'll settle oop when I get back."

A pie and cabbage and a flagon of ale later, father and son were ready for the road. They went out to the cart where Floss barked and ran round Thomas in circles, before she leapt into his arms and licked his face all over.

"I'll drive, Faether. I'm fresh." Thomas had brought a lantern out with him and hung it on the shaft. He took the reins and they trotted away into the night.

Chapter 64
Rescue

There was a candle burning in the window when they reached Joshua's house. John jumped from the cart with Floss and held the lantern to show Thomas into the yard. Joshua must have heard them coming. He was at the back door to meet them, his face grey with worry.

"I'll just put Floss and the horse in the barn and feed them, Josh. This is ma son, Thomas. I'll explain when I come in."

When John came into the house, Thomas had already explained and the two men were shaking hands.

John said, "I had to take Mary and the others to Grantham, to the House of Correction, Josh. On the way we managed to speak. She's being verra courageous, saying it's God's will. But they left the children hiding in Felicity's house. They must still be there. We'd better goo and find them."

The three men took the lantern and went across the street to Felicity's house. Ruth had lit some candles and kept the fire going and they had found bread and milk. The little ones were wrapped in blankets, sleeping on the floor by the fire. Ruth's face lit up when she saw Joshua.

"Oh, I thought thou had been taken too," she said, and burst into tears. One or two of the other children started crying.

Joshua sat on a chair and gathered them together in his arms, saying, "Hush, be still in the presence of the Lord." He looked at John and Thomas. "I'll stay here with them tonight. Thou canst sleep in my house. I'll see ye in the morning."

Thomas tried to take in this strange situation in which he had found his father. He was amazed that he had stayed here for so long. He seemed different. The anger had gone from his eyes. They spent an hour or so sitting by the range in Joshua and Mary's house, telling each other of their adventures. John began to nod off in his chair and Thomas watched him affectionately. His father had aged in the six months since they were in York together, but he also had a look of peace on his face which Thomas had never seen in him before. He got up and shook John by the shoulder.

"Let's get you into bed, Faether. We might have another long day ahead of us."

They stumbled up the narrow stairs together and Thomas was pleased to see that there was room in the bed for two. He did not want to sleep on the floor.

Light filtered through the trees outside the bedroom window. Thomas heard a noise downstairs. He crept down in his stockings. Joshua was rummaging around in the food store. He looked up when Thomas came through the door, and smiled.

"I have to find food for eight hungry little mouths," he said.

"D'you have oats and milk and eggs?" asked Thomas.

"I might have to go and look in the other Quaker houses, but there will be plenty," said Joshua.

"I'll cook a great pot of crowdies for all," Thomas announced. "That will set them up for theday." He stoked up the fire in the range and went to find a large pot.

John appeared at the foot of the stairs. "D'you need any help, Son?"

"Ay, go with Joshua and look for food and bowls and spoons. There are no enough here."

Later, John stood gazing out of the window while Thomas and Joshua prepared the breakfast and set the bowls on the table. He thought how he would miss this peaceful place, until he remembered the events of the previous day. He watched the little troop of children cross the green, rubbing their sleepy eyes, their hair tousled, and he wondered how Joshua was going to manage to look after them on his own. It might be for weeks, possibly months. John felt he should be here to help, though he could not expect Thomas to stay.

The children came into the parlour and sat or stood round the table. There were not enough chairs for all.

Ruth said, "Let us join hands and wait upon the Lord." They linked hands and closed their eyes for a few moments, until Ruth said, "Amen" and their thin voices echoed hers. They peered into their bowls and picked up their spoons, dipping in cautiously, not knowing what to expect. Soon they were eating hungrily.

John joined Joshua and Thomas by the range and filled a bowl for himself. They stood there, eating with the children.

Joshua said, "Thomas, that was delicious, I wish thou wast staying, but I know thou cannot."

"I showed you how to make it," said Thomas. "'Tis no difficult. Faether, come outside a while, I want to talk."

He and John left the kitchen and went to feed Floss and the horse and let them out of the barn.

"I've been thinking, Faether. I'm all set to goo to Sussex theday. I'm hoping you'll be coming with me." He looked questioningly at John.

"I was preparing to continue ma journey, when all this happened." John spread his arms wide. "It dinna feel right leaving Josh to look after all those children, and visit Mary and the others. How will he manage withoot the cart?"

"I was going to buy a horse. That's the best way to travel these roads," said Thomas. "Why dinna we buy a horse for you and leave the horse and cart for Joshua? I have enough siller saved for a couple of nags, and 'twill only take a few days by ma reckoning."

John stroked his beard. "What about Floss? She canna walk all the way. She's no used to it."

"But she was born to travelling on foot with the drovers. She's been mollycoddled," insisted Thomas.

"She's no as fit as she was, with that limp. You know that."

Thomas sighed with exasperation. "You're just as stubborn as ever, Faether. We've no' been together a whole day yet and we're arguing. What would Mother say?"

John looked at his son with a scowl. Floss came and made a fuss of him, nuzzling and pawing.

Thomas said, "If she gets tired I'll carry her across the neck of ma horse. How's that?"

"But what about the plaids and hides and…"

"Leave them behind. We dinna need them now."

Joshua came out of the house. "I have one last favour to ask, before ye start thy journey."

John looked at his friend. "Anything, Josh. I dinna want to leave you like this."

Joshua said, "I'll be fine. Ruth can cook. All I need is a lift into town to get some provisions to start us off. I'll walk back."

Thomas said, "We'll do better than that, Joshua. We'll take you to Grantham where you can buy what you need. You can visit Mary and take them some food. They'll need it, I know. I've been in gaol. We'll goo and get some horses and leave you the cart, so you have use of it." He looked at John and said, "How's that Faether? D'you agree?"

Joshua's face was all wrinkles and a tear or two escaped.

John said, "Surely, that's the least I can do after all you've done for me, Josh. Come, now, let's get ready." He thought he could change his mind and stay with Josh when they reached Grantham. Thomas would be free to go south and follow his own life.

They spread the plaids and hides out in the sun to air. The children took the bonnets and pranced around with them on their heads. John gave Ruth his cooking equipment and bowls and cutlery to augment those in the house. Joshua said that the children could all sleep in the two beds upstairs and he would sleep in the parlour wrapped in the plaids on the hides.

They were about to leave when the blacksmith and his wife came into the yard.

Harold went up to Joshua and said, "We heard what happened yesterday, Joshua. You people don't deserve it. If there's anything at all that ye need, we'll be pleased to help, and there's a few others in the village of the same mind."

"I've been baking bread this morning," said his wife. "Mary's always baking for other people. Now it's my turn. You've got so many mouths to feed... I'll bring it round when it's ready."

Joshua stood with his mouth open. "Thank thee, thank thee, Friends," was all he could say.

Epilogue

1683
Warminghurst

The view from the ridge stretched downhill across woodland and parkland. Thomas sat on his horse taking in the scene. The sun shone warmly on his face. Fluffy white clouds sailed past, driven by an autumn wind. He turned up the collar of his coat and looked to his left. He could see the little church, perched on the end of the ridge, where he was soon to marry his sweet Mary. He thought of her plump little body, her smiling grey blue eyes and her rosy cheeks. He felt the love that had grown up between them, slowly, like a bulb piercing the ground to develop into a beautiful flower, as they fumbled their way through their naïve courtship.

Below him and before the land sloped steeply down to the park, stood the Manor house. Alex MacPherson and his wife lived here, renting it from William Penn, a Quaker, who was away setting up a new colony in America. MacPherson was a good Master. He was also a friend, and treated Thomas with respect. Among the trees he could see glimpses of the big house. A wisp of blue smoke rose above it. There would be a fire lit in the hall against the chill of the evening.

The sinking sun left a pink tinge in the sky, and lit up the woodland: green turning to purple to red and yellow, a final display before releasing their leaves to carpet the ground. Black skeletal branches would be left resting all winter, waiting for the quickening of the earth.

Thomas nudged his horse forward. Floss appeared, panting, back from a rabbit chase, her tongue lolling, her eyes bright and her ears pricked. They walked along the track together and entered the woodland park below the house. He heard the sounds of bustling wildlife, of birds singing their evening song and mice scuttling away from the threat of horse's hooves. A deer froze in front of him before bounding away. Thomas thought of the hunting parties, quite a different experience to the deer hunts in the Highlands, but it was good sport. The dried leaves rustled under their feet, which disturbed the earth, sending up a rich loamy aroma. He loved living here.

The cottage which was his home stood on the boundary of the estate, surrounded by outbuildings and his father's vegetable garden. He caught sight of another wisp of smoke. John would be in his workshop, finishing and polishing his latest piece of furniture: a bed with four carved posts, for the newly-married couple.

Thomas still had difficulty believing the change that had come over his father since their time in York. It was as if he had left all his bitterness and anger behind him. John loved the gentle downs which surrounded them, and spent hours walking or riding in their new surroundings. As Thomas approached the house, he wondered what was in the letter his father had received that morning.

Floss ran on ahead. In the yard Thomas dismounted and took his horse to the stable. He removed the saddle and bridle and groomed the animal while it munched hay from a bag hanging on a hook on the wall.

John appeared in the doorway. "Now you're back, Son, I'll goo and start the dinner." Their eyes met. "I've had some news."

The expression on his face told Thomas that the news was good. The grooming done, he checked the water bucket and shut the lower half of the stable door, then walked across the yard to feed the pigs. The light was fading now. Floss emerged from her shed and followed him round until he gave her some oats and she settled down for the night. He washed his hands and face at the well.

The parlour was warm and bright with the candles lit. Thomas went to pour two mugs of ale and set them down on the range to warm. He sat on the spindle-backed chair nearby and watched the fire. The colours of the flames reminded him of the autumn leaves. He liked this time of the year. The rhythm of life changed; there was less daylight, but more time to be sociable. He would call on Mary when dinner was over, and find out how she was getting on with preparations for the wedding.

John ladled out a portion of stew for each, from the pot on the range. "There's more where that came from," he said as he set the dishes on the table.

Thomas brought the ale and sat down. "Tell me the good news, then, Faether."

John sat facing his son and smiled. "The letter was from Mary and Joshua. The Quakers have been released from prison!"

"That is good news! Maybe you can stop worrying about them now."

"They got ma letter and they say how pleased they are to hear of your betrothal." John raised his mug. "Good health, Son."

Thomas raised his and said, "Thanks be for our good fortune."

Thomas Grant married Mary Finch in Warminghurst Church on 13 November 1683.

Historical Notes

The story passed down my family line was that a tyrannical Scottish Laird banished all his sons in a fit of pique. The descendants believed that there is a castle waiting in chancery for one of us to claim it. The Victorian generation, to whom status was all important, actually attempted to do this, with no success.

The only evidence I have found to support the story was given to me by an aged historian in Grantown in Speyside. He told the story of a laird who disinherited a cadet branch of the Grant clan. They appealed to Captain Hill who was paid by Oliver Cromwell to police that area during the Commonwealth period. Supported by a Macpherson, who was a friend of the Grants, they persuaded Grant to withdraw his punishment. An agreement was drawn up, promising never to banish them. Apparently this document still exists in the archives. I have not discovered it. The laird's son went against this agreement and disinherited the cadet branch.

I have not found any link between this story and our Grants. The first Grants found in the parish records of Sussex were living there several generations earlier. So I have gleaned a history of James Grant, 7th Laird of Freuchie, his wife and family in the 17th century, and fitted in the story given to me by the archivist who is no longer alive. John Grant and his family are entirely fictitious. Their journey was created from studying the history of the towns they passed through, and the customs of the time.

I have brought the date of the first stagecoaches forward a few years to fit in with my plot.

The marriage of Thomas Grant to Mary Finch in 1683 is recorded in the Warminghurst parish records. Their descendants are my ancestors.

Joan Angus alias Clemens Lucke, my spiritual cousin.

Acknowledgements

I am so grateful to be a member of such a lively, supportive and inspirational writing group. Especial thanks to our tutor, Chris Sparkes, who also with meticulous care edited the text of this book and made some very nice comments.

Thanks also to my family who have encouraged me and have contributed to the creation of the cover.

My researches have taken me to various websites: Clan Grant, Scottish Covenanters, The Great North Road, Highland dress, Highland cattle, Alnwick history, Stage Coaching etc.

Books which have been helpful are:
A History of Scotland by Neil Oliver
A History of Clan Grant (Author unknown)
Memoirs of a Highland Lady by Elizabeth Grant of Rothiemurchus
Heart of Midlothian by Sir Walter Scott
The Peaceable Kingdom by Jan de Hartog